Trial
at Grand Marais

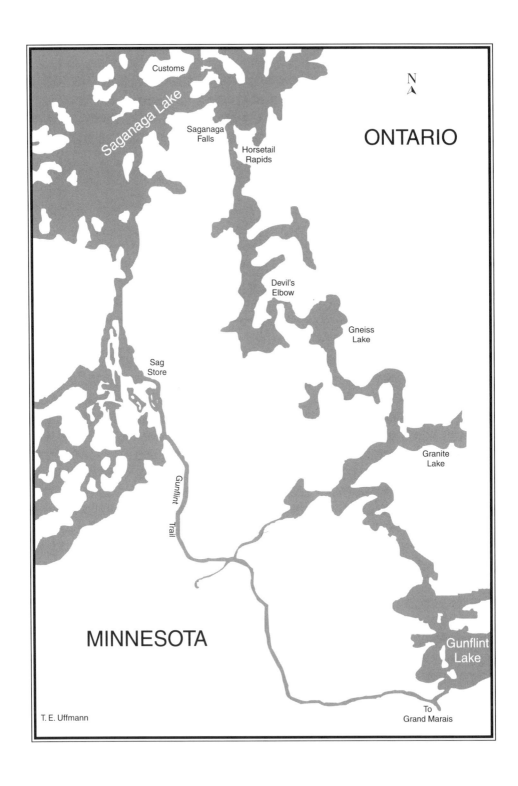

Customs

Saganaga Lake

Saganaga
Falls

Horsetail
Rapids

N

ONTARIO

Devil's
Elbow

Gneiss
Lake

Sag
Store

Granite
Lake

Gunflint

Trail

MINNESOTA

Gunflint
Lake

To
Grand Marais

T. E. Uffmann

A NOVEL

TRIAL
AT GRAND MARAIS

Gene Andereck

ROCK CREEK PRESS

Shawnee Mission, Kansas

All characters in this novel are fictional. Any resemblance to persons living or dead is purely coincidental. Events in the story also are fictitious.

"The Offering," a poem from *The Black Hawk Songs*, by Michael Borich, Springfield, Missouri, is reprinted with the author's permission.

The map was produced by Tom Uffman, Springfield, Missouri.

Published by Rock Creek Press, L.L.C., 10167 Haskins St., Shawnee Mission, Kansas 66215-1857

Andereck, Gene
        Trial at Grand Marais/Gene Andereck

LCCN: 97-68211
ISBN: 1-890826-01-4

Printed in the United States of America
First Edition: September 1997

10 9 8 7 6 5 4 3 2 1

To

Alison
Leslie
Lauren
Nels

The Offering

Come to where the black
bear has left his claws
in the skins of walnut

and sluiceberry, over the foot
hills' tawn breasts, to this
slender underpart of the fall

sky, we bring our gifts.
Our wandering smoke carries up
its black tips of prairie color.

To the far land where the moon
sleeps, to forests of clear water
and proud animals to our final

home we ascend in the arms
of our smoke, in our waiting
hands white-tailed deer, wild

fruit, river otter, pond turtles,
rabbit, walleye, rock bass,
woodcocks, painted pheasant, heron

eggs, stone dove, smooth shells
of corn and beans, in the easy
smoke wingbeat we lose our ground.

from *The Black Hawk Songs*
by Michael Borich

To the Reader

I renamed the Ojibwa Reservation to identify its general geographical location for Canadian and American readers who have never been to the Arrowhead country. My friends in Cook County, Minnesota, who have lined canoes down the Granite River, will discover the palisades described at Gneiss Lake and Devil's Elbow to be higher than they remember; and they might recall there is no rock ledge large enough to accommodate a Boeing Vertrol ACH-47A Chinook. I used literary license to embellish those two places; however, on the whole my descriptions are accurate.

Readers who want to see pristine wilderness the way French-Canadian voyageurs found it hundreds of years ago should take the wonderful canoe trip from Gunflint Lake all the way down to Big Saganaga.

G.A.

CHAPTER 1

WITH WIDE, ARCING SWEEPS OF HER ARMS, Kristen pushed her rock-dented aluminum canoe through choppy waters toward a slot in the low shoreline that she knew would lead them into the Granite River. They were almost home.

The wind shifted, rising with a bellows breath that bucked against the flat of the canoe hull, wrenching the craft into a skid. A sudden gust sliced across the thin tops of waves, shaving off ragged sheets of spray. Overhead, twisting, elephantine clouds and coils of smoke darkened the sky, scrawling a line where the light faded and the dark spread like a bruised welt above the treetops. Another storm was gathering.

Large backpacks weighted the front of the craft and held its prow low in the water. In the bottom of the canoe Kristen's two daughters, Cubby, seven, and Niki, five, their hands gripping the gunwales, huddled like rain-drenched birds, watching their mother, who knelt in the rear, thrusting with strong, swift strokes of a paddle. Their small faces, cowled by rain hoods, glistened with a patina of fine mist. Wind caught the froth of the waves and thrashed it over the bow. The water splashed the girls' backs and ran in erratic rivulets down their yellow plastic rain gear.

The two girls grinned as the canoe dipped into a trough and rose up again, sleek and playful as a seal. Their eyes widened in excitement and they laughed with glee even as the wind snatched away the sound, scattering their laughter beyond the slosh-slap of waves against the silver hull.

Finally, Kristen relaxed as the wind leveled off in a breathless ebb and the canoe scudded silent as a wraith across a momentary calm stretch of water.

Kristen McLean was now a fugitive.

There was a Minnesota law that made mother-love a crime, Kristen thought bitterly, a law that made her decide to steal her own daughters and flee with them into the vast wilderness of the North Woods.

"You were born and reared on the Thunder Bay Indian Reservation?" her husband's lawyer had asked.

"Yes," Kristen had replied.

"And you are full blooded Ojibwa?"

"My parents are Ojibwa. Our tribe is part of the Chippewa Nation." Kristen had remained slender with all the bloom of youth, despite two pregnancies. Her hair was as black as polished obsidian. She was beautiful in an earthy, innocently sensual way, her high cheekbones smooth and rounded, touched with shadows of vermillion, her lips full, precisely chiseled, her nose almost patrician. On the reservation, Kristen was called "Mani," the Ojibwa version of Mary. It was the custom for members of the Ojibwa tribe to take different names at different times in their lives, names that would come and go as their totem would have them do. She chose the name "Kristen" for herself when she began her new life as a student on the university campus in Duluth.

Peter Hauck, the heavy-boned attorney for the McLean family, pressed his point. "And you admit that you have taken both Cubby and Niki up into the Wilderness Area on many occasions?"

"Yes."

"Even though their father objected?"

"Yes." Kristen darted a glance toward Arlesen, seated in the first row next to his mother and father.

Arlie McLean, her husband, had weak eyes and his flesh was sallow from years of desk work under artificial light. He was a decent man, seemingly insecure in the presence of his parents. His objections to the way Kristen was rearing their two girls were acquired from his parents, mostly from his father, Toli McLean.

"And," the lawyer continued, "you did return with the children at times when their clothing was torn and stained as their father described in his testimony?"

"I took the children to teach them how to gather and store blueberries from bushes that grow on the small islands up in the lakes. Their clothes were torn and stained, but they were play clothes and that's what you expect with kids."

"Their father testified that you made the girls stand up in a canoe and one of them fell into the water, and the nearest help was twenty miles away."

"That's not so. I was teaching them to fish the way Indian children fish."

"Standing up in a canoe?" Hauck's eyebrows arched.

"Yes." Kristen, exasperation tensing her facial muscles, thought Hauck wasn't as dense as he acted. Kristen turned to Judge Dorothy Clemens.

"Indian children are taught to fish standing upright in the canoe. They thrust a rod into the water. Fastened to the end of the rod is a net shaped like a pocket. Fish enter the net and when they do, the net is yanked up and the fish are dumped into the canoe. The children must learn to snare the fish without overturning the canoe. My oldest daughter fell into the lake when she was learning to do this and we told her father about it. There was no danger. Both of my girls can swim like fish."

"But you, their mother, told your daughter to stand up in a canoe, in open waters, twenty miles from the end of the trail, and you don't think you were endangering the life of your daughter?"

"Yes, I did, and no, I do not believe I was endangering her life."

"Did you teach your children to swim?"

"Yes."

"Tell the court the ages of your children when you first started to teach them to swim."

"Two months old. When each girl was two months old I started teaching her to swim."

"In cold lake water?"

"No, of course not. I took them to the swimming pool at the university. My husband knows that." Kristen looked out into the courtroom where her husband sat between his parents. "It was a swimming class for infants. Several mothers from the university took their babies to those classes."

Hauck made a check mark on his yellow pad and went on to another subject.

"Your husband and his parents have testified that when you took your children back up to the Indian reservation you taught them pagan beliefs. Do you deny that?"

"Yes, I deny that." Kristen's face contorted with anger. She again turned in the witness chair so she could speak directly to the judge. "I have raised Cubby and Niki in the Christian faith. We are members of the Greek Orthodox Church, the same church their father belongs to. But I have also tried to teach my children to appreciate their native American heritage. Indian children are taught to have their own guardian spirit. Each child, in her early years, takes a spirit which she reveres then for the rest of her days. First the child fasts in order that she may more easily dream in her sleep, for that is when Ojibwas believe the spirit will reveal herself. The purpose is to see in their sleep something extraordinary which takes for them the form of a personal spirit. Thereafter, all her life, the Indian child honors that spirit. That was the tradition I told my girls about. I was not teaching them to be pagans. My girls go to church regularly. I have raised them to be Christians, but I also want them to know about their Ojibwa ancestry."

The canoe jolted with a sudden shock.

The strong current flowing out of Gunflint Lake surged against the canoe. The craft rumbled with a metallic shudder as the hull responded to the abrupt pressure.

For a moment, Kristen thought she might be swept off course. She dipped the oar deep, digging into the swift water, straining to bring the twisting bow about. She wondered if this might be a sign, warning her to turn back. The thought was fleeting, but she wrinkled her forehead as she shoveled water with the flat of her paddle, pushing the canoe back toward the river channel.

Quetico Provincial Park and the Boundary Water Canoe Area encompassed an intricate tangle of paths, lakes, and rivers on a rock foundation that underlies central Canada and the upper Midwest. By mutual decree Canada and the United States required its use to be restricted. Commercial operations, machines, airplanes, and motors were banned from the unspoiled area.

Winding along the three-million-acre Superior National Forest, with its high hills of an ancient mountain chain, the Granite River divided the

United States from four million acres of Canadian wilderness. The river rose at its source in Gunflint Lake on the north slope of the Laurentian Range. The waters flowed out of Gunflint Lake to Granite Lake, and then on to Gneiss, Marabeuf, Saganaga Falls, always north and west until it finally emptied into Saganaga Lake. Eventually its waters flowed into Hudson Bay 400 miles north of Lake Superior.

The river was a gift from the long ice age that sealed the land in white silence. During thousands of years the great glaciers gouged out the lake basins and rimmed them with rocky shores and shifting hills of sand. As the ice retreated, the last glacier left moraines that blocked drainage to the south and carved the river's channel between limestone ledges. Thirty thousand years before, the melting of the ice cover, ten thousand feet deep, gifted the land with blue water flowing to the north and west.

The lake shores darkened with forests, game animals multiplied, the waters swarmed with fish. Indian nations roamed the lake-bordered hunting grounds, using the Granite River as a watery highway for their birch bark canoes. The Menominee, the forest Sioux, and the Chippewa lived in the lake country like deer and foxes, leaving it unchanged by their presence. It was when the white men found the rich country, rich in fish and furs, at first, later in timber, then in copper and iron ore, that the land was changed.

For two centuries the river was the gateway for colorful French-Canadians. The portages around Granite River's waterfalls and rapids felt the tread of moccasined feet as thousands of voyageurs dog-trotted into the interior, carrying trade goods and returning with bales of fur on bent backs held by a strap which reached from forehead to the small of the back.

After the Hudson's Bay Company absorbed John Askin's North West Company the Granite River thoroughfare gave up its traffic, except for Ojibwas who settled on the Thunder Bay Reservation after they put their mark on the white man's Treaty of La Pointe.

This combination of river and lakes was the remote sanctuary Kristen McLean sought for herself and her children. It was the only place she knew where they could hide; a place abundant with wild life, with island-studded lakes.

The Indian woman was certain the area would conceal them. She knew it well, for it had been her childhood home. It was in the network of waterways, edged by impassable inland barriers, that Kristen had taught her girls to net swimming fish while standing in a canoe. It was there that her own father, Mike, dove into the waters and swam alongside her children each time the girls lost their balance and fell into the lake.

The girls loved their grandfather. The most arresting things about the unusual Indian were his piercing eyes and wide, warm smile. Scraggly hair hung down his back. He was smooth-shaven. He always dressed the same, wearing leggings, a breechcloth over torn khaki pants, and boot moccasins that stopped just below his knees. His long-sleeved jacket appeared to have once been a part of a military uniform. The jacket was pierced across the chest by porcupine quills stitched in an erratic pattern. From his belt hung two carrying bags and a knife. Tied also to his belt the leggings the old Indian wore covered the worn trousers. The outer portion of the leggings was punctured and decorated with quillwork. The hip portion was cut higher and slanted to the crotch with the breechcloth providing an apron in both the front and back.

Their grandfather Mike always stripped to his trousers and left the carefully folded quill-worked garments on the shore when they went out on the water for their fishing lessons. Afterwards, at cook fires, the girls sat and listened to their grandfather as he told tales of forest animals, of Ojibwa traditions, and as he patiently explained why he never visited them in Duluth, why he preferred to live off the Indian reservation in the solitude of the wilderness, rather than accept the government dole.

The canoe squirted into the river and bobbed over the ripples of the first shallow rapids.

"Cubby, hang on to your sister," Kristen called as she maneuvered with savage strokes of her paddle.

Niki sat in front of Cubby. The older girl laughed and grabbed Niki around the waist.

"I'm going to throw you out," Cubby teased.

"No, you're not." Niki squealed.

Both had hair as black as Manchester anthracite. The older girl, Cubby, was whippet-thin but Niki was still plump with baby fat. They laughed as a cool spray of water spewed over the bow, drenching them. They looked like rain-soaked quail chicks.

The two girls screamed and rocked as the canoe picked up speed, bobbed through the shallow rapids. Kristen deftly thrust with sharp, quick backstrokes and kept the bow pointed into the slick tongue of water that carried them past jagged blocks of granite, until they again floated in a calm flat pool.

"You're not going to throw me in the water," Niki said.

"I am, too," Cubby threatened.

Kristen rested on her paddle. "Cubby, don't throw your sister out of the canoe," she ordered, playing the game. She knew that her daughters were fearless when they were in the wilderness country.

"Out she goes," Cubby taunted.

"I'll bite you," Niki cried.

"No, you won't."

"If you throw me out, I'll bite you." Niki tossed her head back against her sister's chest.

The craft began to bounce and twist again as it entered a sheet of white water leading out of the pool. The girls continued to rock and squeal.

"Tie Niki's life jacket!" shouted their mother. In their playful struggle Cubby had loosened the ribbon on the front of Niki's life preserver.

Cubby pulled roughly on her sister's tie-ribbon.

"Not so tight," Niki protested as Cubby retied the bow.

The stream deepened. Kristen stopped paddling and let the canoe drift with the current. "God, I love you two," she said aloud. Cubby and Niki returned their mother's adoring look with pixie grins.

CHAPTER 2

KRISTEN KNEW SHE HAD WAITED TOO LONG to leave the McLean household. She should have left after that first pivotal confrontation with her father-in-law. But she was younger then, and pregnant. She recalled her humiliation that time when Toli McLean had invaded her privacy.

That afternoon her naked body was bathed in the brilliant sunlight that filtered through the gauzy curtains of the bathroom window. She reached for a towel as she emerged from the shower. Her finger snagged on the edge of the terrycloth.

"Darn," she said. "A hangnail."

She began to towel off, then opened a drawer on the cabinet. She rummaged in the drawer until she found a nail file. I'll tear my hose if I don't fix this, she thought. She was busy filing off the loose sliver of nail when Toli padded silently into the bathroom.

Until that moment, she had thought her bathroom was sacrosanct, inviolable.

Startled, she stepped back, groped for the wet towel hanging from the sink.

Toli reached out to touch her.

Kristen lashed out with the nail file, jabbed Toli in the arm.

Toli gasped in surprise and jerked back his bleeding forearm.

For a long moment, neither said a word. Kristen glared malevolently at Toli, a rush of thoughts screaming for attention in her mind.

He stared in surprise at the oozing blood on his arm.

Kristen knew that Toli considered himself to be quite popular in the intellectual community, so she reasoned that he was probably astounded by her violent reaction.

With a sudden queasy sinking in the pit of her stomach, Kristen wondered if Toli had expected her to be more of a free spirit just because she'd been one of his graduate students before she'd married his son, Arlie.

"Get out of here!" Kristen shouted. Her voice rose and broke at the top of the scale, quavered with emotion. "If you ever touch me again, I'll make a capon out of you!" Kristen's voice hissed with deadly warning. There had been no other sound in the empty house.

The elder McLean backed out of the room.

"You're crazy," he muttered.

Kristen could see the rage in Toli's eyes just before he left. She stood there, shaking, until the tears came. Then, she hurled the nail file at the bathroom door, heard it strike the wood, then clatter on the aluminum molding at the bottom of the frame.

"Hang on," Kristen called. "We're coming to the first waterfall." She drove her paddle into the stream and pushed for the shore.

She looked up at the seething dark sky. She could smell the coming storm in the heavy air. "We've got to get to shore before the wind comes up."

At that moment, a lightning bolt struck in the woods above the water's edge. Their first sensation was the icy ripple on the edges of their teeth. The bolt was so close it left an acrid taste in their mouths and a prickling sensation in their eyes and nostrils. The air reeked with the tang of ozone. The deafening clap that accompanied the brilliance temporarily stopped all sound. Their eyes swarmed with bouncing, unfocused spots. The children sat stunned as their mother fought to hold the canoe against the rock shore. The current pulled on the craft, trying to drag it out into the channel above the falls.

In the woods where the bolt struck, faint puffs of vapor hung over the land, then smoke began to curl and rise through the evergreens. Wind caught the plume and carried it up into the gray pall that lay like a blanket over the wilderness area. It joined the smoke from countless unchecked fires that had started on the forest floor during the season of dry weather and electrical storms that carried little moisture.

"That was a big one!" the startled Cubby exclaimed.

The eyes of the two girls grew wide with astonishment, but neither appeared frightened.

Kristen wig-wagged the canoe back to the shore. Putting one leg into the shallow water, she dragged the craft up onto the rocks, the aluminum hull thumping on stone.

"A big one," Niki repeated earnestly, as she rocked in the canoe.

"Yes," Kristen agreed. She was shaken by the electrical display, even if the girls were not.

"Mother, that really was a big one," Niki said again.

"Yes, dear, I heard. Now, hop out. We have to portage here."

"Are we almost to Grandpa Mike's?" Niki asked.

"Not yet."

The girls scrambled out of the canoe, their feet drumming hollow booms on the metal hull.

On her first two trips across the portage, Kristen carried the food pack and the pack holding their tent and sleeping bags. The girls carried loose gear and happily stretched their legs. Kristen's third trip with the canoe on her shoulders took a little longer and the two girls sprinted on ahead, skipping over stones in the path.

Feet spread and braced on the ledge of rock, Cubby waited for her mother to arrive with the canoe.

"Niki dropped the fishing rods in the water," Cubby called when she saw her mother coming toward them.

"I did not," Niki protested. "They just rolled off."

Kristen shifted the canoe off her shoulders and eased it down to the ground with her extended leg.

"You did, too, you dropped them in the water."

"I did not!"

Kristen looked down into the clear pool. Reflected tree tops, stirred with the whisper of a warming breeze, swirled green and dark in the depths. The end of the portage pathway was far enough downstream to be away from the main force of current that plunged over the falls. Only in the center did the stream still run swiftly.

The two fishing rods and their reels lay in plain sight in the water below the rock.

"I'll get them, Mother," Cubby said, using her important tone of voice.

The pool where the fishing rods lay was not so deep, nor the current so swift, as to cause Kristen concern.

Cubby took her clothes off. "I'll get them." The seven-year-old was so excited she seemed to glow with an inner radiance. She was, Grandpa Mike had often said, the spitting image of her mother, when Kristen had been her age.

Niki sat down and started untying her shoes. "Me, too." Her straight black hair brushed across her back as she looked first at her sister, then at her mother.

"No, Niki, you keep your shoes on," Kristen ordered. "Cubby can get them."

With a shriek, Cubby plunged into the water and bobbed back to the surface, sputtering. "It's cold!" she shouted. Then, turning, she dove to the sandy bottom of the pool and retrieved the bundle of rods. Rising to the surface, Cubby handed the watersoaked packet to her mother and climbed out onto the shore, shivering as she caught her breath.

Kristen laid the fishing gear on the ground and wrapped her arms around her naked daughter. She rubbed circulation back into Cubby's arms and legs.

"I wanted to go in, too," Niki protested.

Kristen laughed as she dried Cubby with a flannel shirt. "Niki, the next time you drop something in the water, we'll let you go get it," she promised.

Niki beamed.

Cubby screwed up her face. "I'll throw you in the water if you want to go swimming."

"No! I don't want you to throw me in. I just want to do it myself."

"Get dressed," Kristen ordered. "We've got a long way to go before we reach Grandpa Mike's cabin."

At her reminder, the two girls jumped like jack-in-the-boxes and screamed with delight. The children's voices echoed down the river valley like bright tinsel streamers aflutter on a crisp breeze.

As she began to load their gear back into the canoe, Kristen's mind drifted back to the day when the fragile weave of her life began to snarl into tangled knots.

It was on her twenty-ninth birthday that she had finally resolved to leave her ineffectual husband and his stern, impassive parents and to take charge of her own life. The McLean family had retaliated in the courtroom. They fought Kristen's bid for independence by securing a court order that took her two daughters from her and granted temporary custody to the father.

"To do otherwise," the senior counsel for the McLean family had argued, "would be to allow the children to be taken away to live in poor, if not primitive, conditions on the Thunder Bay Indian Reservation."

The court had agreed.

Something had hardened in Kristen that day. Something went out of her that was replaced by a flint hard determination not to allow herself and her daughters to become snared in the court's net.

Something her father had once told her surfaced in her mind that day.

"Democracy is a word found only in the dictionary," Mike had said. "Discrimination is found everywhere."

Bitter words, she thought. They hadn't meant much then, but now she knew what he meant. No court was impartial where Indians were concerned, despite what she had heard in civics class.

Very well, Judge, Kristen thought. You have taken away my citizenship. You have made me an Indian again. You have sentenced me to return to the reservation. I will leave your class-conscious society and return to my Ojibwa place at the bottom of American society. But I will take my daughters with me. If I am Ojibwa, they are Ojibwa.

The loaded canoe drifted away from the portage below the cascading waterfall. Kristen dipped her paddle in the water and they continued their journey. As they floated down the river, all the pain of the past few months resurfaced and the dreamlike lunacy of it all tormented Kristen's mind.

"I had no other choice," she said to herself.

CHAPTER 3

G RAND MARAIS, MINNESOTA, was a collection of wooden buildings on the rocky shore of Lake Superior. It spread up the slope of the Sawtooth Range which was a part of the Laurentian Mountain chain that formed the border between the United States and Canada. The town harbor was divided by two arms of a storm-ravaged seawall that reached out to a shelf rock, a barrier that protected the port from the restless lake. A Coast Guard station and lighthouse stood on the barrier, sentinels facing the row of businesses at the water's edge. The town's streets sprawled up the mountainside past the high school, the hospital, and the Cook County Courthouse.

Errol Joyce was pure lawyer. Not just a member of the bar, not some collection agent who used his law degree and courtroom presence to muscle a fast settlement for a quick buck, but lawyer in blood and bone and sinew, lawyer in heart and brain and soul. In fact, at this time of his life, when he argued the law before the Minnesota bar of justice, he was considered by many of his peers to be the best trial lawyer in the state.

It was Errol's habit to walk every morning from his living quarters to the lighthouse that straddled the seawall of Grand Marais Bay. It was a short stroll from his apartment to the lighthouse, and few people walked the jetty at that early hour. Halfway in his course, he stopped, took off his shoes and socks, and walked barefoot the rest of the way. Nature had laid down a volcanic rock barrier to protect the harbor. Over time, the waters had washed the rock smooth, leaving a texture Joyce had discovered was soft, sensual to the feet. He enjoyed the stroll. The cool air on his face and feet put extra spring in his step. He walked like a boy, free of care and worry, drenched in morning sun. And his was the self-confident walk of a man who knew who he was, who was doing what he wanted to do. He strode with back straight, hips rolling, feet moving like a professional boxer's, in a rhythm that was at once both swaggering and delicate.

Errol, however, now stood still—solemn, dignified, and shoeless. His body was lanky and muscular, like an athlete's. A diamond ring glistened on the small finger of his left hand, simple and elegant. He quickly scanned the rock shore for friends, while a thin, wry smile played on his lips.

"That goddamn sea gull," he muttered.

A bird had interrupted his sun-bask by knocking his shoes and socks off the sea wall. It now clung to the girder above him like a weathervane, its feathers ruffling in the wind blowing across the Minnesota causeway from Lake Superior, a wind that raised goosebumps on the lawyer's skin and made the paper in his hands flap and flutter.

Errol was a man who always looked the part of a trial lawyer, from his neatly-pressed, tailored suit to his gleaming shoes. The shoes he'd lost over the parapet were polished to a high sheen. His hands that held the sheet of paper were rough but carefully manicured. Whether he was in public, or out in the woods, his chin was so closely shaven it seemed glossy. His perfectly waved gray hair added a touch of old world dignity to his youthful mien.

Errol stood under the shadow of the lighthouse at the entrance to the Grand Marais harbor. He looked across the bay toward his office, then glanced down at the letter he'd brought along to study. In neat script, his client had written that she'd decided not to wait for his help. There was more, too. He needed to talk to his old friend, P.M. Gregory. He shook his head and rolled the stiff paper into a cylinder. Turning, he left the seagull to its balancing act on the girder and commenced the quarter-mile walk around the bay, stepping along the flat, smooth ledges and over sharp stones.

Errol could think of no way to avoid the tourists and fishermen, so he ignored them. They stared at his bare feet. The lawyer's bottle-green eyes fixed on a point straight ahead as he strode purposefully toward the converted warehouse that served as his home and office at the harbor dock, as if oblivious to the incongruity of bare feet and immaculate suit.

"It's a lovely morning," called a fisherwoman as he stepped past her like a man walking on hot coals.

"Indeed it is," the lawyer replied affably.

The short, wrinkled Indian woman held a wooden pole in her leathery hands. The lawyer was forty-seven and he judged the woman who spoke to be twice his age.

The others along his path pretended he wasn't shoeless, until after he passed. Then they turned and stared at his naked feet, their faces awash in puzzlement.

Errol climbed the wooden stairs to his office. The remodeled warehouse, a part of the fishing village architecture that nestled at the edge of Grand Marais harbor, had a single loft room next to the lawyer's suite which served as an office for former District Judge, P.M. Gregory. It was Errol's habit, and pleasure, to look in on his friend each day. The retired judge was a small man, wiry, almost elfin. P.M. always dressed as if prepared to attend his own funeral. Errol's eighty-year-old friend was a quiet, pensive man with an acquired judicial temperament.

P.M. had turned his law practice over to a young Errol Joyce when he went on the bench. After he reached mandatory retirement age, the judge returned to private practice, setting up his office in the building with Errol. The elderly widower passed his time examining land titles for banks and insurance companies that foreclosed on delinquent mortgages of timber lands.

Errol walked down the hallway past his friend's open door. P.M. looked over his desk, down at Errol's bare feet. His expression was noncommittal, blank as the inside of a new bowl. Several steps beyond, he stopped, turned, and went back and stood in the doorway of the old man's office.

"I suppose," he said after a moment, "that you're surprised to see me without my shoes on." Errol slapped the rolled paper against his thigh. "And I suppose you want to know why."

P.M. looked up from his desk and grunted. "Errol," he said, peering through his thick eyeglasses, "very few things you do surprise me, and walking shoeless around town in the middle of the morning is not one of them." He turned once again to the business of studying his abstracts.

"I'll be back in a minute." Errol tossed the cylinder of paper atop an open law book on P.M.'s desk. "Like to talk to you about this letter."

P.M. grunted again, made no move to pick up the paper, which rolled back and forth in the crease of the book, curling and uncurling.

Errol shrugged, executed an about-face, and without another word went on down the hall to his own office.

Indifference irritated Errol. He was annoyed by his old friend's unconcern. And maybe that's what bothered him about Toli McLean and his son Arlie. He thought the professor wanted Cubby and Niki in his home, not because Kristen was an unfit mother, but because he considered his son's children to be his own possessions.

"These are my girls—mine!" the professor had repeated outside the Lake County courthouse in Two Harbors where the first contest took place. Toli McLean punched his finger at Errol Joyce's vest, but didn't touch him. Peter Hauck, attorney for the McLean family, restrained his client and turned Toli down the courthouse steps toward the professor's waiting wife and son.

"If the mother wants to come back to the McLean home," Hauck said quietly, "my clients will take her in. But they will fight to keep her from ever seeing those kids outside the McLean home."

Errol knew that Kristen was no ordinary mother. She truly cared about her daughters, and, more than that, she abhorred what they might become if Toli got his hands on them. A child withered under indifference. That's why abused children seldom came forward to sound the alarm. A beating was far better than indifference, although both were cruel.

Errol believed that Kristen had suffered cruelly from Arlie's indifference. He knew what it was to live in that loveless vacuum. Every woman he'd been attracted to had run from him once she discovered that he had a mistress. It made no difference that his mistress was the law, more demanding than a woman. Once his girlfriends learned of his true passion, they treated him with the yawning indifference of silence. He sensed that Kristen had suffered from that same hideous silence in her own marriage. She had tried to reach out and touch her husband, to draw him into the family. Indifference was intolerable from someone you loved deeply.

Errol entered his office, felt the peace of a man completely at home. He scanned the shelves of law books, found comfort in them. They were his life, the food on which he fed during every waking moment.

The clever architect, who remodeled the warehouse and leased space to him, had built an apartment into it for him, as well as a suite of offices.

He went on into his living quarters and rummaged in his closet for another pair of shoes. He was still bristling with anger over the McLean business. Kristen was wrong, dead wrong in the eyes of the law, but she was reacting as a mother, not as a rational individual.

From the highway, the Thunder Bay Reservation filling station, Walt Twohorses' piece of allotment land, appeared as worn and used as the junk cars sitting in the weeds behind it or the rusted pickup truck with a flat tire sitting in front of it. The single service bay at the side of the tiny station office, its door raised in a gaping yawn, looked like the entrance to a mechanical nightmare. An unidentifiable piece of machinery, with parts haphazardly scattered around it, rested on the floor inside. The wind was hot and smelled of tar and the musty scent of floating dust. Dirt from the gravel drive leading to the gasoline pumps drifted over the sill of the open doorway. A cracked concrete porch extended the length of the office beneath its large window, which was lined with posters and handbills.

A faded, hand-lettered sign on the front of the station announced, "Last Chance to Buy Cheap U.S. Gas Before Entering Canada." The words, "Tribal Police Station," had been painted over but were still legible. Walt said the government Indians hadn't been housed in the station for more than five years.

An old man and woman sat on the porch and watched Walt, who squatted at the left front wheel of their pickup.

The visiting couple were southeastern Chippewas, not of the Thunder Bay Ojibwa band. Max and Alma Kadunce had driven from Iroquois Point where the powerful outpour of water at the eastern end of Lake Superior met the Saulte Ste. Marie. There, several broad arms of water separated, united, and divided again. The Kadunces were not reservation Indians. They did not have to live by reservation rules. Their home was a place where masses of primeval rock had been blasted by ingenious white men into a channel, and locks had been built to gentle the water to permit ocean vessels to pass into lower Lake Huron to continue passage to the

St. Lawrence Seaway and finally the Atlantic Ocean.

Near the Saulte locks, the combination of the variously formed waters repeatedly collected in large pools where they became calm and then shot in narrow passages from one lake to another, forming the great rapids that the shipping locks bypassed. In this manner, a labyrinth of large and small islands was formed. The shores of the islands and continent were covered with dense forests of evergreens. On the Canadian side coursed the final spires of the Canadian chain of mountains, which were broken through by the water gods, as the Indians said, to give the lake its air.

In some places the islands and shores at the eastern end of Lake Superior were still as feral as the border lakes near the Thunder Bay Reservation, where Max and Alma had driven.

Before his mandatory retirement, Max had worked for the government in the warehouse of the port authority at the Saulte locks. The homeland of the Indian couple was as exquisite as the border lakes they were visiting.

The Thunder Bay Reservation had been home to Alma until her tenth summer, when her parents gave up their band registration cards and moved to the east end of the lake to find work. Max claimed that for two generations his Kadunce clan had not been registered on any Indian reservation. His family, he said, were southeastern Chippewa, residents of upper Michigan, who long ago gave up the government bait. After Max retired, Alma persuaded him to take her back to visit the border lakes, her ancestral home, and the family she had left behind.

Max Kadunce sat on the concrete porch beside his wife and watched Alma's cousin, the youngest member of the Thunder Bay tribal council, a big boy with eyes black as obsidian beads, snapping with sparks, change the front tire on the truck. Alma listened to the two men talk while her cousin, Walt Twohorses, methodically went about replacing the truck's flat tire with a spare.

Sticking out from the pickup bed was the worm-eaten, weather-beaten bow of the old couple's fishing boat. They had hauled it all the way from Iroquois Point. A borrowed fifteen-horsepower Mercury motor lay in the bottom of the old craft, wedged between two logs to keep it from rocking from side to side. The unlatched tailgate hung loosely at the back to accommodate the fishing boat.

Walt grunted as he wedged the tire beneath the rusted fender. Sweat had darkened patches on his workshirt beneath the arms. Once he had the tire positioned he screwed on the lug nuts.

"Why don't you get rid of that wooden scow and buy my Alumacraft?"

Walt asked. He jerked his thumb toward the battered sixteen-foot boat tipped against the wall beneath the filling station's large front window.

"Nothing wrong with my boat."

"Too damn heavy." The younger Indian pounded on the tire with the heel of his hand.

"Had that boat for thirty years."

"Too damn heavy."

"I can get it in and out of the truck all right," Max said.

"Sure," Alma agreed, "with my help."

Walt laughed. "That's what I mean. If you're going back on the lakes to search for the rice beds and you want to take that Alumacraft of mine, I'll let you have it for a good price." The big man stood and kicked the tire. "Besides, you and Alma can't carry that thing on a portage."

"Hell," Max waved his hands helplessly, "where are we going to portage a boat and motor now'days? It's all canoes. They've got those damn regulations now, so the only place we can run a motor is on Saganaga and Northern Light lake and we can use railroad portage to cross there."

"I'll let you have the boat over there for a hundred dollars even."

"Where would I get a hundred dollars?"

"Let you have it for eighty bucks and your old scow."

"Where the hell would I get eighty bucks?"

Walt stopped his work on the tire and watched as a car with Canadian license plates pulled off the highway, moving fast, hit a pothole and bottomed out as it slid up to the gasoline pumps.

Walt operated the only filling station on the reservation, and once visiting Canadians crossed the border at Pigeon River bridge they bought the cheaper gas on the state's side from him or drove another twenty miles down the shore to the town of Hoveland.

Walt walked to the pumps.

The old Indian turned to his wife. "We're going to be late getting started, but I don't think we better go back up on the end of the trail without a spare tire. We better wait until Walt gets it fixed."

Alma ignored his statement. She looked up at the overcast scrim that hid the sun. Her eyes were deeply watchful, watery and red. Old-woman eyes, sad and wise. "We're going to get a change in the weather," she announced, "but that haze is smoke, not rain clouds." Her voice was low and brittle as a dried corn husk. She measured the heaviness of the air, the smell.

Max didn't answer. He watched Walt return and the Canadian car spin out of the driveway. "No sale?"

Walt shook his head and clenched his jaw. "Nope." He knelt at the tire on the ground beside the truck. "These Canadians don't know the difference between the Imperial gallon and the American gallon." Walt's white teeth glared. "They think we're cheating Indians when we tell them they're going to get four quarts to a gallon instead of five like they get on their side of the border. I told them if they thought they could do any better with white men, to drive on down to Hoveland."

The younger Indian started wedging open the nail hole in the tire and lathering it with glue to hold the plug. "You better use this tire for a spare. The one I put on has better tread than this one."

Max grunted.

For a few moments the old couple sat and watched the younger man work on the spare. Finally Max asked, "Who are you going to support on casino gambling? Engel or Marie?" Max had heard the two Indian leaders debate the new law when Alma's cousin invited him to their tribal government meeting.

"Hell," exploded Walt, "Marie, of course. Engel Tormudson has got no business arguing with Marie for putting gaming machines in the hotel. When Congress passed the Gaming Act back in '88, that wasn't just to give us more government paper. It was to help the economy of the Indian tribes by letting us put in casino gambling."

"It's not real gambling, only government bait," Max said. "Just lets the tribe put in electronic games that imitate poker, black jack, slot machines, roulette and craps."

"I know, but ours is the first of the tribes to enter into a compact with the State of Minnesota to have gaming operations. Hell, it's better than nothing. Eighty casino games will create twenty or thirty jobs for our people."

"If you can draw a crowd. You're going to need players from off the Agency."

"Marie's planning on doing some room renovations in the lodge. It's the best chance we've got for economic development up here," Walt added. "Engel hasn't come up with anything better. He's opposing it because it was Marie Saulturs' idea."

"Well, I wouldn't say that," Max said. "Engel says he is just trying to keep some of the older traditions. I think he's afraid of what'll happen if Marie's plan for high stakes bingo and video casino games goes in. I had a long talk with Engel the other night after your tribal council meeting. The man's got some strong arguments against Marie's plans."

"What was Engel complaining to you about?"

"He says Marie is the one who came up with the idea for the tribe to create two subsidiary corporations under Minnesota law. One to build the Hotel and Convention Center. The other to buy the Wedgewood-Ben truck line."

"So?"

"Engel's argument is that after doing that, the hotel costs were more than expected, and that caused the tribe to take on more debt than planned. He says the tribe then refinanced the hotel with bankers back east to get in the trucking business. Engel says she's mortgaged the tribe to where it will never get out of debt. Bankruptcy, that's where he says she's headed . . . bankruptcy."

"What did Engel say the tribe should do?"

"Engel's idea is the tribe should have stayed like it was. He says the tribe needs to attract tourists but not by getting so far in debt it goes broke."

"Did he say he had a plan?"

"Get out of the trucking business! Then he wants to refinance the debt so the tribe can handle the hotel payments without going broke. He says everyone on the reservation should just tighten their belts and look to developing the fishing industry and get back to the simpler way of doing things."

Alma spoke up, her tone challenging. "You mean like taking the electricity out of the reservation houses and having the women carry the water like my mother used to do?"

"He says that's better than living the way the white population lives, polluting streams, cutting down forests for pulpwood, poisoning the lakes with mining tailings dumped into the harbors. He says a return to the old ways would be better than that."

"When you've lived on the reservation as long as I have," Walt Twohorses said, "you realize we're never goin' to go back to the old ways. In fact, we'll be lucky to make our allotment payments and not get caught by the Agency termination policy and lose our land. That's the reason I voted for Marie Saulturs to be chairman and chief of the tribal council. The woman's smart. She's got a college degree. She's worked for the tribe since before the riots in the Dakotas, when we all went over there to support the civil rights marches.

"That woman's got a lot on the ball. If we had elected somebody like

Engel Tormudson as council chairman, we would never have gotten the money for our hotel and truck line. Even if it is more government bait, this plan of hers to put in video gaming in the hotel is going to add more jobs for our people."

"Engel says Marie is going to get the tribe into trouble with the government over forming the hotel and truck line corporations."

"Shit! Engel's just saying that because he wasn't smart enough to think of it."

Max leaned back and wrapped his arm around his knee. "Engel's no dumbbell. He graduated from college, too. He's had one year in law school and he's just about as smart as Marie is."

"I doubt that," Alma said. She was ready to defend the woman who had been elected chief of the Thunder Bay tribe.

Walt walked over and got the air hose. He knelt again at the tire. Over the sound of the air rushing, he shouted, "Alma, you're prejudiced."

"Well," she said, "that was one time you men on the tribal council did something right."

Walt laughed. "When we elected Marie chief, we made every woman in the tribe happy." Again Walt laughed. "My old woman is just like Alma. She thinks Marie Saulturs can do no wrong." The big Indian rose and kicked the tire. "There, that ought to get you down to Grand Marais and up to the end of the Gunflint Trail."

"As long as I get only one more flat."

Walt rolled up his air hose. He picked up the tire and deposited it in the pickup truck behind the cab. "You two going to be back tonight?"

"Maybe. Maybe not." Max and Alma stood up.

"If you stay over, ask Thor Elmgren at Sag store to let you borrow a tent and sleeping bags. Alma and you can sack out at the end of the trail and come back some time tomorrow."

"We don't plan to stay over."

Walt wiped his hands on a rag and walked to the truck cab. Max and Alma climbed in and shut the doors.

"Seriously, Walt," the older Indian said, leaning out the window. "Chippewa politics is your game. I know you think a lot of Marie Saulturs, but if she keeps going the way she is, the tribe may get so overextended, the bankers will take everything the tribe's got. You've got your necks stuck way out with those loans. Engel tells me the tribe's in deep financial trouble."

"Max, we don't have any choice. We can't pay our allotment fees without money. There isn't anything the federal government or the State of Minnesota, with all their economic projects, is going to do for the Ojibwa band stuck off up here. Government money is going to be spent in the big cities. Minneapolis, Chicago or back east. Any place except here. The tribe is only going to get what money it makes for itself."

Max Kadunce fired up the engine on the truck.

Walt shouted. "Engel Tormudson is just pissed off because we elected a woman as chief of the tribe, rather than him."

Max gunned the engine and started rolling across the filling station drive.

Walt waved. "Let's talk some more."

As the old truck bounced onto Highway 61 and headed down the north shore toward Grand Marais, Alma looked out the rear window. The wooden boat and the motor they had borrowed had not shifted.

As they rolled down the highway, Alma settled back on the bench seat. "Let's go see if we can find the rice beds."

Max tromped his foot down on the accelerator.

After Errol put on fresh-laundered socks and slipped on a pair of polished dress shoes, he walked down the hall and stopped at his friend's doorway again. "Damn it, P.M.," he said, "aren't you going to ask me why I wasn't wearing my shoes this morning?"

The old man continued to peer down at his desk through the magnifying glass he was holding. But Errol saw that he had read Kristen's letter. It had been smoothed out and laid flat on an uncluttered spot atop the desk next to that week's copy of the *Cook County News-Herald*.

"Nope."

"Well, I wouldn't tell you even if you did ask."

"I'll hear about it from someone who saw you tiptoeing around barefoot," growled the old man. P.M. looked up at Errol, cocked an elfin eye at him. "Now, do you want to talk about this letter?"

Errol slid into a chair.

P.M. was born in an Ely, Minnesota logging camp to the camp cook who had married his father, the chief timber spotter. He graduated from Hibbing Normal School and read law in Duluth before passing the bar and establishing his office on the north shore of Lake Superior. Here, Errol thought, was a rock he could sit on when the tide got too high. From his octogenarian perch, the sly old bird had the ability to make the thoughts of others seem shallow, trivial, although he did it without condescension. Those who knew him simply regarded P.M. as a man worth listening to. Errol counted himself as one of those who valued P.M.'s opinion.

Errol's glance drifted to the certificate that hung on P.M.'s wall certifying the former judge to be a Senior Counselor, no longer required to pay annual bar dues to the State of Minnesota. That's what Kristen McLean needs, Errol thought, a senior counselor.

"Errol, if your client does what she says she's going to do, what you've got here," P.M. pointed to Kristen's letter, "is an admission of guilt. What are you going to do about it?"

"I'd like to reopen the case. What she wrote puts an entirely different light on the court's initial decision."

"You lost the first time. What makes you think you can win this second time?"

"A hunch?"

"You can't win lawsuits on hunches. You need evidence, Errol."

"Something, or somebody, made that woman think about running. Made her think she must take her girls and run for her life."

"Do you want to know what I think?"

"That's why I'm here."

"You don't have a snowball's chance in hell of winning this case if you reopen it." The little man arched his eyebrows.

"Thanks," Errol said, cracking a wry grin. "I needed that."

"Glad to help." P.M. picked up Kristen's letter, rolled it back up again like a scroll and handed it to Errol. "Talk to me any time, son."

The Indian driver and Jan Kiel were standing beside a Wedgewood-Ben tractor-trailer unit when Errol arrived. He carried a thermos tucked under his arm. The driver was explaining, "Our tractors are Peterbilts, top of the line, and the tanks and trailer chassis are manufactured by the Collier Steel Company down at Terre Haute—"

Jan interrupted the man and turned to the approaching lawyer. "You're late," she said in an accusing tone of voice. She spoke as if the evening she and Errol had spent together the night before had never happened.

Over dinner, Errol had found that Jan could be gracious, gentle, sympathetic, a very charming partner. But when she was at her job as the
Assistant Attorney General for the State of Minnesota, she was thought by
most lawyers to be an intransigent bitch, an image she cultivated after she
had commenced her work in the profession that heretofore had been dominated by men.

"I had problems," Errol answered. He nodded to the driver in greeting.

"So I heard." Jan climbed up into the cab. "And, if what I heard about
you this morning is true, you'd better start taking some counseling sessions before Judge Clemens orders you locked up."

Errol rankled at Jan's words. He grabbed the handhold and swung up
on the seat in the cab beside her. He set the thermos bottle on the floor by
his feet, then slammed the tractor's door shut. "Did you ever stop to think
that there might be a logical explanation for why I walked back from the
lighthouse today without my shoes on?"

"Of course, Errol," Jan said brightly. Her eyes opened wide in feigned
innocence. "That's perfectly normal conduct for a bright lawyer—walking
around fully dressed except for his shoes. That really gives your clients a
lot of assurance. 'Not a bad attorney,' they'll say, 'except he forgets to put
on his shoes.' Dumb, Errol. Real dumb."

With a gesture of irritation, Errol signaled the grinning truck driver to
start their trip. If Jan expected that she was going to get an explanation
about the morning incident, then she would be disappointed. P.M. Gregory
had been indifferent, but the woman who had charmed him the night
before was being sarcastic, and Errol could handle that. Sarcasm was just
one of any good lawyer's valuable stocks-in-trade.

"Touchè," Errol said, *sotto voce*.

The truck lurched away, the roar of its engine drowning out all
conversation.

CHAPTER 4

EAST OF THE TOWN OF HOVELAND, on the north shore highway, repair work by road construction crews had been suspended and the workmen and their machinery had been sent off into the national forest preserve to fight the summer fires. The tractor-trailer unit carrying the two lawyers and their Indian driver, John Whitehorse, snaked through construction barricades and followed a single line of automobiles as serpentine traffic made its way along the cliffs of Lake Superior and climbed the long grade to the palisade at Five-Mile-Rock. Before reaching the summit, the procession of cars stopped. Whitehorse barely had room to pass them, as he shifted gears and prepared to pick up speed for their downhill run.

"Oh, my!" Jan gasped.

As the tractor began its descent toward the valley floor, Whitehorse and his passengers saw the reason the other vehicles had stopped. Spread out below, a raging fire, whipped by surface wind and eating its way through trees and scrub undergrowth, spewed flame and smoke out of the interior of the forest. The smaller vehicles had ground to a halt and were backing up and turning away from the surging fire line.

Whitehorse twisted his steering wheel to avoid crashing his fuel load into a recreational vehicle sitting in the middle of the road. The trailer and tank scraped the guard rail and Whitehorse accelerated to prevent the unit from sliding. The burst of speed sent the tractor-trailer careening forward toward the flames.

"Hang on," yelled Whitehorse.

The Indian skillfully shifted gears and aimed the rig for the open center of the blacktop highway. The road tar had begun to soften and bubble like volcanic lava at the edge of the pavement.

The tractor-trailer raced across the valley floor where the violent blaze burned fallen trees leveled by windstorms and disease. Jan clung to Errol and braced her feet against the floorboard to keep her slender body from sliding off the bench seat. Both lawyers and their Ojibwa driver swayed from side to side as the tanker sped past the exploding inferno toward a granite palisade that overlooked Lake Superior's north shore. The thermos rattled and banged against the door until Errol trapped it between his feet. Woodsmoke engulfed the highway. The three people gasped and began to choke.

"Jesus Christ!" exclaimed Errol as Whitehorse downshifted and started a climb that would take their volatile cargo out onto a ledge of rock where the roadway would put them beyond the reach of the flames.

The conflagration was, in part, a crownfire, one that consumed the topmost foliage. Gusting winds relentlessly drove embers from the doomed trees. An unexpected shift in the blaze had sent it raging out of the deep woods and onto the edge of the coastal highway. The freight-train roar of the heat storm assaulted their ears.

"Is this the fastest this sonofabitch will run?" Errol muttered, his face a grim mask of concern. The stoic driver wrestling with the steering wheel didn't reply.

The tractor unit pulled the tank over the top of the grade. The tractor entered a cut in the granite bluff and the two lawyers sagged in the seat with a sudden sense of relief. Whitehorse brought the rig to a halt alongside the sheer cliff. Hot orange sparks, burning clusters of vegetation, blew off the rock face above them and out into Lake Superior, winking out before they landed or sputtering to gray ash as they struck the water.

The three occupants leaped from the cab and ran to the far edge of the protecting cliff. Below, the blue expanse of water churned in winds generated by the fire storm.

"God damn, that was close!" Errol exclaimed.

Jan shook a flake of clinging gray ash from her blonde hair. "This has to be the dumbest thing I have ever done in my whole life!"

The State's Attorney was startlingly attractive, tall and slender, with compelling features, nice lips, strong and full, good facial structure, yet open and wholesome, as if she'd scrubbed her face with sunshine and cream. But at that moment she was unaware of her own good looks as she thought how great it was just to be alive.

Whitehorse, a short, muscular man with a pleasant, burnished wooden face that never revealed emotion, scraped a match on his boot and touched it to a cigarette. He squatted at the side of the road and looked back down into the valley of fire through which he had just wrestled his cargo of fuel. Flames had crossed the two lanes and both sides of Highway 61 were now ablaze. The fire danced crazily in the shifting wind, scattering sparks and smoke in all directions.

Whitehorse pointed. "Even the trees that only have their crowns burned off will die." He took a drag on his cigarette. He didn't really speak to his two passengers. He was just talking out loud, as if mesmerized by the flames. "The pine will die, except for the jack pines. Usually jack pines, aspen, and birch will survive a fire. Next spring that entire area down there will be waist high in vegetation again—grasses, sedges, fern, sprouts, jack pine seedlings. Nature is wonderful."

"We damn near get caught in a fire with four thousand gallons of gasoline and you say, 'nature is wonderful'?"

Whitehorse nodded. "Sure, life changes and fire is part of it. Everything's gotta adapt, even us. Next spring there will be little shoots of aspen . . . rabbits and mice'll come back, followed by bobcats and fox, and they'll be followed by the moose and the wolves. Fire in the forest always brings new life."

As he said the words, Whitehorse thought of the Indian woman, Kristen McLean.

He took another pull on his cigarette and continued to stare off into the valley. His cropped hair was black, his skin pale as sand, thick and rough. Mani! He thought of the name he called Kristen when they were growing up on the reservation. He wondered if she and her kids would find a new life. The Ojibwa mother had come to him for help. Whitehorse knew Kristen would find the canoe and camp gear on the shore of Gunflint Lake where he had left them. But he wondered if the fire that Kristen was igniting by her flight would put in motion a surge of new life. Or would she be consumed by its blaze?

Highway traffic in both directions was stopped well back from the palisade where the fuel truck was parked. The drivers of all the other vehicles had given the gasoline tanker a wide berth when they realized that it could not turn around in the narrow road and was forced to run the gauntlet of fire.

A black streak of soot marred the giant "W-B" logo on the side of the tanker.

Jan watched as Errol walked back to the truck cab and retrieved the thermos of coffee.

Throughout his career Errol had been a sole practitioner with an office in Grand Marais, Minnesota, but with a practice that extended as far south as Albert Lea. The lawyer was a difficult man to get along with. Some said he was not well liked. However, no member of the bar doubted that Errol was one of Minnesota's best trial counsels. Some thought him to be the best.

His representation of members of the Indian community dated from early civil disobedience cases on South Dakota's Mandan Indian Reservation. He was the young lawyer the tribal council brought into the state to defend unpopular lawsuits when Bismark lawyers refused representation.

Although Errol could be described as being a loner, lawyer Jan Kiel was best described as simply being alone. Errol lived the solitary life by choice. He had chosen the law for a mistress. But an alcoholic father and a demanding mother motivated Jan to build her defensive barriers against those who would intrude on her privacy.

Jan wasn't certain of Errol's age, but knew that he had graduated from the University of Minnesota Law School twelve years before she had, and she was thirty-two. Jan had tried several criminal cases against Errol, but this Wedgewood-Ben litigation was their first confrontation in a civil case. For safety reasons, the trucking line's permit to use state highways was at risk. Jan's relationship with Errol was different from those she had had with other men. Professionally, she held Errol at arm's length, and her determination in that regard intruded into their social life. She could not bring herself to put her emotions at risk.

Jan Kiel had worked her way through law school, employed by an air charter service at the Minneapolis airport. She was acknowledged to be an expert on aviation law, and she had been employed for the past seven years as Assistant Attorney General of the State of Minnesota, working out of the Duluth regional office. Many considered her to be one of the State's best trial counsels.

While Jan watched Errol cross the highway to the gasoline rig, she thought back to the State Bar meeting when she'd first felt a strong magnetic attraction to the man, a tide-pull on her senses, a surging in her veins like the sea under a full moon, a skip-beat of her heart that left her breathless and unsettled.

Jan remembered the spring morning when the meeting of the Minnesota Bar had been held on the Duluth campus of the university, overlooking the twin ports. Both she and Errol had been scheduled to speak to the assembly. Errol had waited for her at the edge of the speaker's platform.

Errol scanned the printed program he held in his hands.

> Air Traffic Analysis and Reconstruction
> of Air Craft Accidents and Incidents.
> Speaker: Jan Kiel, corporate jet pilot, A.T.C.O.;
> Assistant Attorney General, State of Minnesota;
> graduate University of Minnesota, School of Law, 1977.

Jan scurried up to the platform and flashed him a bright smile. "I'm not late," she said, pointing to her watch.

"No, we have plenty of time."

Jan peered out into the auditorium. "I hope I don't screw this up."

"No way that can happen. There aren't five lawyers out there who know a damn thing about aviation law."

"Then I can speak freely."

"I didn't know you were a pilot."

"I have a De Havilland Beaver with amphib floats, or," she corrected herself, "I should say the bank and I have a De Havilland Beaver. I'll take you up for a ride some time, if you like."

"Are you really licensed to fly corporate jets?" he asked.

"Sure am, mister. What you read there is what you get." She had tapped her finger on his printed program. "That's how I paid my way through law school."

"How did that happen?"

Jan shrugged. "When I was a kid in high school, I worked as a secretary part time for a charter outfit in exchange for flying lessons. They let me stay on as one of their pilots when I was studying to be a lawyer. By the time I got through seven years of college I qualified for my Air Taxi/Commercial Operator's rating and had enough IFR and night hours to qualify to fly their corporate jet. During my last year in law school, two overnight flights to the west coast would about pay my expenses for a month."

The audience began to file into the rows and take their seats.

"Why did you study law?" Errol asked.

"Why did you?"

"I always wanted to be a lawyer."

"So did I. Does that surprise you?"

"No, It's just hard for me to think of you as growing up wanting to be a lawyer or a pilot."

"What do you think I should have wanted to be? A nurse? A house-wife? A mother with a half a dozen kids?"

"Well." She caught him off guard. "Damn it, Jan, you know what I mean."

"Errol, you mean you think women have no business being either lawyers or pilots."

"I never said that."

Jan stood close and tilted her face to him. "I know what you're think-ing, but I'm still willing to give you a ride in my airplane."

"Now why would I let you get me in an airplane with you?"

"I'm pretty good, mister. Want to take a chance?" she asked brightly.

"I'm willing to talk," Errol said with a laugh. "With me everything is negotiable."

Jan smiled provocatively. "With me some things are not negotiable at any price."

"You are a tease."

"Nope, just telling it like it is." She smiled.

Errol changed the subject. "What are you going to say in your speech? Should I stick around after I introduce you?"

"Of course," Jan said. "How are you going to know how to sue me when we crash in the Beaver if you haven't learned about aviation law?"

"I don't think you're going to get me up in your airplane."

"We'll see." She smiled again.

As Errol prepared to escort the speaker onto the stage of the auditori-um, he confided, "I prefer canoes."

The morning following the session of the State Bar meeting, the DHC-2 Amphibian Beaver hurtled along two hundred feet above the sur-face of Lake Superior at a hundred and thirty-five miles per hour.

"For Christ's sake, Jan, these things are supposed to fly higher than this!" Errol shouted, gripping the metal edge of his seat. He could hardly make himself heard above the throb of the radial engine. Looking out the window, he could see the water racing below the aircraft's high wing, which was held in place by its massive single brace.

"Don't sweat it," Jan shouted back as she deftly maneuvered the aircraft parallel to the coastal highway. "We have a hundred miles of runway to land on right in front of us, under our pontoons."

The surface of Lake Superior that morning was glass smooth, marred only in a few spots by thinning early morning fog where waters cascading off the Masabe Range spilled into the lake. At the time, Jan did not know that Errol, who had ridden with bush pilots on fishing trips out of Ely, wasn't keen about flying in her ancient De Havilland. But the weather was ideal, and Errol didn't want her to entertain doubts about his masculinity. He later confessed that he felt she was putting him to the test.

Jan flew the aircraft offshore, holding it low to the water as she overtook the vehicle traffic driving Highway 61. Their view of the rocks at Castle Danger and Gooseberry Falls was stunning, with the morning sun reflecting off the water in showers of spun gold. Tourists inside the Split Rock Lighthouse were startled to see the airplane pass below them. Truckers driving the highway on the palisades waved and called on their CB radios for others to watch for the crazy pilot who was flying up the lake at an altitude lower than the roadbed.

Jan pulled the throttle wide open, lifted the nose of the airplane and climbed at a steep angle. Then, with a breathtaking slide off of one wing, she dropped over a point of land and at the last minute leveled off for a landing in the bay at Grand Marais. As they sliced across the harbor and settled onto the pontoons, Errol released his white knuckled grip on the seat.

Jan taxied past the Coast Guard station and shut off the engine. The pontoons carried them to sheltered waters inside the sea wall, where they had a breathtaking view of the town sprawled up the side of the mountain.

"You know my car and my luggage are back in Duluth," Errol said.

Jan nodded. "I know. I just wanted to fly up here this morning. The north shore is so beautiful and I love your town."

They rocked gently on the surface and for a few moments neither spoke.

"What happened to what's-her-name? I thought you and she were pretty thick."

"You mean my artist friend from Duluth? She left."

"Are you that hard to get along with?" Jan asked bluntly.

"Probably," Errol admitted. He glanced over at her. "How about you? Why haven't you ever married?"

Jan shrugged. "I've never met the right man I guess—maybe I'm not the marrying type."

It bothered the lawyer to talk about herself. She was curious about Errol Joyce, but she didn't want to discuss her own life. The memories of her father were too bitter. Her dreams of having a child of her own were too haunting. Turning on the switch, she made the engine kick over the propeller and the aircraft began to plow through the water of the harbor.

Neither had been completely frank that spring morning.

Ever since Errol left his family's hard-scrabble farm near New Ulm, Minnesota, his one true love had been the law. For her part, Jan wanted to be loved and to have a child of her own; and there had been many men in her life who wanted to have her and make a child. But she thought marriage was fragile and she could never commit herself to raising a family.

"This has been some trip!" Errol shouted. "Not only do you scare me half to death with your flying, but you land in the Grand Marais harbor just to ask me why I never married; and then take off again."

Jan laughed. "We have to get back to the bar meeting," she shouted.

As the De Havilland rose from the harbor, Errol leaned over to Jan. "Before the canoe season is over, I'm going up into the Quetico Park for a few days," he shouted. "Want to come along? We can talk up there."

Jan thought for a moment. "All right."

"I have only a two-man tent to sleep in," he yelled.

"That's all right."

"And I have only one sleeping bag."

"Now that, we will have to talk about," she said, laughing.

The pontoon plane rose above the coast, and as the harbor and town dropped away behind it, the aircraft turned west toward Duluth.

Jan Kiel was jarred from her musing by the voice of Errol Joyce.

"Coffee?" he offered.

"Yes, thanks."

Errol sat on the rock beside Jan and opened the thermos he had retrieved from the cab of the W-B tractor trailer unit. As they sipped scalding coffee from plastic cups, they watched the Ojibwa driver inspect his rig. The flames in the valley began to die down after crossing the road and reaching the water's edge. There was no morning sun in the sky, only haze.

Jan saw a vagrant blaze shoot up through a stand of pines and shuddered. She closed her eyes for a moment as if to shake off a bad feeling.

"The fire bother you that much?"

Jan sighed. "I was thinking about my father. When he was drunk, he was very careless with fire. He smoked and would fall asleep with lit cigarettes when he was drinking. He set a workroom on fire once when he was carving a wooden toy for my birthday, and another time he caused our back yard to burn up. I always wondered what would happen if he ever got drunk in the woods."

"I'm sorry."

"It was just a passing thought. I don't even know where my father is."

Whitehorse walked back to the rock where the couple sat. "Is there anything else you two want to know about tractor-trailer units that haul tanks of high octane gasoline?"

"I've already learned more than I want to know about driving fuel tankers. I was just plain dumb to let you persuade me to take this trip," she said to Errol.

"It was a hairy ride," Errol admitted, looking down into the smoking valley, "but you told Judge Clemens you wanted to know how these units operated and the best way to find out is to take a ride in one."

"Did you feel the fuel load surge to one side as we rounded the curves?" asked the Indian.

"I could feel the swaying from side to side."

The Ojibwa squatted and with a stick drew a diagram in the sand at the edge of the road. "The tanks are built with four compartments. The walls and baffles run crossways. This allows the fuel, once it starts surging, to flow in a looping motion in each compartment. All they need is a baffle to divide each compartment lengthwise to lessen that effect when we are rounding curves and climbing hills."

The Ojibwa tribe has come a long way, thought Errol. He knew the story of Wedgewood-Ben well. He had researched for this court case with the zeal of a cartographer.

"May it please the court," Errol had argued, in support of his pre-trial motion, "the statement of facts in this case is as follows:

"In 1885 Viscount James Wedgewood-Ben founded the drayage business and became its namesake. First with draft animals, later with trucks imported from stateside, the company built a reputation on the notion that it would, for a price, haul anything that would move, anywhere. In 1935, after the shore road between Duluth and Fort William was completed, the corporation received authority to do business in the United States and started its border crossings. It received the first transportation license issued by the State to a motorized carrier. Following World War II the depressed Canadian economy forced many company changes. When the heirs of James Wedgewood-Ben chose to squander the remaining assets of the company in family quarrels and litigation, part of the company was sold off and only the transportation license for the route between Fort William and Minneapolis, via Duluth, was retained as an asset. It is this license that is in danger of being revoked by the State of Minnesota.

"In the spring of 1988, Marie Croche Saulturs was elected leader of her Ojibwa tribe. She negotiated the purchase of Wedgewood-Ben to provide employment for Indian drivers from the reservation. Marie Saulturs holds a master's degree from the University of Chicago, School of Economics, and she has led her tribe to make two investments that provide jobs for her people in Northern Minnesota's depressed economy. The first was the hotel and convention center that has been constructed on reservation land at the Pigeon River border crossing. The second was securing control of the Wedgewood-Ben corporation and its permits that allow the tribe to bring aviation fuel across the border into the United States.

"Marie Saulturs also negotiated the price for the aviation fuel the tribe takes from the trans-continental pipeline which was constructed from Canada's Northwest Territories to the Fort William shipping terminal; and she negotiated a sale of the fuel to airlines that service Minneapolis and Duluth."

Errol argued that the tribe was a model for other native Americans who had not done so well. The judge listened with interest, but did not dismiss the State's charge that the tribe's tractors were pulling tanks that were defective and dangerous across Minnesota highways. The State's Attorney, Jan Kiel, insisted on a demonstration of the tractor-trailer tankers.

"These units are as safe to pull across Minnesota highways as any other tanker manufactured by Collier Steel," Errol said to Jan. "All they need is a fix to stop the fuel in the tank from surging, and my client will do that."

"Will your client agree to the payment of a fine without a hearing?" Jan asked.

"How much of a fine?" Errol bargained.

"Twenty-five hundred dollars, and court costs. Your client has operated these units on the highways in violation of the Department of Transportation regulations," Jan reminded him.

"We fix the baffles, pay a twenty-five-hundred-dollar fine and court costs and my client gets a waiver of the regulations to give it time to make the fix without shutting down its operation."

"How long?"

"Ninety days."

"Sixty."

"Done." Errol closed the negotiations.

"Good, then that settles our lawsuit."

"Do you want to draw up the settlement papers, or shall I?"

"My office will prepare a stipulation and the form of judgment and send it up to you to look at before we show it to the judge."

Errol nodded his agreement.

Jan stood and handed the thermos cup back to him.

"Are you ready to ride back to Grand Marais?" he asked.

Jan shook her head. "No way! You two aren't going to get me back in that rig again. Now that we've got the case settled, I'm going down the highway to see if I can catch a ride back to my car with one of the tourists."

The two men watched in amusement as Jan started down the hill toward the line of vehicles that had stopped a quarter of a mile away.

"She's a beautiful woman." The Indian driver grinned.

Errol nodded. "I think so."

CHAPTER 5

THE LINE OF TRAFFIC CREPT SLUGGISHLY FORWARD, crawling south along the shore road away from the fireline, a rusted pickup lumbering valiantly in the lead.

Jan sat between the heavy-set couple whose ages she guessed to be in the late sixties. When Max consented to give Jan a ride to Grand Marais, Alma didn't object, but she refused to give up her side of the seat. Alma was round-faced, muscular, rotund as a wooden keg, with a fixed scowl that Jan thought was a sign of ill-temperament.

Jan pulled her skirt under her legs and placed a knee on each side of the pickup truck's gear shift. "I appreciate very much your giving me a ride back to my car."

"Glad to."

"I couldn't see myself getting back in that tanker rig again, after the ride I had."

"We didn't see you people come through the fire. I couldn't believe it when that gasoline tanker drove out of the smoke and stopped up there on the palisade. That must have been some ride."

"It was and I don't want to repeat it."

"Well, we're happy to give you a lift back down to Grand Marais." Max gripped the steering wheel with both hands.

The traffic picked up speed. The woman beside Jan said nothing.

Jan looked out the window at the scenic view, listening to the comforting

drone of the engine. The pickup followed the contour of Highway 61, a ribbon of asphalt that hugged the north shore of Lake Superior. Most of the
shoreline was rugged and rocky with beautifully wooded sections of high
bluffs and gravel beaches famous for their yield of agates and other gem
stones. Along the shore, rivers spilled fresh water from the south slope of
the wilderness into the lake.

For several miles they drove in silence. Max stared mindlessly at the
road. He was a fine figure of a man, Jan thought, with all his hair, a beak
like a hawk, and cheeks as sharply defined as the blade of a hatchet. Once
Jan saw the woman give her husband a quick glance, but mostly she sat
prim, her big, placid face as stoic and forbidding as a bulldog's rumpled
countenance.

"Where are you going now?" Jan asked the woman.

"We're going up on Lake Saganaga to look for ma-no-nien, our wild
rice."

"And to fish," Max added.

"With a motor?"

"The end of the Gunflint Trail is the one place where we are told we can
still take a fifteen-horse motorboat and go up into Canada. The old treaty
that established the border says that equal access to the border lakes has
to be given to citizens on both sides. That includes transportation back and
forth. So there's an area from the end of the Gunflint Trail to the Canadian
Customs Island, and beyond, where we can use a motorboat."

"I guess I should have known that."

"We can't go any farther west than the American Point or any farther
east than Saganaga Falls, with a motor, but that's an area some twenty
miles long and ten miles wide where we don't have to use a canoe."

Max started slowing the truck as they approached a roadside rest area
in a setting of tall pine trees. "I've got to stop for a minute."

"He has a spastic colon. He got shot in the butt during the war."

Max stopped the truck and got out.

The old Indian was robust, powerfully built, with block-square shoulders, sinewy arms, strong, bulky hands. He thought he was as fit as when
he served his time in the army. His eyes were still speckled with little
chips of quartz as they had been when he was eighteen. Max's mouth,
however, had become set in a thin tight line. Postwar years of manual
labor in a warehouse had kept his 180-pound frame lean as a bullwhip,
with little fat showing.

"Alma knows I wasn't shot in the ass," Max muttered.

He strode away, moving with a loose-boned, easy gait.

Jan and Alma sat in the truck in silence. The sun was high overhead. Haze from the fires turned the clouds in the sky gold and pink and gray. Cloud tatters hung in shifting layers of raw hot wind like strips of cotton batting, wispy storm-warning pennants.

After a few moments the old woman spoke. "The winters can be so harsh up here that the sap in the trees will freeze." Alma pointed to the stand of pine trees surrounding the rest area. "There is snow and ice all over but the water for the tree trunk is locked away," she continued, as if musing to herself. "The trees up here have to endure as much a drought in the winter as plants down south in the deserts."

"I never heard that before and I've lived in Minnesota all my life."

"It's true," Alma said, nodding to acknowledge Jan's interest. "It takes a special kind of leaf to withstand those conditions." The old woman continued to look out at the trees. "The pine needles are thin and long and snow doesn't set on them very easy and weigh them down. And, they contain little sap that can freeze. They're dark. They absorb heat from the sun."

"How did you know that?"

"The woods is our home." Alma said with a grin that flashed wolf-white.

"Let me show you something." Alma motioned Jan out of the cab and led her across the grader ditch.

As she followed the woman, Jan noted that Alma concealed the fullness of her body under a formless dress and loose jacket. Alma had a white halo of hair, blue eyes, and a sad, round face. She had masculine hands and heavy features, a broad frame. Thick ankles showed above her sturdy walking shoes.

The Indian woman picked up a handful of pine cones. "This is our oldest form of life. Only the rocks are older than the pine cone."

Glancing upward at the tree tops, she chanted, "I come from above and I am holy. The cone is my sister who will be with me to the end of my days."

Jan listened in fascination.

"Where do you think paradise lies, in the east or in the west?" Alma asked thoughtfully.

Again she startled Jan by her words.

"Paradise?"

Alma nodded. "After our death, in what direction does our soul travel to reach paradise?"

"I've never thought about it. East, I suppose, if there is any direction, east toward the rising sun, toward the Holy Land." Jan was confused by Alma's philosophical turn. "Why did you ask that?"

The old Indian woman spoke quietly. "Max and I have just been talking about it while driving back here from Michigan." She smiled shyly at Jan. Gone was the stoic mask, the waxen frown. "When you reach our age that gets to be a topic to talk about—who is right in this religious thing."

Jan thought for a moment before she replied. "I consider myself a Christian. I guess, like my Jewish friends, I think of the east when I try to fix a home for my beliefs, don't you?"

Alma gave Jan an embarrassed smile and shook her head. "This trip is a homecoming for me. Max and I are getting old. For a week now, while we've been on the road, my husband and I have had this running discussion, sometimes argument, about the differences between the white man's paradise and the Indian's paradise."

"Oh?" Jan's tone was soft, inquisitive.

"The pine cones," Alma said, gesturing to the ground litter, "remind me of our mortality, of how little we know about death."

"Where do Indians say paradise is after death?" Jan continued to be puzzled by the woman's preoccupation with the morbid subject.

"Indians believe their paradise is in the west," Alma answered quietly. "Max and I were baptized in the Christian's church when we were kids, and like most in the white man's faith we grew up accustomed to connecting the idea of paradise with the east and the rising sun, but our Indian heritage tells us that it's to the west."

"Does it make any difference after we die?" Jan asked softly.

With her finger Alma traced a design, a crude map, in the grime that covered the truck's hood panel. "This is the earth," she said as she made a rectangle. "On the earth God has planted his law, like a tree straight upwards or like a path straight forward." She drew a line above the rectangle. "Some of us wander the right path, but many of us get on to the side-paths of the lane." Alma drew branches off the straight line. "These run into the desert."

"When the Indian dies," Alma continued, "he goes, after death, along the path of souls." Alma drew another straight line from the rectangle to two waving lines that she said represented a river beyond which lay the Indian paradise. "On the center of the path of souls there is a strawberry lying on one side. It is very large and is said to taste very sweet. A man who stands by it invites all passers-by to taste it. But they must not accept it, for whatever soul does so, is lost at once. Those who resist continue their journey prosperously till they come near paradise. Altogether, it is a journey of from three to four days. Then a large river bars the way."

"Is there a bridge to the Indian paradise like the Christian's pearly gates?"

"No." Alma shook her head. "No regular bridge—a great tree stump lies across it. Its roots are fastened on the other shore. On this side it raises its head, but doesn't reach clear across. There is a gap which our souls must hop over. The log is constantly shaking. Most of the souls are able to spring across and save themselves. Those who jump short or slip off the tree-bridge fall into the waters and are converted into toads or fishes."

When Alma finished she stood staring past Jan as if lost in thought. Jan started to speak, but before she did, Alma added softly, "Indian mothers can never be consoled when their children die before the time when they can help themselves along the road to paradise. Little children are not good jumpers. They perish in great numbers off the bridge." She continued to stare off into the woods.

"Where did you ever hear such a story?"

"That's what I was taught when I was a little girl. Max doesn't believe in an Indian paradise. He's always been a Baptist, but that's what I was taught."

Alma threw back her shoulders and lifted her chin. "I don't usually talk about things like this to strangers," she admitted, looking into Jan's eyes, "but it was on my mind, and you're here. It's a bad thing to grow old and not be sure in your faith. If that ever happens to you, you'll get desperate to find answers that aren't there, and pour your feelings out before a stranger."

Jan didn't have the words she needed to offer a reply. Her heart went out to the old woman who was torn between her Christian beliefs and the teachings from her childhood that she could not shake.

Nodding toward her returning husband, Alma said, "And the end of our days is not so very far away. We have come back to look at our homeland for a last time before we die."

Alma and Jan climbed back into the cab. Jan did not understand Alma's reference to the couple's mortality. Then she heard the woman's breath, a slow animal wheeze.

Alma and Jan were silent as Max started up the truck and pulled back onto the road.

Half an hour later, Max Kadunce stopped his pickup in front of Errol Joyce's leased waterfront office.

Jan climbed out of the truck. She held Alma's arm as the large woman stepped back up into the cab.

Before the door closed, Jan squeezed Alma's arm. "I believe what you said about the pine cone, Alma," Jan said, for the first time using the woman's name. "But you do not seem to be near the end of your days."

Alma gave her a faint smile and closed the door.

Jan felt strangely depressed as she stood in the middle of the roadway and watched the truck drive away. There was a little corner of darkness pervading her senses as if a cloud had crawled across the sun.

Tom Boushey called to her. "Do you know where Errol Joyce is?" the Indian asked. Errol's bright Indian friend taught science classes at the Bureau school on the reservation during the winter and guided canoe parties up on the border lakes during the summer.

Jan walked over to the sidewalk. "Errol is in one of the Wedgewood-Ben rigs. I left him up on the other side of Hoveland. They're probably about half an hour behind me. Why? You got problems?"

"Errol does."

"Why?"

"Errol's got a client who stole her two kids and ran off. The judge is mad. The sheriff has been trying to get in touch with him to find out if he knows where his client took her kids. Judge Clemens has a warrant out for her arrest."

"The McLean case?"

Boushey nodded.

"Errol's not going to be happy to hear that news," Jan said. She turned to her car and opened the door. "When he gets here will you tell him I went on down to Duluth and that I'll call him from my office in the morning?"

Boushey nodded. With almost animal-like stoicism, the Indian crouched on the step to wait for the Wedgewood-Ben truck.

Two wildlife research biologists met a float plane at the forest service dock in Ely, Minnesota. The forestry service plane had made one last sweep of the wilderness area to the east before being forced by the weather front moving down from Canada to take shelter at the Ely base.

Predatory bears that will charge a human being are rare. Typically, the rogue is an animal with little or no contact with people. They are unlike camp-wise bruins that are nuisances and almost never prey on humans.

The U.S.D.A. Forest Service on the state's side employs a small cadre of wardens and biologists whose duty it is to investigate incidents involving encounters with rogues and to keep track of them in order to forewarn canoeists and campers of any suspect bear's whereabouts. Man is required to show deference to the animals, for he is a visitor in their homeland.

"Did you find the bear?" one of the biologists asked as the plane's door opened.

"No. No luck at all," the pilot called as he jumped down to the dock. "We never saw it and we got nothing on the scanner."

"Damn," the older biologist said. "He's either slipped the collar or the batteries are dead."

"Probably dead batteries," the pilot said. "If the bear got the collar off, it would be lying out there and we would have picked up some kind of reading on the scanner. We got nothing."

"Dead batteries," the biologist agreed. He turned to his partner. "Let's go call in our report." He shook his head. "I hate to lose track of that bear."

The rogue, on two different days, had injured campers in unprovoked predatory attacks. A summer of forest fires had driven the animal from its isolated habitat eastward toward the Gunflint Trail. The gaunt bear entered a campsite, approached a camper, hesitated, then attacked, biting the camper on the head and neck until the man's companion flailed it with a canoe paddle and drove it off. A second attack at another campsite followed the same pattern. A day after the second attack, the wardens located the animal and shot drug darts into its hide. While it was unconscious, the bear was measured and weighed. Samples of its blood were taken, and an electronic collar was affixed around its neck to provide the service with clues that might indicate the extent of the predator's range.

The rogue's only punishment for its attacks was banishment to the edge of the border in the Boundary Water Canoe Area, where its wanderings were electronically monitored. But after two weeks of charting by the two biologists, the rogue's radio signal had mysteriously stopped. All the biologists knew now was that a dangerous storm was approaching and the predator was moving eastward toward Lake Saganaga.

There was no vehicular traffic on the Gunflint Trail when the rogue crossed the blacktop at the Seagull River bridge and started a lumbering climb to the height-of-land overlooking the shoreline of Marabeuf Lake.

Behind it, voracious swaths of fire that the animal avoided in its wanderings, continued to blaze.

CHAPTER 6

A S THEIR CANOE CARRIED THEM DOWN THE GRANITE RIVER in a valley where high, rocky ridges rose from both shores in hushed majesty, Kristen thought of Arlesen McLean. If she had ever loved him she had forgotten it. But as soon as the thought took form, she knew that it was not so.

Their first date was a disaster, she remembered.

The two had argued over how long Arlie should stay out their first night. Arlesen had parked his father's car on Skyline Drive, scarcely a quarter of a mile from the university campus and his home. The overlook where they stopped gave the couple a view across the harbor to the lights of Superior, Wisconsin. Below them were the bright dancing lights of the city of Duluth. During her last year on the Duluth campus, at the request of Toli McLean, the head of the Biology Department, Kristen worked in the laboratory as one of the assistants.

Before Kristen went to work in the lab, her relationship with Arlie had been a cordial friendship. Toli's son, Arlesen, was a semester ahead of her in her class. After she commenced her part-time work, both the head of the department and his son flattered her with attention. Toli McLean made it a point each day to come to her table and be solicitous about her work. He insisted on helping her, even at times when she didn't need help. He plied her with questions about her finances, offering to assist her if necessary. Kristen was surprised by the older man's attention. She assumed that his attentiveness was because of the interest his son Arlesen had shown in her and the feelings she had begun to experience toward his son.

Once Toli took her and Arlie to lunch in a nearby restaurant. On another occasion the professor asked Kristen to join him for lunch, when he knew his son was not available to go with them. She politely declined.

Arlie had thick black hair and dusky, Mediterranean-hued skin. He was a short, slender man, with eyes as dark as olive pits. When Kristen stood in front of him, she looked down at him, for she was two inches taller. Arlie's facial features, like his father's, were square but not strong.

In the fall of their senior year, Arlie's last semester, his visits each afternoon, and his father's visits as well, to Kristen's laboratory table became longer and more frequent. Consequently she told both men they weren't letting her get her work done for the university.

The afternoon of their first date, Arlesen had stopped by the laboratory and whispered his dinner invitation. Kristen had accepted. Following their dinner at a seafood restaurant on the wharf in the Duluth harbor, Arlesen drove his father's car back up on Skyline Drive and parked.

Kristen innocently suggested that they see a late movie at the theater complex on the mall. With a shy grin Arlie turned to her and said, "I can't."

"It's only nine o'clock," Kristen said. "The university isn't going to flunk you out of your last semester in college if you miss one evening of study. You don't have to spend all your time at the books."

Arlie shook his head. "It's not that. I must have the car back to the house by 10:30."

"You mean your father won't let you stay out after 10:30 at night?" Kristen teased.

In the darkness the girl did not see the flush of color on Arlesen's face. "I must be in by 10:30," he repeated.

"Come on, Arlie," Kristen pleaded. "Your father knows you're with me. We're not going to wreck his car. If he's worried about his car being out after 10:30, let's take it back to him and walk over to the mall. It's not all that far."

Arlesen shook his head. "It's not the car. My father has a rule that, except for special occasions, everyone in our household must be home when he locks the front door."

Kristen laughed. "You mean to tell me that your father locks the door to your home every night at 10:30, like the security people lock up our dormitories?"

Arlie nodded. "He always has."

"Don't you have a key to get in?"

"Yes."

"Well, why don't you use it?"

"I can get in all right. It's just that at our house, everyone is to be home at that time each night."

"Even your mother?"

Arlie nodded. "Yes, and the servants."

"That's a strange rule. In the dorms they don't lock our doors until midnight. And even then we can get passes from our housemother to come in later than that."

Arlie shrugged. "My parents are from the old country, they do things different from other people."

"They sure do," Kristen said with a laugh. "Your father is always telling me he wishes he had a daughter like me. If I were his daughter I would drive him crazy breaking his curfew rules."

"You know my father. It's easier to follow his rules than to have an argument with him. I didn't ask about being out past 10:30 this evening. I better get the car back. Maybe we can go out another time and catch an earlier show."

Kristen looked at his face in the shadows cast by the street light. She liked the man. She liked his innocence. Arlie, she thought, was not like the others she had dated on the campus. Scandinavian-blooded students of northern Minnesota were very much different from the sensitive scholar sitting beside her. Kristen thought he was a shy and caring person, and she liked him for that.

As the weeks passed, the couple dated more frequently. Kristen was amused by the attentions Arlie's father gave her. She assumed that he knew that her relationship with his son had taken a serious turn. As the end of the fall semester arrived and Arlesen graduated, she was pleased to learn that his father's influence had enabled Arlie to land the job of assistant principal at the elementary laboratory school operated on the campus by the university's Department of Education. This permitted them to continue dating through the winter and spring of her last year in college.

After Kristen's graduation, Toli arranged for her to teach science classes in the same school where his son was assistant principal. She did not return to the Indian reservation, but remained in Duluth. The following summer, she and Arlie married, and she moved into the household that had a 10:30 curfew.

Kristen loved Arlie. She developed an affection for all the members of the McLean household. However, she could not understand why her mother-in-law, a very kind and gracious woman, allowed the professor to treat her like chattel. But, she thought, there were probably compensations in her in-laws' marriage that she couldn't see. It was obvious to her that Selma McLean adored her husband.

Toli's authoritarian house rules irritated Kristen, but did not particularly concern her because she obeyed them when it was convenient for her to do so and ignored them when it was not.

Kristen insisted that she have a key to the front door, and even threatened to move out if Arlie didn't give her one. Finally, the professor had a key made for her and she came and went as she pleased.

The love that Kristen experienced for Arlesen had peaked the night she gave birth to her first child, Cubby. The professor and his wife were away on the east coast attending a conference at one of his academic societies. Kristen missed Selma's presence. She became frightened at the hospital when a rapid onset of labor pains convulsed her body.

Arlesen had clasped her hand and whispered, "I'll be with you every moment."

As they wheeled her down the corridor to the delivery room, Kristen wished that she had taken the birthing classes recommended by her doctor. Classes which Toli, the professor, had insisted were unnecessary.

"I am a biologist," Toli reminded Kristen. "Your studies should make you aware that having babies is a natural process. It is not necessary for you to attend classes to learn how to have them."

Damn you, thought Kristen. Nothing had prepared her for the violent muscle contractions over which she had no control.

As Kristen was being positioned on the delivery table, she looked up at the sensitive face above her. Clearly she and Arlie were of one soul. They were bound by a simple, unquestioning devotion to each other. A contraction seized her and caused her to close her eyes and grit her teeth with pain. When she looked again she saw a nurse fasten a face mask on her husband. Before it covered his mouth, Arlie lifted her fingers to his lips and kissed them. Kristen clutched his hand tightly and felt her baby move. As she fell into the rhythm of her labor, she thought, the father of my child is different from his own father, Toli McLean. This man, she knew, was a man of compassion who would help her raise their beautiful child. Kristen began to push. She felt the comforting grip of Arlie's hand and the strength of his presence. His love and encouragement soothed her, calmed her in the stormy sea-swirl agony of giving birth to their first child.

In the intervening years between the birth of Cubby and of her second daughter, Niki, Kristen's relationship with her father-in-law became more strained. They argued about money, about the way she conducted herself. But mostly they argued about the rearing of Cubby.

In other subtle ways, Toli McLean also had changed. His attention toward his daughter-in-law, which had started out of genuine concern for her, became a fawning possessiveness, an insidious domination over her. His manner and behavior progressed from ambiguous innuendo to suggestive conversations and unnecessary touching. His hands reached out for her so often that Kristen sensed his repeated advances were purposeful.

When Arlesen was in the home, even in their bed at night, he was reluctant to take part in any discussion which was counter to the actions or wishes of his parents.

Outside the home, however, he was different. On the campus, at their work, the couple talked and discussed plans for their future. But no matter how insistent Kristen was, and despite the progressive antagonism that developed between her and her father-in-law, Arlie would not move his family out of the large, sprawling home. As the years passed, Kristen began to realize the hold that Toli McLean had on his son. She knew the old man and his son would never let her leave their household and take her daughters with her.

Kristen stayed and tolerated her father-in-law, but she was determined that her daughters would not be caught up in the subservient female culture that he insisted was their natural lot in life.

At every opportunity Kristen took her daughters up onto the Thunder Bay Reservation and back into the wilds of the Boundary Waters Canoe country so they could see that there was more to life for a woman than to serve the men of their household.

"I know you don't like the Wilderness Country and don't want to go up there," Kristen had said to Arlie one day, following one of their regular minor disagreements.

Arlie insisted. "I just don't think that's a place to take our kids."

Kristen put her hand on her husband's arm. "You don't know what it's like up there. It's absolutely beautiful. It's a gift God has given to us and I want our children to know it."

Arlie shrugged. "Kris, I don't like to camp out with bears and mosquitoes.

And after growing up in the poverty of the reservation, I can't understand why you would want our kids to go up there."

The Northern Lights, the seasons, especially the fall, Kristen thought. For no good reason, her husband's mention of poverty brought to her mind the Northern Lights on cold, wet nights, a scene which no amount of money could buy for her children. Pale green licks of light pulsing, fading across the reservation's dark ghostly sky as if an invisible master painter was painting the heavens. Living lights. The wavering fires that pulse and fountain higher, higher, then die out in blackness. At times the whole sky ranged wildly with dancing colors, in shooting points and puckers of light gathering and falling, vibrating, fading, flowing like water colors on a canvas, rhythmical as breathing, yet mystical and mysterious as magnetism or electricity.

And the antics of the common loon, Kristen thought. A free show for which money was not needed, a show that made her girls laugh so hard their bellies shook like jiggled gelatin.

And the moral tales that condemned extravagance, told to her by Agnab, the man-who-is-in-front-of-all. And the songs sung to her by old-woman Kanik, the pipe-maker, who sang of the corn spirit and of the tribe's customs, laws and traditions.

God, she thought, how can I make Arlie understand?

Kristen dropped her hand from her husband's arm. "I just want Cubby and Niki to see a place where money isn't important, where animals are so innocent and untouched by civilization that they'll walk up and eat out of your hand, where there is food for the taking without having to go to a supermarket, where the water is so pure you can drink right out of the lakes. I want our girls to see those things before they grow up and lose their innocence."

Arlie McLean took his wife in his arms and held her. He pressed his face against her black silken hair and murmured into her ear. "Kris, sometimes I think I don't even know you. I love you so very much. There are times I feel that we're so close we are inseparable, and there are other times that there is this great gap between us. And, when you take Cubby and Niki back and forth across that gap, I'm afraid it's going to hurt them."

"Nothing in the Wilderness Country or on the reservation will hurt Niki and Cubby," she whispered. "I promise you that. This was my home. Up there on the lakes is where I grew up. It's a part of me and I want it to be a part of Niki and Cubby."

She looked into the eyes of her husband. "And, Arlie, I wish that it could be a part of you, too."

He squeezed her arms and stepped back. "It's not for me."

Kristen tried to choose her words carefully so her husband would not think she was arguing again. "Do you remember when we were in college, that spring when we were both sophomores, and on Earth Day, you read your term paper to the crowd of students who were celebrating our environment on the steps of the administration building?"

Arlie laughed. "We had the university administration excited that day, didn't we?"

She nodded. "You contrasted the beauty of the lakes and trees in Minnesota with the stark, barren, worn-out landscape of Greece that you visited while you were in high school, when your father took you to his homeland. Do you remember that?"

Arlie remembered.

"That's what I'm talking about now. The values you said we should live by to preserve our planet are the values the Anishinibe have lived by for centuries. That's why I take our children up there. I don't want them to someday read a book about it or write a term paper about it. I want them to feel it, taste it, live it, be a part of it. It's up there waiting for them now, it's waiting for you, it's waiting for all of us. I want our kids to know that there is something more beyond our front yard than the university campus and the shopping mall up by the airport. I want them to know what it is that God has given us, and money can't buy for us, before it's all gone. I want them to feel what I felt and to learn what every Indian child learns about life that will never be taught in school. Things I wish you could experience and learn. I know your father doesn't like it when I take Cubby and Niki up there. But, Arlie, will you talk to him and try to make him understand?"

He shook his head. "I don't think it will do any good, but I'll try."

Kristen kissed her husband.

"But," he added, "don't try to get me in the other end of your canoe."

The last time Kristen and Arlesen slept together was the night he asked for the return of the house key.

"You want what?" Kristen tried to control the hysterical lilt of her voice, to maintain complete control so as not to awaken their children. The entire second floor of the ugly house was home for their family. But she let the girls sleep in the next room rather than at the far end of the house.

Arlesen swallowed hard. "The key. Father wants the key back."

"And you're going to take it from me?" Kristen was outraged by her husband's suggestion. Her face blazed and quivered with a violent tic.

"Kris, I'm not going to take it from you. I'm just asking you to give it back to him."

She heard the coaxing timbre of his voice. "Why?" Her voice was laced with rage, but controlled.

Arlesen in freshly laundered pajamas sat in the overstuffed chair beside the bed. Lamplight sprawled over the ceiling and lit their faces. Kristen was seated on the edge of the bed where she had been brushing her blue-black hair. The children were asleep in their room.

Lowering his voice, he leaned toward her. "Father says that you have been abusing household privileges and he has asked for your front door key. He's just angry tonight." He shrugged. "He'll get over it. He'll give you the key back."

"And he sent you to ask me for the key?" Her voice seethed with a deadly undertone. She laid her hair brush on the nightstand beside the bed.

"I'm your husband. It is my duty." He moved in his chair with stiff, brittle dignity.

"Your duty to do what?" Her eyes flashed. They were so black the irises bristled with jagged blue flames.

Arlesen lifted his chin and spoke as if reciting memorized pap from a political tract. "It is my duty to see that there is harmony in my family." He held his head at an arrogant angle.

"Shit!" she hissed with disgust. "You're just repeating something your father told you."

"Kris," he coaxed, "he's just mad tonight. He'll get over it. Just let me give him your key. When he has made his point, he'll give it back."

Kristen's voice tightened. Her face became set and drawn. "You go downstairs," she said in a flat tone, "and tell your father that as long as my babies and I are locked in this house, I shall keep the key to the front door. And you tell him that if he changes the lock on the door, I'll throw a chair through the front window!"

Arlesen McLean rose stiffly. "You should not talk to me like that, Kristen. I am your husband."

Tears glistened in Kristen's eyes as she looked up at him like a wounded mink, hurt but still fighting. "And I am your wife." Inclining her head toward the next room she said in a thin whisper, "and they are your children."

He stared down at her stonily. For the first time, she realized how much like his father he looked. He wheeled and left the bedroom without a word.

At that moment, Kristen felt a creeping uneasiness at the bottom of her heart, a wrenching from her center that left her rootless, uncertain and terribly afraid.

CHAPTER 7

THE CANOE RODE THE CURRENT AND BOILING EDDIES, and Kristen was one with its every motion. The young Indian mother had paddled the wilderness lakes for as long as she could remember. Her paddle was an extension of her arm and mind. The craft glided like a silver-skinned trout, silk-smooth and graceful, responding to her every whim and thought, each deft dip of the paddle blade.

The Granite River was a spectacular work of nature like its neighbor, the Quetico, whose name came from the Ojibwa Indian word that loosely translated into "place of exceptional beauty." But the river was also very dangerous.

The water around Swamp portage was strewn with sharp rocks and ran in shallow troughs. Kristen dipped her paddle from side to side, adjusting the bow to avoid rocks that could puncture the craft's fragile bottom.

"Now girls, sit still," Kristen ordered.

The two youngsters sensed the tenseness of the moment and grasped the sides of the canoe. They watched as their mother slowly swung around toward the lip of the roaring waters that would lead them down to the lake above Devil's Elbow.

Large V's of streaming water pointed the way above the breakers. Ahead were swirls and smooth, slick sweeps. The three could feel the canoe being taken by an unseen power. With fierce abandon, the canoe leaped toward the spume and the sprouting minefield of treacherous rocks. In the grip of the river it entered the maelstrom. The three people in the canoe were at the mercy of the rapids until the flow-through had spent its strength. Through reaching snags and ragged phalanxes of rocks and surging billows of boiling water they sped. Kristen used all her cunning and skill with the paddle to ride the narrow ribbon of clear water. The storm churned up by the river matched the roiling clouds and haze in the sky overhead. They plunged on until they broke from the Granite's grip and coasted into the dead calm waters of Gneiss Lake.

Exhausted by the exhilarating effort, Kristen bent over her paddle, and her daughters looked back at her, grinning. Both girls still held onto the sides of the canoe, and Cubby's legs were wrapped around her sister's waist in a scissors lock.

"That was fun!" Cubby called out.

"Can we do it again, Mother?" Niki asked. "Can we?"

"Not right now." Kristen breathed the words.

"Why not?" the five-year-old asked. "Why can't we?"

"Our mother is tired," Cubby said in her important tone of voice.

"After you rest, can we? I want to do it again," Niki insisted.

Kristen laughed and put her paddle back in the water and started a slow push across Gneiss Lake. The circular body of water was almost a mile wide. High palisades rose in all directions from its edges. The cliffs protected its waters from gusting winds like those that impeded their passage across Gunflint Lake.

Now the river had spread out into the lake and lost the force of its current. To the north was a small rocky outcropping of land, the lake's only island, covered with lichen and scrub pine. On one side of the island there was an opening in the face of the cliff where the river gathered its strength again and plunged out of the lake into a narrow canyon—the entry into Devil's Elbow.

The Elbow, like the wilderness lakes, had been given its name by white men. It was a crook in the river where Gneiss Lake joined the lake of the Marabeuf. The water ran deep, but at its narrowest point it was scarcely the width of two canoes. There, all of the force of the stream was concentrated, and it burst into a sweeping turn that carved out the crook of the elbow. Over eons of time water had polished a smooth flat surface along one side of the hidden canyon. The flat shelf lay beside the stream like a manmade highway. Canoeists who paddled the Granite River were always amazed when they shot down between the cliffs and on the sweeping turn found the isolated roadway that had no entrance and no exit. Above, the cliffs towered three hundred feet into the air. Occasionally, canoeists stopped long enough to walk the curving ledge, but mostly canoe parties sped by on the tongue of the water and dropped down into the lower canyon without pause.

The Elbow was a loop of almost three miles of water, all of it confined within the high canyon walls. The beginning and end of the loop were barely four hundred yards apart, separated by a high, tree-lined ridge of broken granite. At the bottom, the Elbow straightened. The stream became wider and emptied into the Marabeuf.

Angling the bow of the craft toward the shore, Kristen worked the canoe along the rocks as she made her cautious approach to the opening that poured water out of Gneiss Lake.

"Girls," she called, "do you have to potty?"

"I sure do," Cubby announced.

"I sure do, too," Niki echoed.

"You're just saying that because I have to go."

"I do, too. You're not the only one who has to go, is she, Mother?"

"Wait till I pull the canoe up to the rocks," Kristen said. "We'll stop here before we go down into the canyon."

Kristen maneuvered the craft parallel to the shore and put a leg over the side to hold it against the rocks. Below, they heard the sounds of rushing water reverberate off the canyon walls. A fine spray of mist, laced with miniature rainbows and sparkling with sunlight, rose above the opening into the river.

"Don't step on the paddles," Kristen warned.

First Cubby, then Niki, crawled across the backpacks past their mother, avoiding the two paddles, and stepped out on the shore.

"Why does Niki have to do everything I do?"

"And don't argue," Kristen said. Picking up the paddles, she climbed out of the canoe and carefully placed them on a rock shelf where the girls wouldn't walk over them when they returned. Then, lifting the front of the craft, she pulled it onto a flat rock. The hull grated with a metallic sound.

She called to the girls. "Don't go too far!"

"Do we take this path to Grandpa Mike's cabin?" Cubby asked, eyeing the faint trail that led away from the water's edge.

"No, we'll go to Grandpa Mike's in the canoe."

"Because Niki is too little to walk?"

"I'm not too little to walk to Grandpa Mike's."

"Girls, will you please hurry up and finish or we'll never get to Grandpa Mike's."

"I can't undo it," Niki said, struggling to unfasten her clothes.

"Let me," Kristen said.

With a mother's reflex, she released the canoe and turned to help her daughter. One end of the craft swung away from the shore. With a scraping sound the bow slipped off the rock and the canoe floated free.

"Oh, damn," Kristen exclaimed. Without hesitating she turned and waded out into the water to retrieve the craft, but it floated just beyond her grasp. "Oh, shit," she cried, and plowed out into the shallow waters to grab it, but the bow of the craft swung away from her as the current caught it. Now, the water rose above her knees and she realized the desperate mistake she'd made in releasing the canoe.

The Wilderness Country, Kristen knew, was totally unforgiving of mistakes. Never did you dare lose your equipment, your food, your shelter, and above all, never your transportation. The Superior National Forest was one of the few places in the United States where there were absolutely none of the conveniences of civilization, except those carried into the woods on the traveler's back.

Kristen ignored the drag of her wet boots and clothing. She plunged into the cold water and swam after the drifting canoe. The bewildered youngsters stood on the shore and waited. The canoe began to bounce and pitch and pick up speed. The girls went to the water's edge as the current swept the canoe and their mother out past a tree-lined point of land.

"Don't step on the paddles," Cubby said, pulling her sister back from the ledge. "Mother said don't step on the paddles."

When the girls looked again, the canoe and the swimmer were out of sight.

The two girls waited for their mother to reappear.

"Cubby, will you help me?" Niki asked, tugging at her clothes. "I have to go to the toilet."

"All right," Cubby said, "but hurry, because Mother is going to be right back."

Kristen knew the seriousness of her situation. She was a strong swimmer, but she was fully clothed and the weight, especially the boots, slowed her progress. The canoe continued to tantalize her by drifting ahead, just beyond her reach. Then, as if plunged into a flash flood, the craft and the woman were thrown into the swift deep channel. Kristen quickened her strokes in an anxious burst of strength. Her tangled wet hair blinded her as she finally touched the cold aluminum hull. Flailing out with her right arm, she touched it a second time, then she brought her left arm over and grasped at the stern. Her hand slipped on its wet surface and her left wrist was torn with a deep laceration as it dragged over a jagged piece of aluminum seam.

She lunged at the craft again as it twisted sideways in the erratic current. Finally, she managed to get her right hand on the gunwale, and dragging her body up to the side of the craft, she reached over and hooked her arm under the thwart. The floating craft held her head above the turbulent waters and, exhausted, she closed her eyes and held on tightly as she and the canoe rode the center of the chute down the river.

Despite the numbing cold, Kristen felt pain in her left wrist. Lifting it out of the water, she saw a wriggling stream of blood coursing from the torn tendons in her wrist. The blood streamed into the water, swirling streamers of pink froth like a pinwheel. In panic, she clamped her body against her wrist, pressing it to the side of the canoe, trying to apply pressure that would staunch the flow of blood. She clung to the gunwale with her arm looped under the thwart. She tried to push her hair out of her eyes by rubbing her forehead against the canoe. Kristen knew it wasn't only a matter of losing their equipment now. Her very life was in danger.

She shuddered and felt lightheaded. Daring to hesitate no longer, she freed her left arm and ignored the pain. She grasped the thwart with both hands and tried to haul herself over the side. The pain as she stretched the torn tendons was excruciating. She had almost levered her body over the side when her hand grip slipped on the oozing blood. Kristen fell back into the water. The canoe floated out of her grasp.

The icy water numbed her body, but kept her revived as she frantically dog-paddled with both arms. She fought to keep her head above the surface and when she did start to sink, her boots touched the bottom. Bouncing on her toes and pushing with her arms, as blood continued to flow out of her wrist, Kristen finally dragged herself up on the flat expanse of rock that nature had carved into Devil's Elbow. At first she crawled, then she rolled, but as she tried to rise to her knees she pitched forward and her left arm twisted under her body. As she lay still on the isolated rock shelf, the weight of her body stopped the flow of blood.

Out of the sky above Devil's Elbow, an osprey folded its wings and plunged down, down, down into the river. Its talons kicked up a wild spray of water as it caught a fish that was feeding on the blood spilled along the shore. The sky filled with shrill cries as a gangster eagle, its snowy crown glistening in the sun, boldly wrested the fish from the osprey. Two sea gulls ignored the contesting birds and circled above the still form that lay on the shelf below. Finally the gulls flapped down onto the smooth rock ledge and strutted about, waiting for the Indian woman to die.

CHAPTER 8

"Your Honor, you do not have the authority to do what the McLean family is asking." Errol Joyce spoke bluntly. The lawyer was obligated to represent his absent client. He had no choice. He had accepted employment by Kristen McLean, and until the court or his client relieved him of that responsibility, Errol was required to appear in the courtroom on her behalf, whenever and wherever the court directed.

Judge Clemens turned to the other lawyer standing in the courtroom beside Errol. "What do you say to that?" she asked, tonelessly.

Peter Hauck stood ramrod straight. "That is Mr. Joyce's opinion," he replied, with a wry smile on his lips. Hauck was confident that Judge Clemens' anger over Kristen McLean's actions had inclined the judge to show a favorable bias toward his client.

"No," Errol said, "that is the opinion of the Minnesota Supreme Court in *Riley v. Riley*."

The Cook County Courthouse in Grand Marais sat halfway up the side of the mountain in singular majesty, its grandeur assured by the six weathered granite columns that held its lofty roof solidly in place. The courtroom, located on the third floor—the top floor—was drab. Some said it resembled a graceless mausoleum. The acoustics were atrocious, despite sound-absorbing squares placed on the walls. The judge's bench and witness box were raised above the level at which jury, lawyers, court reporter, and clerk did their work. A single railing with two swinging gates divided litigants from ornate oak pews. An aisle down the center and one on each side separated the pews into two sections. High narrow windows lined the walls, except for the one behind the judge's bench where a partition enclosed smaller offices and the court's inner chambers. During winter sessions, radiators clanked and hissed and constantly spit out steam and water. But the heat of the summer day required that all the windows be propped open to allow a lake breeze to flow through.

In some ways the Cook County courtroom was more of a home for Errol than the waterfront apartment where he now lived. It was in this courtroom that he gave his oath of fidelity as a member of the Minnesota Bar. And it was here that he and Jan Kiel had surprised themselves with new and compelling feelings one day when her father had shown up drunk at the courthouse. The incident had embarrassed Jan and, after her father left, she ended up sobbing in Errol's arms.

Despite the frenzied disorder of blackboards, tables, chairs, books, mechanical recording devices, and flags of the state and nation, the great room felt marvelously comfortable to Errol.

Peter Hauck, the elderly lawyer who represented the McLean family, took the offensive. The former law professor looked forty, not seventy years old. Under his creased blue suit he wore, as always, a ribbed and cable-trimmed vest. His hair was salt and pepper gray. The lawyer was a big, thick man, congenial and shrewd. He exuded an air of dignity and graciousness.

Hauck referred to his handwritten notes. "I had time to do only a quick search in my library before I drove up to Grand Marais today with my clients. I think, however, I found the citation that bears most directly on the issue here. *In Re: Noeltinger* is also a State Supreme Court decision. The court there said it has been repeatedly stated and accepted that a parent's moral fitness is a vital factor in determining custody of a child. And I submit to you, Your Honor, that the mother in this case has demonstrated a complete failure of morality by defying the temporary custody order of this court and by kidnapping my client's children."

"I remind counsel that they are Kristen McLean's children also," Errol said.

Judge Dorothy Clemens ignored the bickering. Clemens was an honors graduate from the University of Minnesota School of Law who had had a successful career as a trial lawyer herself before her appointment to the bench. She had an innate knack for sifting through tangled jungles of rhetoric. Turning to the Errol, she said, "You are arguing that I have no jurisdiction to sustain the McLean motion and issue sanctions against the mother and award permanent custody to the father. Is that in substance your argument?"

"It is, Your Honor."

"Are you saying that because the venue of the McLean divorce action is at Two Harbors down in Lake County, not here at Grand Marais in Cook County?" the judge asked.

"No. I'm not quarreling about the venue. Until I got back to town I didn't even know that my client had run off with her children; nor that Hauck had brought his clients up here to try to get you to change the temporary custody order to a permanent custody order. My reason for saying you have no authority at this time to issue sanctions against my client and make the custody order a permanent one is not a technical reason. Today was your regular Law Day here at the Grand Marais Courthouse. If I stood on a venue technicality, all you would have to do is drive forty-five miles down to Two Harbors and enter your order there."

Errol reached for the law book he had carried into the courtroom. "The real issue is one of due process. You must conduct a formal hearing and afford Kristen McLean the opportunity to present evidence before you can issue sanctions against her, or change the form of your custody order. In the Riley case the court said," Errol quoted, "'only on hearing, and determination that the change in the custody order would be for the best interest of the child, may a court act to change its order.'"

"Errol, that's simply a delaying tactic," Hauck protested. "It is necessary to the welfare of the children that the custody order be made permanent today."

"Why?" Errol asked. "If the children are with their mother now, how does changing the custody order today do anything?"

"My clients have reason to believe that Kristen McLean is an unstable and violent person. She could do bodily harm to her own children. After all, she stabbed her own father-in-law during a fit of rage."

Judge Clemens interrupted their argument. "We're not going to get into the facts surrounding the divorce proceedings," she said.

Errol addressed himself to the judge. "How can any act of the court today have an effect on the children, for good or bad? None of us knows where they are or what they're doing. Signing an order isn't going to change that."

"Let's get back to the matter you raised." Judge Clemens turned to

Peter Hauck. "Mr. Joyce has cited authority which says I must first conduct a formal hearing before I can rule on your motion. Do you have any authority to the contrary?"

"No, not with me," Hauck said.

"Do you agree that it is a due process issue?" the judge asked.

"Before you can issue sanctions? Probably yes, because sanctions are in the nature of a civil punishment. I suppose we must go through the motions of a contempt proceeding," Hauck admitted, "but no hearing is necessary to change the custody order."

"What basis do I have to change the custody order from temporary to permanent if I do not first make a finding that sanctions are proper?"

"None, I suppose, but it all is such a waste of time. There is no question but what you signed the temporary custody order, and Kristen McLean violated it by taking the children out of the McLean home."

"Unless," Errol interjected, "the judge determines that her original order was improper and should be set aside. In that event the mother was entitled to take her children out of her father-in-law's home."

"That's already been litigated," Hauck argued. "The judge has already signed the temporary custody order."

"By asking the court to vacate the temporary order and to make a permanent order, the McLean family has re-opened the entire matter of child custody. I am now entitled to relitigate that issue."

"Are you saying that because the McLean family has filed this motion, we are again back to fighting over custody of the children, pending the divorce?" the judge asked.

"Exactly," Errol said.

"And you want me to set this whole custody matter down for a formal hearing again?" the judge asked.

"Yes."

"And at the hearing Mr. Hauck is going to attempt to show that the father is entitled to permanent custody of the children because of the mother's actions; and you are going to try to show that the mother was entitled to take off with her children because my original temporary custody order was wrong?"

"Yes."

"Other than delay, what do you think you're going to accomplish?" Hauck asked.

Errol leaned back against the empty jury box. "The burden of proof is upon your clients to show that it is in the best interests of the children that they be taken from their mother, in whose custody we believe them now to be." IIe gestured expansively. "All of the cases say the court's primary concern in child custody litigation is to reach a decision which is in the best interest and welfare of the child. Custody has been denied parents whose attitude toward the children, though not lacking in parental love, was lacking in parental responsibility."

"The McLean family has certainly demonstrated that responsibility," Hauck pointed out.

"The grandparents have," Errol admitted. "They've promoted and financed this custody fight, but it's the children's father the law is talking about."

Out in the courtroom Kristen's husband squirmed in the seat between his parents. Toli, the elder McLean, could hardly restrain himself from speaking out.

Errol continued, "It has been the mother, Kristen, who taught Cubby and Niki the use of eating utensils, to distinguish colors, to recite nursery rhymes, to learn parts for their school plays. She took the children to church and taught them of their heritage. She is the one who has given care and supervision and attention for all the years since they were born. And all of these kinds of things the mother gave the children are a demonstration of her ability as a parent, which, according to our courts, must be given preference."

"What does your research show you about proof of home environment?" Judge Clemens asked.

"The home environment in which a child will live has been held to be the most important single factor in child custody," Errol admitted, "but it's not enough for the McLeans to say life on an Indian reservation is primitive. The father must show that the environment is detrimental to the best interests of the children. He hasn't done that. Consequently, I think that on re-hearing this matter, the court will permit the children to stay with their mother, even if she does take them up on the Thunder Bay Reservation to live."

"Very well," Judge Clemens said. "I'm going to call a recess now so that I can check my notes."

The judge swept her notes up and left the bench. Her empty chair rocked on its springs in the sudden silence.

In the wake of her departure, the two attorneys stood for a long moment exchanging looks like two strangers who suddenly find themselves stranded on the same small island.

CHAPTER 9

MAX SLOWED THE PICKUP SO ALMA COULD ENJOY the grandeur of the land, the exquisite expanse of sky and water. The highway they drove had evolved over the years from an old logging track to a serviceable road, blasted, hacked and cleared between Superior and the border lakes.

"It's beautiful," Alma said above the groan of the engine.

"Mighty nice."

The homely, rustic road once ended at Gunflint Lake, and beyond that tourists, continuing along the stretch of the trail to Saganaga, paid a toll. Later, highway engineers widened the entire road to two lanes, made travel free to the public, and by early 1980 the jolting rock bed was overlaid with asphalt for its entire sixty-three miles.

Rising from the harbor on the north shore, the blacktop climbed two thousand feet into the Sawtooth Range and wound gracefully through lush timber. Along the way stands of virgin pine glistened emerald in the sun. Spectacular scenic overlooks appeared at intervals. Patient travelers might see wolf, lynx, and loon and occasionally bear, deer, and fox. Alongside the road, for the picking, were clutches of thimbleberries and wild blueberries. The streams that the trail crossed not only had an abundance of fish, but shimmered, on close scrutiny, with agates and thompsonite as well.

Near Brule River the road passed east of Minnesota's highest point, Eagle Mountain.

At the Brule River bridge, Max and Alma's pickup truck met, and passed below, a lumbering helicopter marked with the maple leaf of the Canadian Forestry Service. Wild ducks and gulls, disturbed by the flapping rotors, flew ahead of the pickup, skimming the empty road like vagrant kites. The helicopter passed out of sight and the pickup sped north into the wilderness country.

The couple checked in at the forestry station.

"Hello folks," the ranger said, a cordial tone to his voice. "Going into the BWCA?"

"Yes," Max said. "We'd like a permit."

"That's what I'm here for," the ranger said.

The eastern portion of the Boundary Water Canoe Area wilderness was under the jurisdiction of the Grand Marais Ranger Station.

The ranger set a form down on the counter. He began asking questions, filling in the blanks. When he was finished, the young biologist-attendant handed them their camping permit and a list of precautionary suggestions.

"Pay particular attention to the warning about bears," he said, as Max paid him the fee.

"Bears?" Alma asked.

"This has been a dry summer. The stunted berry crop and the fires have caused an unusual amount of movement among our bear population," he cautioned. "They're hungry and they can tear up your equipment searching for food."

"Will they try to bother us in the truck?" Max asked.

"Probably not. Bears are like humans. They can be shy as well as extroverts, easy-going as well as cantankerous. Some are clowns. Some are thieves, panhandlers, even killers, or they can be all of these things, just like humans. There are blacks that are foolish, others are smart. But be especially careful at the garbage dumps. The most dangerous are the black bears that feed out of the dumpsters in the solid waste disposal stations maintained by the park service. They've learned to be indifferent and almost contemptuous of man's presence."

"I heard they mostly feed on berries and fish," Alma said.

"Bears eat like pigs. They'll eat anything they can find: plants, insects, rodents, carrion. They'll even eat humans, and they'll eat each other."

"Is it safe to go back there?" Max asked. He liked this young man.

"Oh, sure." The young park attendant lifted his palm. "Just don't leave food outside your vehicle, and stay inside your truck when you see bears roaming about."

Max looked over at his wife. Her eyes sparkled as if the ranger's words had given her a jolt of renewed vitality. She smiled at her husband, and he wondered if she was thrilled by the anticipation of danger.

"What if we come across one when we're outside the truck?" Max asked.

"Avoid the sows with young cubs. Back off and give them lots of space to get away from you. And," he added, "be careful where you walk. Don't go near a bear's kill."

Alma turned to Max. Her eyes widened. "Is that right?"

The ranger lifted his hand in a cautionary gesture. "Once a bear makes a kill it usually covers it in a pile of vegetation and dirt and then allows nature to take its course in a sort of tenderization process. Usually the bear will rest where it can view or be near its aging carrion and protect it from intruders. It's under these circumstances that most bears will attack. Just watch where you're stepping."

Max turned and leaned toward Alma. "Do you still want to go up into the woods?"

"Don't you, old fearless leader?" There was a spontaneous air of *joie de vivre* about her that surprised him. Alma's audacity caught Max off guard.

"I will, if you will." Max smiled, accepting her challenge.

Tilting her shoulders, pooching her lips in a half-moue', the large woman leaned back and said nonchalantly, "Hell, let's do it, mister!"

The ranger and Max laughed.

Max and Alma's love for each other was real. Despite an occasional undercurrent of antagonism that sometimes threatened their usually happy marriage, their love continued to exist and to flourish. This was one of those moments when an attack of mutual affection splashed over them like a freshet of spring water. Alma's antics caused them both to beam.

They drove from the end of Gunflint Trail into the parking lot at Sag Store. They got out of their truck and went inside.

Sag Store was not an ordinary shop, but a home. It was located at the northernmost point of Gunflint Trail, northwest of Grand Marais on

Saganaga, deep in the heart of the canoe country. Lakes with names like Seagull, Round, Ham, Magnetic, and Popular were within hiking distance.

The interior of the two-story building was as ordinary as its owners. The dwelling, with its tarpaper roof and sprained doors, perched at the water's edge like a box washed in by the tide and anchored there by some passing Gulliver. Some thought it had once been painted but no one knew that to be a fact.

Sleeping quarters were upstairs, reached from the outside by an open stair. Downstairs, the kitchen also served as a dining area for the public. Most of the lower side was open, its walls lined with shelves that displayed retail goods hauled in from Grand Marais. On either side of a wood stove, overstuffed chairs with slightly frayed upholstery covered with needle-point pillows occupied a prominent place. All of the other furniture was made of old boards planed smooth. The building exuded an ambience of comfortable decay.

"We'd like to rent some fishing gear." Max shook the hand of the man behind the counter.

"Come on, I'll show you what I've got."

The proprietor, Thor Elmgren, led them back outside.

There was no porch. Wooden steps led directly down to the dock where rental canoes were stacked like cordwood, and, tied to the shore, some with motors, a few fishing boats bobbed like headless decoys.

Max and Alma looked over the surroundings.

A homely, flat-bottomed boat carrying two overturned canoes on its upright rack sat at the dock where a party and their guide loaded it with gear. It was the canoe party's transportation up to the Canadian Customs Island.

"After they clear customs, the tow will take them up to the portage into Northern Light Lake and off-load them," Elmgren told Max and Alma. "That way, for a forty-dollar tow, they will save themselves a day of paddling."

"I thought they came up here to paddle."

Thor Elmgren laughed. He had a heavy Scandinavian body, sturdy and ample, that shook all over. "None of us are purists. We still use gas-fired campstoves and foam mattresses under our sleeping bags. A tow up through the narrows to Customs Island," he explained, "gives a party an extra day out in the wilderness area away from civilization's boats and motors."

Returning to his business with Max and Alma, the store owner pointed to a shed where the fishing gear was stored.

"What do you need?"

"A spinning rod, some rooster tails, a stringer, maybe some crankbait. We're starting out a little late, but we plan to be back before nightfall. We'll go out tomorrow and look for the rice beds."

"Maybe we'd better take a lunch along," Alma said.

"My wife can fix you up."

"That'd be fine."

Elmgren nodded toward the bay. "Remember, there's a lot of open water between here and Sag Falls. If it gets windy and the waves start whitecapping, no one goes out on the lake. A good wind can swamp a boat, even your heavy wooden one with a fifteen-horse motor. So if you get lost and the wind is blowing, you'll just have to sit and wait wherever you are until the wind lays. If it gets too hairy, we can come and get you."

Alma reached out and touched her husband's arm. Her gesture contained an intimacy she hadn't intended. "Max," she said with a laugh, "I think this may turn out to be quite an adventure."

A gust of air blew off the lake and washed against their faces.

CHAPTER 10

THE TWO LAWYERS, PETER HAUCK AND ERROL JOYCE, sat in the jury box as they waited for Judge Clemens to return or call them to her chambers. The clerk and court reporter remained at their stations like diners at tables, idly conversing before the main course.

"Don't you think your client could have an accident or get lost up there?" Hauck had moved his knees so Errol could take the juror chair beside him.

"Not Kristen," Errol said. "The BWCA wilderness is home to that woman. Members of her tribe know that area like you know your own back yard."

"Taking her kids up there wasn't very smart."

"If she wanted to keep them from harm, it might have been her smartest move."

"That's no place to raise children. She took them from the home they grew up in, a wealthy home, if you will, where they had lots of advantages, to a primitive Indian camp. It's like going backwards in time."

Errol's jaw tensed. A muscle along his cheekbone quivered like an exposed nerve.

"Peter, for Christ's sake, calling the reservation primitive is hogwash. Have you ever been up there?"

Hauck shook his head. "No."

"It's beautiful, and mostly modern. The Ojibwa are now business people, just like us. They have a local government. They live in houses just like we do. Most have electricity, indoor plumbing, and telephones. Ojibwas hardly ever sleep in tepees or beat the drums to communicate with one another anymore."

"There's no need for you to be sarcastic," Hauck said, testily.

"What I'm saying, Peter, is that Kristen wasn't taking those girls to the bush to live like naked savages. She was taking them to the only safe place she knew, where her people have a different attitude toward children than we do."

"Oh? How's that?" Hauck was still bristling like an aroused porcupine.

"The Indians consider themselves responsible for all children, not just their own. I think Kristen left and took her girls with her for a very sound reason. There was something, or someone, in Duluth who might have harmed them if she left them with her husband and his family."

"That's nonsense. In Duluth the girls had a good home, a better home than the mother can give up there."

"Kristen was raised on the reservation," Errol argued, "and, like many of her people, she was educated there before she went off to college. Like others of her tribe, she tries to preserve the Ojibwa culture and traditions while helping her people cope with our modern society."

"The girls had all that down in Duluth."

"Yes, but they didn't have something else, something you and I value above all else."

"What's that?"

"Freedom. Justice."

"Where do you get off saying something like that, Errol? It sounds so noble."

"Those girls were prisoners in that household, the same as Kristen. They sought relief in our court system and they were denied it."

"For good reason."

"No, damn it, no!" Joyce brought his clenched fist down hard on the jury box railing in front of Hauck. Across the room the clerk and reporter looked up, startled.

"The law has failed Kristen and her girls," Errol said, dropping his voice. "I can't let it fail them again, even in absentia. I want them to have justice. I want freedom for her and her children."

There was a blaze in Errol Joyce's eyes.

Peter Hauck shook his head. "That's your opinion." Leaning back in the jury chair, the former law professor added, "If you can't abide by a court ruling once it has been made, maybe you're in the wrong profession."

Errol's eyes turned to flint, the green depths swirled with an emerald flame that sparkled with danger. His tone rippled with a deadly calm. "Listen, Peter, don't ever accuse me of being in the wrong profession."

Hauck looked at the younger lawyer without changing his expression.

"I am one of the lucky people," Errol said, his voice dropping to a husky pitch. He leaned toward Hauck, speaking softly. "Every morning when I get up, my feet hit the floor running. I don't luxuriate in my bed or soak in the tub. While I'm soaping up for a shampoo, or shaving the side of my face, my mind searches through the first teasing tangle of law that I must unravel that day. I look at all the puzzles of modern law.

"New puzzles, Peter, like escrowing the source code for my client's computer software so that he can resolve any post-contract disputes, the developing law for new technology. And old puzzles for the ancient common law, like adverse possession, or actions *in quantum meruit*.

"I question the legality of disclaimers on parking lot receipts. The tort doctrine of last clear chance flickers through my head when I have a near-miss at an intersection in my automobile. I savor the chase for the elusive word or legal phrase that will give my law briefs their completeness.

"No matter how acrimonious my relationship with the court, I am pleased to rise when the judge takes his seat on the bench and address him with the centuries-old salutation: 'May it please the court.'"

"You're one of the best," Hauck said drily. "But maybe you're too caught up in principles instead of practicalities."

"That's the difference between you and me, Peter. You walk out of the courtroom and for you, it's over."

Hauck swept a hand through the air. "No use in carrying excess baggage, Errol. When it's over, it's over. When I get out of court, I leave the case behind me."

"Time passes all too quickly for me in the courtroom," Errol said, shaking his head. "When my day is over, my yellow legal pad and pencil are on the nightstand beside my bed. When I finally turn out the light, I have to know, I have to believe, the system works. Despite what anyone else writes or says, despite the complaints about our legal system, I must believe it works. And I believe it works because no one has found anything better to bring us equity and fair play. It's not a perfect system, but I love it.

"And I grieve at those times when our law fails to right a wrong. I grieve for the Kristen McLeans and her daughters; I grieve for those for whom the system does not bring equity and justice because technical rules add to the weight of evidence that is necessary to grant a person what is fair and just and right."

"You're making too much of this, Errol," Hauck said. "You're taking too much onto your shoulders. You're worried about those rare instances when the system fails. This thing with the McLean family is a fairly uncomplicated hearing. Take your fee, do your best, and leave philosophy to law school scholars."

"You just don't hear what I'm saying, do you?" Errol rubbed the bony ridges above his eyes. "The law is different for me than it is for you and those members of the bar who think of it as a job or a way to making a living."

"The law is a job, a way to make a living. That's the bottom line."

"No, Peter, the law is much more than a job. We have this wonderful unique system designed to adjust the conflicts in our lives. It isn't perfect. It doesn't work all the time. It didn't work for Kristen the first time and I don't know that it will work for her the second time.

"But, it's all we have and I've got to believe in the system and believe that it'll work, because without that kind of belief, I can't be a lawyer. I can't practice law just to make a living. It truly is an article of faith with me.

"It's the law that calls me out of bed each morning. It awakens me. At the end of each day, it puts me to bed at night."

Peter Hauck rocked back in his jury chair.

Errol knew that the man hadn't understood a god damned word he'd said.

CHAPTER 11

O N EASTER DAY, 1972, IN SOUTHEAST ASIA, an exceptional aircraft, a
Boeing Vertrol ACH-47A Chinook, performed an unusual evacua-
tion mission. The Chinook, originally designed to carry only forty-
four soldiers in combat gear, took on board one hundred forty-seven men,
almost four times the load envisaged by its manufacturers. Military ver-
sions of this large helicopter were credited with rescuing some eleven
thousand helicopters and planes that had been immobilized either by
crashing accidentally or being hit by enemy fire in landing operations.

The aircraft was never manufactured in great numbers; however, the
Forestry Service of Canada was able to secure one rebuilt version for a
variety of activities involving men and materials, but chiefly for transport
in the fire zones of the Canadian wilderness.

The Chinook, ninety-nine feet long with two rotors, each sixty feet in
diameter, is the big brother of the Huey, Vietnam's all-purpose helicopter,
but requires only a two-man crew to operate it. The American craft was
chosen by the Canadians because of its exceptional ability to operate in all
kinds of adverse conditions.

First Officer Shaw and his Second Officer, Lacrosse, had flown the
Chinook from its home base in Toronto to Thunder Bay at an average
speed of more then two hundred kilometers per hour, but that day they
had no headwind and carried no cargo.

At the docks in Thunder Bay, twenty thousand pounds of chemicals and equipment were loaded into the aircraft's bay, nearly its maximum take-off weight. Fires in the Kenora district, inaccessible to ground-based vehicles, burned out of control, endangering homes and lives on the Lake of the Woods.

Once the chopper was loaded, Shaw plotted a course that would take them along the United States border south of Atikokan to International Falls, then northwest to the Lake of the Woods. The bulk of their cargo were drums of fire-retardant chemicals, but they also carried a number of high volume pumps strapped to wooden pallets and packing crates filled with hundreds of feet of canvas hose, couplings and nozzles.

Wedgewood-Ben tractor-trailer units had left two days earlier with the crated gasoline engines that would be used to power the pumps. After off-loading its cargo in the Lake of the Woods fire zone, the Chinook was scheduled to go on to Kenora where it would transfer, by lowering suspension slings, the engines from the W-B's to the site of the fires.

"We will stay below two thousand feet and try to get under the clouds and smoke," Shaw said. "I filed an IFR flight plan, but we have clearance to ignore the altitude restrictions over the Quetico, and I want to fly VFR for as long as we can."

It had been Second Officer Lacrosse's job to supervise the loading of the cargo and to make sure weight and balance were within allowable limits.

The Lycoming turbines began to whine as the rotors slapped the air in preparation for lift-off from the docks. As the transport lumbered into the air, Shaw set his radio to the designated frequencies and followed the required voice procedures to report his position and state his intentions regarding their flight. Airport Advisory Services passed along to him pertinent information and confirmed clearances as the Chinook rose, made a pirouette over the harbor and skirted around grain elevators that lined the shipping bays. The Chinook turned west on a course that would take them across the route the French voyageurs had traveled in canoes three centuries before. Their flight path was to take them over Pigeon River, past Mountain Lake and West Bearskin Lake, then to Lake Saganaga, Hunter Island, Lac La Croix and finally, International Falls.

Flashes of lightning burnished the clouds and limned the smoke from the fires with glowing copper and silver and gold. Ashes from the forest flames sailed aloft for miles on winds generated by the heat. By holding a course to the south along the border, the Chinook avoided the turbulence set off by the electrical storms. Valkyrian winds gusted against the craft nevertheless, and the spectacular light show in the sky gave the scene an eerie resemblance to a Wagnerian opera, complete with the thunder of kettledrums, the gothic smoke of destruction, and the wild fires lit by ghost torches in some maddened version of a twilight of the gods.

"We used to fight those fires in the woods," the senior pilot said, gesturing toward a distant plume of smoke rising to the right of the aircraft, "but not anymore. The botany people now say it's better to let them burn, unless they threaten human habitations."

"There's a difference of opinion about that policy," Lacrosse shouted.

"Did you ever hear how the theory of letting fires burn themselves out got started?"

Lacrosse shook his head.

"The closed-cone characteristic of the jack pine started it."

"What the hell is that?"

Shaw leaned over so that he could make himself heard above the roar of the engines. "Some years back, botanists discovered that the cones of the jack pine are borne high in the crown of the trees and remain closed for years. When a fire rages through the stands, the trees may be killed but usually, even in crown fires, the temperature inside the cones remains below lethal levels, and the waxes that seal the cone scales melt. After the fire passes, the cones open and release thousands of seeds to regenerate a new jack pine forest."

"Does it really happen that way?"

"That's what the pro-fire people argue. They say the black spruce does pretty much the same, although its cones are not as tightly sealed."

"What about the aspen and birch?"

"The botanists claim that the paper birch and the aspen adapt and regenerate from their root systems after the fire dies out."

"Do you think that's so?" The co-pilot sounded skeptical.

"I'm no botanist, but that's where the idea came from to let these fires burn themselves out unless they endanger property or lives."

As the Chinook labored west and north, the clouds and haze thickened and the pilot wrestled the craft to a lower altitude, finally holding it to a course at twelve hundred feet above the forest floor.

Suddenly, Lacrosse tapped Shaw's shoulder and pointed. "Look down there," he shouted.

Below them, between the frothing rapids of the Granite River, the pilot could see the curve of Devil's Elbow and its deep canyon walls.

"There." Lacrosse pointed downward. "See? On the ledge."

Carefully, the pilot banked the Chinook and did a complete circle over the river so the two men could have a closer look at the object below.

"It's a body," Lacrosse said, peering through his binoculars.

"Alive?"

"I can't tell—doesn't appear to be. Let's come around again."

The pilot made a second and lower circular maneuver with the large helicopter, then adding more thrust from the engines, he brought the Chinook into a hovering mode above the curve in the river.

Shaw did not take his eyes off his instrument panel. They were at five hundred feet. He left it to his co-pilot to determine if the person lying on the ledge was alive. If so, they would risk their cargo and craft in an attempt to pick up the person from the narrow canyon; or if the subject was already dead they could avoid the risk and call for the body to be recovered from the ground or by a smaller helicopter.

"I can't tell," Lacrosse said. "But it looks like a woman and she appears to be down there alone. No gear, no nothing else."

"Any movement?"

"I don't see any."

Shaw continued to watch his instruments and hold the Chinook hovering, twisting it like a weather vane into the wind. "Get on the horn," he instructed, "and tell Thunder Bay what we've found and that we're going in to try to lift her out."

"You better take a look first," the co-pilot said. "That canyon is pretty damn narrow."

Lacrosse took over the controls and held the aircraft poised, watching the instrument panel, while Officer Shaw took the binoculars and peered down at the rushing water.

"It's a woman."

Her black hair was spread out over the ledge where she lay doubled up. He saw no sign of life, but he knew that didn't mean she was dead.

Raising the binoculars, he surveyed the canyon walls. It would be a tight fit, but Shaw thought he could get the Chinook in and out without the tip of the rotors touching the granite face. He would have preferred to make the maneuver without his load. The weight would make the controls sluggish, slower to respond than if the Chinook were empty. The high palisades, however, would cut off the wind once he got the helicopter down in the valley. Coming back out he would need to stay as far downstream as he could take the Chinook, because once they rose above the rim of the canyon, the winds would throw them about and he would need air space behind him in which to maneuver.

"Get on the horn," he ordered, again taking the controls. "Tell Thunder Bay we're going down after her, and find out the nearest hospital on either side of the border. Once we get back out—if she's alive—I want to get her to medical help as soon as we can."

While Lacrosse was talking on the radio, the pilot began to prepare for the tricky maneuver. Easing back on the controls, he took the Chinook higher and turned it away from the river. Coming around again, he held the aircraft poised so he could look out the window and survey the curving valley.

"I sure wish I had my old Iroquois," he muttered, referring to the helicopter in which he had learned to fly. That model, one of the first Hueys, was half the size of a Chinook, highly maneuverable.

At the downstream end of the Elbow, the flat ledge extended out into shallow water. The pilot tried to calculate how far out into the stream he would have to land to permit his rotors to clear the granite palisade. The depth of the water was no problem. The flat ledge extended out a long way, but if he miscalculated and the force of the current caught the side of the aircraft, they could overturn, despite the weight of their cargo.

As he planned his descent, he decided that he was better off with the Chinook than with the old Huey. Once the craft settled into the water, he would need its bulk and ballast and the thrust of its powerful turbines to stay in position long enough for Lacrosse to get the woman's body back to the cargo bay.

"Grand Marais Hospital!" shouted Lacrosse. "They say if we can get her out, we're to take her stateside to the town of Grand Marais. It's about seventy kilometers."

The pilot nodded.

"Okay, let's go down and get her."

Cubby sat on an old log, soft and spongy with decay. Both girls were hot and sweating from their long climb, for neither had taken off the life preserver she wore.

The faint trail led to the top of a high ridge that separated Gneiss Lake from the Marabeuf. At first the trail took them through a swamp where the woods were dark, austere, abounding in mystery. Then the path began its climb to the pinnacle of land where, despite the haze, the two children had a spectacular view of the curving Devil's Elbow, although they could neither see nor hear the water.

After waiting a long time for the return of their mother, because of the impatience of her younger sister, Cubby felt compelled to tell Niki where their mother had gone.

"I suppose you won't stop asking unless I tell you." Using her important tone of voice, Cubby explained to Niki. "Mother has gone to Grandpa Mike's cabin in the canoe. She has left me here to take care of you. You are the baby and I am the mother. I am supposed to take you on this path to Grandpa Mike's house."

"Did Mother tell you that?"

"No, but that's what she would say," Cubby replied earnestly.

"Really?"

"Yes, and you have to obey me. Mother said this is the path to Grandpa Mike's house, so come on now."

"She didn't say that."

"Well, I think she did, so you come on!"

The girls followed an old game trail worn through the wilderness by countless deer, moose and bear that had taken the shortcut over the ridge to Marabeuf Lake.

Cubby was confused by the disappearance of their mother. She believed all that their mother had taught them about the woods and the animals, even though she didn't understand everything she believed. While that wouldn't make sense to an adult, to a seven-year-old it had enough logic to start them fearlessly on the path through the woods to find the cabin of their Grandpa Mike; the cabin where their mother had proposed they go; the cabin Cubby somehow thought was at the end of the forest trail.

Niki was standing on a protruding stone ledge covered with gray lichen and fern clusters when the giant helicopter flew over. She lifted her arm to wave.

"No, Niki," Cubby ordered. "Come back down here. You know what Mother told you. You're not supposed to wave at strangers."

"It's just a helicopter." Niki jumped down from the rock in disgust. "I was just going to wave at a helicopter."

"That's the same thing." Cubby rose to continue their climb. "You're not supposed to wave at strangers, or cars, or helicopters."

Niki trudged along behind her sister and muttered, "Not at cars, or helicopters, or buses, or trains, or bicycles, or wagons, or roller skates..."

"Be quiet and come on. It's not much farther to the top."

"Is that where Grandpa Mike lives?"

"I don't know. We'll see."

As the children set off, a black hulk rose from the forest floor and followed them.

Kristen's unattended canoe rocked gently on the waters of the Marabeuf. The river current had carried it through the canyon like a bobbing cork. It lay in calm waters, next to the shoreline under an overhanging pine near a beaver lodge that had been constructed in the bay.

An injured squirrel, stranded on top of the beaver lodge, waited as the canoe drifted up against the mud and wood structure, then, dragging its mangled leg behind it, the animal dropped down into the canoe onto one of the Duluth packs. It exhibited none of a squirrel's usual busyness or chatter. The injured animal set about to gnaw its way into the food pack. The small creature was heather brown with a rim of white around the eyes and a cream-colored underbelly. Its tail switched in jerky animation, but the injured leg showed nature had marked it for death. In its healthier days the squirrel had helped perpetuate the forest by burying pine cones. Now it was hurt and starving. The leg flopped behind it as it wormed its way into the hole in the canvas and disappeared into the food pack.

Shaw took a sighting on a lone tree standing on the bare cliff, and 180 degrees in the other direction, he sighted on a peculiar rock formation. These were to be his two reference points as the Chinook began its perilous descent. Looking back and forth at the reference points, he let the aircraft sink below the rim of the canyon, while his co-pilot peered through the window that curved below their feet and called out the distances to the water. As the spinning rotor blades began to churn up a spray, Shaw carefully rotated the Chinook so that the cockpit pointed out into the river. The rear rotary blade was sixty feet in diameter. Half the blade turning on its axis extended over the part of the rock ledge that was not under water.

Easing the Chinook farther out into the stream, Shaw finally let it settle with a splash. The cockpit pitched forward as the undercarriage touched down. Water rose part-way up the windows that curved down to the deck.

"Go!" the pilot shouted.

Lacrosse unfastened his harness and bolted out of the cockpit. Climbing up on top of the cargo, he squirmed along the ceiling of the bay until he reached the rear of the craft. He threw the latches and kicked open the rear cargo bay door. Then he jumped to the rock ledge without getting his feet wet. Ducking under the whirling rotor blades, he ran across the rock to the motionless body.

"Oh, my God," he said under his breath as he turned the woman over on her back and saw the blood and her slashed wrist. He whipped off his belt and made a tourniquet for the woman's arm.

Lacrosse gently picked her up and, keeping his head low, ducked under the rotors and climbed into the cargo bay. There he laid the woman on top of a packing crate and wedged her feet and the uninjured arm under cargo straps. He closed and latched the cargo doors and crawled back to the cockpit.

"She's alive," Lacrosse shouted, strapping himself in his seat, "but we better hurry. Her wrist is bleeding pretty badly."

Shaw powered up the turbines. The Chinook trembled and pulled free from the river, blasting a pair of plumed rooster-tails from its stern. Carefully, the pilot inched the aircraft upward, constantly sighting on the two reference points he had chosen for the descent. Then, breaking free of the canyon, the aircraft half spun before the pilot made his recovery. Shaw brought the nose up, pointed the Chinook south for the border and the hospital at Grand Marais.

Judge Dorothy Clemens returned to the courtroom and motioned for Errol Joyce and Peter Hauck to approach the bench.

"That was a short recess," Errol said.

"I just had a telephone call from the sheriff," Judge Clemens spoke in a low voice. "He received a call from U.S. Customs at Pigeon River. Kristen McLean has been found up on the Canadian side. Her wrist was slashed. The sheriff hinted that he's looking into a possible suicide. They say she's pretty bad off and they're bringing her out in a helicopter to the hospital here in Grand Marais." Her eyes clouded with sadness as she spoke in a husky whisper. "The crew that's bringing her out has radioed that they found pictures of her kids in her wallet, but they didn't see any sign of her children or of her equipment. The sheriff thinks she may have drowned her children and then tried to take her own life."

"Oh my God!" Peter Hauck exclaimed under his breath.

Errol Joyce, for once, was speechless.

CHAPTER 12

A TALL, WHIP-THIN MAN, emaciated from drink and undernourishment, struggled up the steep, tree-stippled slope, a tattered knapsack of foraged food and a bottle of whiskey strapped to his back. His face was veined like a road map, his once-handsome features now lumpy from the ravages of cheap whiskey. His eyes were rheumy, the whites muddy with brown smudges, the pupils murky. He breathed hard from the exertion. His rumpled clothes reeked of night sweat and stale liquor. His shirt was caked with dirt and vomit, his coat torn and patched. The seat of his pants was stiff and shiny, the trouser legs wrinkled with haphazard pleats that showed he had slept in them, again and again.

The man was a derelict, a victim of indifference and his own alcoholism. Over time, he had lost his family, his job, his home, his self-respect. Unlike the urban street people, who gravitated downward to skid row, the man had taken to the woods, there to nurse his guilt and shame, to feed the terrible habit that he could not shake, could not control.

When he was hungry, the man scoured the campsites that dotted the shore of Lake Saganaga or the Gunflint Trail. Or he walked the portages of the Granite River or haunted the public campgrounds. He searched for driftwood, pieces with unique shapes, and sold them to artists and tourists, or traded them for whiskey and sandwiches. Some pieces he kept for himself and whittled into sinewy, smooth sculptures of bears, deer, elk, marten, squirrels, owls, somehow finding in the grain of the wood a strange and vivid beauty. He had a knack for saving for himself just the right piece of wood that would hold an animal's essence, and his knife would find the soul of the creature and bring it to light, make it rise up out of the wood and breathe like some living thing.

The man, his legs wobbly from drink, weak from hunger, stumbled over the rise. He looked furtively back over his shoulder at the dim trail, then lurched through the trees to a clearing where he had made a home for the past two or three years. He had built a crude shelter, a fire ring of various sized stones, fashioned a bed of pine boughs over which he had placed a flattened cardboard box so the needles didn't sting him while he slept. Discarded tin cans, styrofoam food cartons, and empty whiskey and wine bottles littered the campsite.

The man slipped off his knapsack and sank to a fallen log that was his bench, his couch, his work table, his kitchen counter. He had chopped up most of the log for firewood, leaving himself ten feet for rustic camp furniture. A rusted axe, filed to a keen edge, leaned against the log. He opened the pack and dug out a bottle of whiskey, held it up to the light. He measured the amount left in the quart with his eye, spun the top off and poured whiskey down his throat. He coughed and his eyes misted over, but the scorch of the alcohol steadied his craving, quelled it for a moment.

It would be night soon, and he had traded a piece of driftwood for two pork chops wrapped in aluminum foil. This would be his supper, and he had a bottle of Tokay that he had bought from a town wino down in Grand Marais for two dollars. The bottle was half-full, but it would get him through the night, help him keep the pork chops down. He upended the pack and watched as his hoard of supplies tumbled out: week-old sandwiches wrapped in cellophane, a crumpled loaf of bread, an open bag of soggy potato chips, French fries retrieved from a dumpster at the Harbor Inn restaurant, a fresh box of wooden matches, some lunch meats that were turning gray from age, soup bones that had been thrown out by a butcher, a small bottle of instant coffee, remnants of barbecued chicken and ribs retrieved from another restaurant's garbage bin.

He stood up, hauled down a canvas bag tied to a tree limb. He left out the pork chops, the matches, and the wine, put the rest of the food in the bag and hoisted it back up, out of reach of animals. He picked up the axe and walked a couple of hundred yards to a lightning-struck tree that had fallen and begun to rot.

He cut wood for his fire from the tree, hauled the kindling back to camp in two trips. He reached for the buck knife on his worn belt and shaved a stick of wood into thin splinters. He built a cone of small pieces with some larger dead twigs around the pyramid. He knelt down close to the wood, retrieved the box of matches. He struck a match on the sandpaper side and held it to the shavings. The wood caught and he watched it flame.

As the fire grew, the man added larger pieces of wood. When it was going well on its own, he went back in the woods for larger logs. He hacked dead limbs with the axe, carried three loads back to his camp.

He would be drunk for at least three days, he knew, and unable to cut wood. The nights were cold and the mornings so chilly only the whiskey could keep his teeth from rattling. If he built the fire big enough this night, he would have coals in the morning, and he could keep them all day long. He could have his wake-up coffee laced with whiskey and do some whittling when the sun had warmed his fingers so that he could feel the contour of the wood.

The man had lived so long in the woods, no one in Grand Marais remembered his name. Although he was a familiar sight to the outfitters, the guides, and to a few of the residents, he was known to be harmless, and so was ignored. He never got drunk in town, so he had no brushes with the law.

Some said he had come up from Duluth, years ago, and some said he was from Minneapolis or St. Paul, or from some place in Iowa or Illinois. Still others thought he might have lived in Grand Marais for a time and gone broke, or lost his family in some unmentioned tragedy. Occasionally, the man brought in a rental canoe that had gone adrift and was paid some small reward, but no one bothered to ask his name.

It was as if they knew he had long since shed all trappings of society. They knew he lived in the woods and that he was some sort of artist, but no one ever offered him a job.

Maybe it was his smell, or the look in his eyes, but they tolerated him only so long as he kept moving and didn't loiter. His kind was bad for business. If he had dealings with certain people, it was always off the back porch, in the alleys, or behind the business establishments. He was like a shadow that drifted into town and then drifted back out again. Nobody in Grand Marais cared where he had come from or where he went when he left.

The fire blazed bright and high and the man kept putting more wood on it, too much wood, as he sucked on the bottle of whiskey, reaching for that plateau of oblivion where he felt no pain, had no memory, cared not for the future.

There was a point, he knew, where his mind would blot out all previous existence and just float him on a dark sea just above pain and unconsciousness.

The sun sank behind the tall spires of pines and left a glow in the sky. The man kept drinking, a swallow, then another. He sang a little song only half-remembered and he drank some more. He put more wood on the fire and set the pork chops on top of coals at the edge of the blaze. The bottle of whiskey he stashed inside his pine shelter, next to his crude bed. He broke open the bottle of Tokay and took a slug. The wine hit him with a jolt. He drank half of it, then gnawed on the almost cooked pork chops.

He lost all sense of time, and the flickering landscape began to tilt and waver in and out of focus. His fogged mind darkened with the creeping effects of alcohol. He wasn't sure whether or not he had finished the two pork chops. It didn't matter. He was no longer hungry and the wine was making his veins hum.

He stood up and the trees spun around him, faster and faster until he lost his balance. He staggered, tried to regain steady footing, but the gyroscope in his brain teetered out of kilter.

The man staggered under the weight of the alcohol and he felt himself falling. He half-turned and saw the flames roaring up at him, but it was too late to escape. He screamed as he fell face down into the blazing fire, a moment of clarity snatched from the dark jump of his alcohol-soaked mind. He screamed and sucked flames into his throat. Fire cooked the side of his face and seared one eye. He convulsed in a savage pain as the flames licked at his flesh and he heard the terrible sound of his skin crackling under the heat.

The man clawed at the fire and singed his hands. He tried to get up, but couldn't, and he kicked and rolled to get away from the flames eating at his loins. Somehow, he managed to roll out of the fire, but the heat wouldn't leave him and his nostrils filled with the stench of his own burnt flesh.

He crawled away, his coat and trousers still smoking and the pain was so intense he could not touch his face to find out if it was still burning. He could no longer scream through his fire-ravaged larynx, but the pain screamed for him and later, he heard someone sobbing from far off and he wondered who it was, and then he realized that it was his own voice and his own tears were burning the open wounds of his face with salt. He prayed that God would kill him or that he would die before morning and float out of the pain, out of the horror, forever.

CHAPTER 13

THE CHILDREN PICKED THEIR WAY ALONG THE TRAIL. Cubby knew of no other place to go. As she climbed, she thought on it. If their mother took the canoe, she must have meant for them to follow the path.

Cubby didn't like for the animal to follow them. "Come on," she said when Niki stopped again and waved to the bear in the shadows. It was different when their mother was with them and they met forest creatures in the clearings or on the paths. For then they would stand quietly as their mother told them and listen while she softly spoke the incantation that expressed to the forest creatures their oneness with them, an incantation that kept them safe.

Without their mother Cubby knew that because she was bigger it was her place to protect herself and Niki from the animals and she wasn't certain she could remember all the words.

"For as long as man had memories the forest Sioux possessed the lakes." Their mother's recitation of native American history to Cubby and Niki had been uttered in stilted Chippewa phrases translated into English by earlier generations.

"The Cree and their brothers the Monsoni and the Chippewas, who are also known as Ojibwa, forced the Sioux out on the plains to the west. The Monsoni and the Cree moved to lakes farther north, but the Ojibwa remained and became masters of the wilderness waters." That was what Kristen had told her children, "masters" not "owners."

When Canada and the United States declared the rich lands to be public domain it was of no consequence to the tribes. To native North Americans none of the Wilderness Country could be owned by anyone. All of it was common property, a place where both men and animals were intended to live.

The girls did not remember all of what their mother had related to them about the beautiful country, but that was the sense of what Cubby had in her mind when she cautioned her little sister. Cubby sang the chant their mother taught them, their talisman; the totem that protected them against harm from woods animals. "I came from above. I am holy. This is my second life. At another time I, too, was a bear. We are sisters."

"Hi, Mrs. Bear," Niki said.

"I'm going to tell Mother you bothered the animals."

Niki pretended not to hear.

"Come on, Mrs. Bear," she coaxed. The younger girl looked back down the trail at the rubbery-nosed animal that followed in the shadows. The bear had been behind them since they topped the ridge and started their downhill journey.

Cubby thrashed through the brush, plodding along the faint trail, jumping down from the rock outcroppings.

"Stop bothering her," Cubby ordered, "you'll scare her."

Niki stepped across a crevice and jumped down beside her sister. "I will not," she said, lifting her chin. "She likes me. She just likes to follow me."

"You're trying to get her to come home with us. I'm going to tell Mother you tried to get the bear to come home with us."

"We're supposed to be friends." Niki followed her sister over a tree trunk that lay across the path. "Mother says animals are our friends. I'm going to tell Mother you aren't being nice to the bear."

Cubby stopped in the middle of the trail and turned to her sister. "I am, too. I just don't want to take her home with us. She's supposed to live out here in the woods."

Up in the forest above the girls, the stealthy animal waited and watched. Every time the girls moved, the bear moved. When they stopped, the bear stopped. It had massive shoulders and powerful legs. Its pigeon-toed claws were hooked, each talon razor sharp. Its powerful neck, nearly the width of a man's shoulders, supported a keg-shaped head. Nickel-sized pig eyes, six inches apart, peered at objects with piercing but nearsighted vision.

The climb had been difficult for the children. They still wore their plastic rain gear and the bulky life jackets. The pathway was a trail for long-legged animals.

It was not by sight that the black bear tracked the girls as they worked their way down the side of the ridge toward Marabeuf Lake; rather it did so with twitching nostrils that constantly tested the air.

The children started down the trail again. The animal moved off its haunches and stalked after them.

"I think I will throw her in a pot and cook her," the younger girl muttered, stepping in the tracks of her sister.

"Come on."

"I'll make her into bear soup," Niki said, laughing.

Cubby didn't answer.

"I'll make bear soup and potatoes. Bear soup, potatoes and Kool-Aid."

"I'm going to tell Mother you talked about doing mean things to the animals." Cubby bent aside a tree limb.

The Black slipped off to one side of the trail. Quietly the bear began to overtake the two girls who were thrashing along ahead of it.

After a silence, Niki made a plaintive plea. "Cubby," she said, her voice cracking with weariness.

"What?" her sister asked sharply.

"I'm hungry."

"Be quiet, Niki." The sister wrestled with another branch blocking their path.

"I'm hungry," she whined again.

The black bear had silently worked its way abreast of them, out of their sight, and off to one side, when Cubby called, "Look, Niki, a swing!"

The older girl pulled back on a long, thick branch, then lying across it on her belly, using her life preserver as a cushion, she lifted her feet from the ground and let it swing her off the ledge over an open space with a ten foot drop. "Look at me, Niki."

The branch reached the end of its arc and sprang back to the ledge where she landed on her feet.

"Let me, let me," Niki cried as she scrambled up on the ledge.

"Not yet." Cubby launched off on a second swing.

"Let me," Niki called.

The change in the movement of its quarry startled the black bear. It couldn't discern the reason. The animal rose on its hind legs in a classic stance, its massive shoulders and front paws cocked at either side. Testing the wind with its nose skyward, it moved from side to side. The animal was unsure. The happy sounds that filtered through the trees confused its senses. Lowering itself on all fours the black bear bounded off into the underbrush and circled around between the children and the lake. Silently it sought out the trail above the water's edge, and lay in the brush beside it.

The girls soon tired of their playing.

Cubby turned to jump down from the ledge but her little sister slid down the other side and worked her way through the trees to another out-cropping of rock.

"This way," Cubby called. "The path is over here."

Niki called back, "I want to see something down here."

Cubby stood for a moment, then she, too, slid on the soft, mossy side of the rock and landed on her feet below the ledge. She caught up with her sister who was standing out on a promontory that gave them a broad view of a lake.

The Marabeuf was dotted with floating islands. Seagulls turned in lazy circles on invisible air currents high above the specks of land.

Cubby looked down to the bay below where her sister was pointing. There, drifting like the seagulls on their airy carousels, was their mother's canoe.

"That's our canoe!"

Niki turned and looked at Cubby. "I don't see Mother."

Cubby stared down at the craft. She saw only their gear in the canoe. The narrow boat was trapped in an eddy of water created by the force of the current flowing out of Devil's Elbow. Part of the current broke away from the main stream and swept along the edge of the shore to a large beaver hut that was some thirty feet wide and extended four or five feet out of the water. The bulk of the mud and wood hut was submerged, concealing the entrance used by the beaver family. The beaver's home deflected the water and turned it back into the main stream where it made a circle around the eddy. The canoe was caught in the loop, first bouncing against the beaver hut, then slowly pulling out to enter the main body of the Marabeuf where it was struck by the strong current out of Devil's Elbow and shuttled back again toward land. There it scraped along large rocks until it drifted back to the beaver hut.

Cubby stood, puzzled. She watched the craft wander to and fro in a seemingly endless journey. Then as if making up her mind, she grabbed Niki's life jacket at the shoulders and pulled her down the slope to the lake.

At the water's edge they waited until the canoe completed its turn and came back to the rocks where they were standing.

Cubby grabbed the canoe and held it tightly against the shore.

"Where's Mother?" Niki asked.

"Climb in."

"But where's Mother?"

"Climb in. Mother sent the canoe back for us."

Grumbling, Niki crawled into the boat and waited for her sister to climb across the gear after her. The canoe floated away from the shoreline and continued to circle in the swirling eddy of water.

Niki looked down at the food pack. "I'm hungry, Cubby."

Cubby unfastened the straps of the large Duluth pack. "Mother has sent the canoe back to us so we can ride down to Grandpa Mike's. That's what we're supposed to do."

Niki screwed up her face and looked at her sister. "Really?"

Cubby curtly nodded her head. "That's right. Now be quiet."

Cubby flipped back the top of the pack and was startled to see a small head with bright eyes pop out at her.

Niki immediately forgot her hunger and scrambled to see Cubby's find. The squirrel looked up in defiance but didn't make a sound, only bared its fangs. "It's hurt," Niki said.

"Its leg is broken."

Niki peered over Cubby's shoulder at the injured squirrel.

"Be careful," Cubby said, "It'll bite."

"He won't bite."

Cubby took the end of the strap on the Duluth pack and put it against the nose of the squirrel. "See," she said when the animal fastened its teeth on the strap.

Niki shrugged. "I guess he's hungry, too."

Cubby picked up their fishnet from the bottom of the boat and carefully placed it on top of the squirrel so the animal was confined. Then, cautiously, she reached into the food bag and pulled out a box of candy bars.

The girls munched candy and watched their new friend as the canoe completed another revolution around the eddy. Thoughts of their mother were crowded out of their minds.

Hidden in the brush on the shore, the black bear lifted its head and sniffed the air. The faint smell of chocolate assailed its nostrils. Quietly the animal rose on all fours and slipped through the brush to the water's edge. Squinting its small eyes, the bear saw an apparition floating on the water. The animal's nostrils told it that whatever the object was, it was fit to eat. The bear let out a roar and reared up on its hind legs, stretching its front claws apart.

The girls looked up, startled by the sudden noise. Slowly the canoe touched the beaver hut and began again its circular journey back to the shore.

The bear roared and reared up in an effort to get a better look at its quarry, then dropping down on all fours, it trotted pigeon-toed a short ways down the shore toward the end of the game trail. Turning, it made a rushing charge to leap into the water and take the canoe. Short of the edge it stopped and turned back.

Twice it made unsuccessful charges as the canoe lazily turned in the eddy. The girls were amazed that the bear was putting on such a show for them.

As the canoe again touched the beaver hut and bounced away toward the main current, the large Black turned and, gathering speed, leaped through the air into the water with an enormous splash. As the bear started to swim toward its quarry, the wave created by the wash shoved the canoe into the force of the current and sent the craft spinning out of the bay. The plunging bear had upset the careful balance of swirling water which had captured the canoe and forced it onto the main body of Marabeuf Lake.

First the bear paddled toward them like a dog, and then as quickly as it had attacked, it abandoned the chase. Turning, the animal paddled back to shore and dragged itself, dripping, up on the rocks. With a loud roar of defiance, the bear slunk off into the underbrush.

Cubby and Niki sat speechless, munching their candy. They had never seen a show like that put on by any of the woods animals.

A light appeared in Niki's eyes. Turning to her sister, she said, "She was mad at you, Cubby, 'cause you wouldn't let her come with us."

On the opposite shore a thin, long-legged figure with a half-burnt face watched and trembled in excruciating pain. The canoe turned and drifted backward toward the shoreline where the man was standing in the trees.

One side of his face and neck was covered with a crust that oozed colorless fluid through cracks from under scorched tissue. The eye on the charred side was swollen shut and the lid crusted. Chalk-white skin lay over the cheek bone where charred flesh had flaked away.

Infection caused the grotesque lopsided swelling that pulled at the edge of the man's mouth and exposed a yellow tooth. Beads of fever sweat ran down the unmarred side of his face.

The one undamaged eye, a hard, gelatinous eye, darted from side to side unblinking, watching the craft float and bob in the current. When the man finally moved his stiff muscles, he stumbled. Then he recovered his balance.

There was a stalking, purposeful intent in his stride as he set out to intercept the canoe at its landfall. He knew with pulse-pounding certainty that he had to have it.

CHAPTER 14

MAX AND ALMA SAT IN THE FADING LIGHT of late afternoon and drifted in the bay in front of Sag Store, getting the feel of their wooden boat that they would use the next morning.

"Do you think the fight between Engel Tormudson and Marie Saulturs is going to get out of hand?"

"It already has," Max said. Alma's question turned back his thoughts to the tribal council meeting he had attended. The disagreement was the result of Engel's attempt to abide by Agency rules and Marie's effort to find a way around them. Rules that denied native Americans even-handed justice and did not apply to any other group of citizens.

Alma let out a sigh. "I'm glad we haven't had to live our lives on the reservation."

"The Agency rules are the price for taking the government dole."

The setting sun splashed a flaxen glow across the bottom side of the pall of smoke that hung over the Iron Range. Waters in the Grand Marais harbor reflected the sky's tint. Some of the color brushed the fuselage and pontoons of the De Havilland Beaver as it started its final approach into the bay.

Jan Kiel flew airplanes by instinct and habit, although she was ever mindful of her instrument panel. However, neither her experience nor her instruments warned her of the pulpwood log lurking beneath the surface directly in the path of the landing aircraft. Months earlier, the water-soaked timber had fallen through the ice from a dockside rick awaiting the spring thaw and transport to a Wisconsin paper mill.

Jan adjusted the trim to let the De Havilland's pontoons clear the top of the harbor's breakwaters and settle down onto the surface. A shuddering thump caused her to cringe and exclaim, "Shit!" Quickly she opened the throttle and kept the float plane moving on the step of its pontoons, not daring to let it settle into the water until she reached the rock beach. Maintaining her speed, she skimmed across the harbor and glided up to the shore below a warehouse sign that read, "Errol Joyce, Attorney at Law."

The roar of the engine brought Errol out onto his balcony. By the time Errol got down to the shoreline, Jan had switched off the engine and was standing out on the sinking pontoon.

"This is all I need," Jan yelled, "to spend $6,000 for a pontoon!"

"What the hell are you doing up here?" Errol shouted. "Boushey told me you went on down to Duluth and would call me tomorrow morning."

"I know," she said. Jan stepped off into the water and waded to the strut that supported the wing. She shoved the craft around so that the damaged float settled onto the rock beach and stabilized. With Errol's help she tied the airplane to a pier supporting the warehouse. She handed him her suitcase and locked the plane's cabin door before jumping down to the beach.

Upstairs, Errol watched Jan drip on his carpet.

"Why did you come back up?"

"I heard on the radio that they found Kristen McLean and that her children are missing up on the Granite River," she said, her voice soft, almost sad. "How's Kristen?"

"I went to the hospital to see her. She's in a coma. So, we still don't know what happened to her kids."

"I thought maybe you might want to fly up there tomorrow and look for those kids, so I brought the De Havilland up. But now that I've messed up my pontoon, I'll have to see about it before I can do anything."

"I appreciate your effort, Jan." Errol was pleased by his friend's gesture. "The sheriff has a party up on the range now. They're going back in from Gunflint Lake and are setting up a radio base at Kerfoot's Lodge. Tonight they'll start searching the river's shoreline but it will be slow going because they must do it from canoes. There are too many rocks and portages to take a motor boat into those waters. The sheriff has arranged for a helicopter to come in tomorrow to overfly the river."

"God, I hope they find those kids alive. I hope the mother knew what she was doing out there in the woods."

"She knows the woods," Errol assured her. "Tom Boushey told me that when Kristen was a kid, she kept a hunter, who had accidentally shot himself, alive for forty-eight hours, while her father walked out of the woods to get help. She's an expert woodsman."

Jan smiled. "Woodsperson, you chauvinist."

From a distance the couple heard the cry of a loon. It was a brilliant, clear sound followed by a silence that astonished them. Then, farther away, there was the sound of a motor boat completing its journey on the lake. But mostly it was a quiet evening of shadows. The rest of the harbor was still, except for the slapping of the waves against the shore, the wooden piers, the hollow hulls of boats.

"Tomorrow morning I must call the airport at Ely to see if I can get a mechanic to come over and look at my pontoon. I'll ask them to let me use their plane while he's inspecting my damage, and I'll take you up over the range. Perhaps we can find Kristen's campsite."

Errol leaned over and kissed her on the forehead. "You're a nice person. Want to stay here tonight?"

"No, I'll go over to the Harbor Inn and get a room."

"Not like that, you look a mess."

Jan glanced down at her clothes and grinned. "I do, don't I?"

"Let me give you a bath."

Jan shook her head. "That's the last thing I need."

"That's the first thing you need," Errol said with a wry smile. He led her into the bedroom.

Although Errol had agreed that his old friend, the former District Judge P.M. Gregory, might occupy a one-room office on the third floor during the day, Errol used the rest of the loft for his own office and living quarters. The arrangement permitted Errol to have two wooden balconies. The larger deck opened off his office and the smaller deck opened off his bedroom. Both balconies offered spectacular views of the lake and were connected by a skywalk.

Errol had chosen pastel peach and greens for the suite's color scheme. A small kitchenette opened onto a dining area at the end of the living space which was furnished with department-store furniture.

That room also had a window view of the water.

It was the bath, however, that impressed the very few persons he allowed into his home. It was a large room tiled in bright ceramics, set off by a skylight that opened up half the ceiling. The room was proportioned for a tall man and equipped with mirrored walls and a king-sized whirlpool bathtub. A cushioned chair sat in a corner of the room.

Except for the four-poster bed, the rest of the living quarters, and all of his office space, leaned toward the ordinary, but not the bath. When Errol had grown up on the farm near New Ulm, his home did not have indoor plumbing. Because of that, he had designed the fancy bath he'd always dreamed of as a boy. His tiled bathroom was the most extravagant on Minnesota's north shore.

Jan sat on the edge of the bed and began to remove her wet boots.

Errol went on into the bathroom and drew her bath, adjusting the jets of water by spinning the dial of the faucet, adding scented oil and some granules of bubble bath. The two lights on the sides of the mirror were dimmed and he lit a candle on a shelf beside the tub. The burning candle laced the air with the heady fragrance of wild flowers.

Satisfied, he walked back to the bedroom and escorted Jan to the bathroom. He spread a large peach-colored towel over the floor tiles.

"So your feet won't get cold."

"Are you going to undress me, too?"

"If you let me." He grinned.

"No, I'll bathe alone." Jan motioned him back into the bedroom and closed the door behind him.

She took off all her clothes and laid them neatly on the chair in the corner of the room. Slowly, she eased herself down into the water. It was too hot and her skin flushed pink, but the warmth felt good and soon she was luxuriating in the steamy heat.

A few minutes later, there was a quiet tap on the door. Errol opened the door just a crack and set a radio on the floor. It was tuned to a station playing Chopin's Nocturne in E flat minor. It sounded, Jan thought, like Eugene Istomín at the piano, his touch both delicate and masterly.

"I thought you might be ready for some music."

Jan laughed and invited him in. "If that's Istomín playing Chopin, you've stolen my heart."

"It is. I saw him in Toronto once." He stared at the sleek islands of flesh rising out of the bubbles. Bare shoulders, a knee, a pair of toes.

She lifted a soapy foot, flexed her toes.

"Nice," he said, as the top of one of her breasts surfaced for a moment. She thought she was safely submerged in water and bubbles.

Errol turned the volume down on the radio and sat down on the floor across from her.

"Water feel good?"

"Yes," Jan said softly, sliding in deeper, "delicious." She felt the challenge of his nearness.

"May I get in?"

Before Jan could answer he started undressing. She shut her eyes. She opened them when he put his foot into the tub.

Errol bent his knees and laid his feet on either side of her hips. Her legs were under his. The tub was large enough for Jan to stretch her legs out full-length and still keep her chest under water. But her breasts tended to float to the top.

"May I wash you?" He was already soaping the cloth.

Jan closed her eyes and listened to the music and basked in the glow kindled by the delicious strokes of Errol's hands. Her body tingled as she felt the rough edges of the wash cloth slide and sweep all over her.

He began with her arms, all the way from her shoulders to her fingertips. Then he washed her legs, calves first, then thighs, and worked his way down to her feet.

Then, beginning with her hips, he washed up to her waist and slid across her breasts, finally running the warm, wet cloth over her neck and shoulders. Jan bowed her head, subservient to his gentle caresses.

With his bare fingers he washed her face, kneading the outline of her bones, smoothing her cheeks. He had her face in his hands when he stopped moving. As Jan opened her eyes, he kissed her gently on the lips, licking the sensitive inner flesh.

Errol got out of the tub. He wrapped Jan in a towel and led her to the bed in the adjoining room. He slid down beside her and put his arm around her.

They came together, as lovers, and he sank into her wordlessly. His volcanic desire consumed him with a gentle flow of lava in his veins, and he stemmed the tide that would release him.

And he waited for her, so it would be like nothing else in the whole world.

CHAPTER 15

T HE ROOM WAS VERY QUIET. Green hospital walls flickered like sea waters in the glow of the reading lamp. The soft night light above Kristen McLean's narrow bed threw a yellowish cone onto the headboard. Sheets that draped her form bore an antiseptic viridian cast. They rose and fell with the patient's shallow breathing. The nurse who attended her silently read a novel and watched for signs that she had regained consciousness. Until then, there was no further need for the physician. Doctor Jens Erickson had performed all of the medical miracles he knew. So the staff took turns watching and waiting.

When the two girls had been confronted by the stranger below Devil's Elbow, Niki had innocently pointed at the man's swollen face and asked, "Does that hurt?"

"Yes," Cubby answered, speaking for the stranger. She admonished her little sister, "You shouldn't ask the man about his face. He can't help it that he has an ugly face." She turned to the man. "Can you?" she asked politely.

"I just wanted to know if it hurt."

The open eye stared wildly at them. The man tried to speak but his seared throat would not let the words come out. A big ham of a hand held the canoe tightly against the shore. Then he crabbed out of the brush and slid down the rock ledge into the canoe. Slowly at first, then faster, the canoe left the shoreline and drifted out onto the moving waters of the lake.

The man shook involuntarily as he searched through the craft for the canoe paddles. Neither girl understood what he was looking for. They drifted with the current. Finally, exhausted, the man sat as quietly as his injury would permit at the opposite end of the canoe.

He again tried to speak, but no words would come between the burnt lips.

"Do you know where Grandpa Mike lives?" Cubby asked, finally.

The man slowly digested her question, then shook his head. His lips mouthed the word "No."

For the length of the Marabeuf the girls, from their end of the canoe, watched the man, and his one eye stared back.

As they drifted, the disfigured man shook with a chill, partly because of the fever and partly because of the delirium tremens that had gripped him at his campsite. After falling into his campfire, he had wandered in half-blind agony to the water's edge below Devil's Elbow.

The hint of another late summer storm was in the air. Smoke from many fires drifted across the long narrow valley. Loons swam in front of the children's canoe above and below the surface of the water, like iron silhouettes in a shooting gallery. Manic laughter signaled that they were going to serenade.

Cubby and Niki forgot the strange man who drifted with them. The two girls leaned over the edge of the craft and tried to touch the wet backs of the birds. First there was the wild, excited calling of a group of birds dashing across the water, then answers from other groups, until the entire expanse of the lake was full of their music, a wild harmony.

Niki beamed and clapped her hands.

In open water the current and breeze pointed the canoe toward the outlet of the lake at Horsetail Rapids. Without paddles, the canoe floated freely, sometimes twisting, but always moving north, away from Devil's Elbow.

Once, late in the day, Cubby saw the black bear. Niki was asleep with her head on her sister's chest. The stranger was also silent, his good eye was closed. Cubby watched as the big animal swam across the distant cove. It was far away, but its black hulk left no doubt in the little girl's mind.

It was their black bear, and it was following them to their home.

Cubby's lips moved. Silently she mouthed the words, "this is my second life . . . we are sisters."

The black bear pulled itself out of the cove. Sopping wet, it disappeared into the woods, continuing to move in the same direction as the drifting canoe.

Later, after the stranger had put into shore, Cubby and Niki huddled together on a log in night air that was washed by moisture spraying up from the Granite River. He sat opposite them on the other side of the fire. His face and shoulders jerked in spastic convulsions. He had finally gotten the tent erected.

The canoe lay back from the shore among the trees and was overturned. One side of it was hung with the canvas cook fly the stranger stretched to provide a makeshift shelter.

Above Horsetail Rapids, the woods rose thick on high ground. There at the end of the Marabeuf, the rock outcropping protruded abruptly and divided to form a flat tributary choked with granite slabs and large boulders—six hundred rods of plunging waters and dangerous obstacles that blockaded passage, except by land, along a narrow path that French voyageurs, centuries before, carved in the rock ledge. The high ground caught the night breeze and blew away the mosquitoes in skidding swarms, made the flames of the campfire waver like supple wands and flicker with shades of fiery gold and tawny copper.

Niki leaned against her sister. "He doesn't know where Grandpa Mike lives," she said with childish disdain.

The girls watched the man with frank curiosity.

The stranger was one of civilization's forgotten people who poured his life through the neck of a liquor bottle. In a city like Duluth he would have been pointed out as one of the street people. There he could have found an urban shelter or public kitchen in which to sober up. But the men, and some women like him who took to the woods, had to make their own shelter and fire to curl around. His kind reappeared at the edge of Grand Marais, in Cook County, only long enough to trade what they scavenged in the woods for cheap bottles of whiskey.

Later, the two girls lay down to sleep. The stranger stayed awake.

The light from the campfire flared brightly when the shavings carved by the stranger's buck knife dropped into hot coals. The wind had died down and noisy mosquitoes returned outside the tent.

Niki slept. But for a time Cubby watched, barely able to keep her own eyes open. The strange man outside the tent's screened opening appeared to be shaping an intricate design in the wood that he laid, from time to time, beside the injured leg of the squirrel. Cubby had watched as the thin shaking figure with large hands gently placed the squirrel, still entangled in the fishnet, at his feet beside the warmth of the fire.

The stranger sat beside the flickering light in the same place he had occupied all evening. Carefully and slowly he drew the knife blade along the length of the small cylinder of wood, making deft strokes, sometimes pausing until a body tremor passed, preserving most of the wood's outer edge. He carved a smooth rounded groove to shape it into a tiny splint. After every few strokes with the blade he laid the wood alongside the animal's leg without touching the white of its belly, as if to painlessly judge the fit.

Finally Cubby also closed her eyes and nodded off to sleep.

The stranger took a long time to finish his carving, and by then, the campfire had burned to a pulsing bed of coals. When he was satisfied with his work, he picked up the squirrel and lightly held it as he carefully disentangled the cords of the fish net. Holding it in the flat of his palm, he fitted the tiny wooden splint to the animal's injured leg. The creature struggled to get away and in doing so sank its teeth in his thumb. He winced. Carefully clamping his other hand on the animal's jaw, he slowly forced the squirrel to release its grip. Blood drops formed on the puncture wound. Ignoring his injury, he wrapped a dishcloth around the animal's furry head, and again set about attaching the tiny splint. Twice more he had to pause when fever made his hands shake. Finally, satisfied that the leg was protected, he gently placed the squirrel on the ground and watched it crawl into the underbrush.

The two girls slept a placid, dreamless sleep inside their mother's tent, unaware of their small forest friend's release from captivity.

CHAPTER 16

TOLI MCLEAN DECIDED TO STAY AT THE HARBOR INN on the north shore rather than drive back to Duluth.

He paced the hotel room like a caged lion. His rage spilled out in a stream of unreasoning words. He spoke with an emotionally charged voice that sporadically lapsed into a thick accent.

"Woman!" the professor screamed, "did you hear what your son said? He wants to go up to the hospital to visit the Indian bitch! She killed his children and he wants to go visit her!"

"Well, what would that hurt . . ."

In the grip of his fury, Toli struck his wife with the backside of his hand.

Usually his blows left only red marks, but this time his knuckles raised four dark swollen bruises on his wife's cheek. Selma Itbitissam McLean accepted her punishment dutifully. She was one in a succession of Persian women for whom shouting and arm twisting often were not enough to uphold the veneration that a man like Toli demanded from the females under his care. The brilliant Mideastern professor never revealed the origin of his Scotch surname. But his temper was distilled from his vague ancestry, both Scotch and Islam, which reinforced his perception of the exalted position of males in the home.

Of late, Toli had come to expect Selma and their son to side against him. It was partially a result of her exposure to the culture of an American university, he supposed.

But tonight's proposition was unforgivable and was particularly galling because it concerned Kristen McLean. Even though Kristen was not his wife, she was a female of his household—under his care—and he was offended by her leaving, by her slight to his position of authority. That would never happen with the granddaughters, Toli had resolved when Judge Clemens' order placed them temporarily in his household.

Selma, he felt, should have been aware of that, even if his son was not, and she should never have sided with the boy.

For her part, Selma McLean stood in the middle of the room servile, obsequious. She felt her face draw and quiver from the first blow. Appearance was important to her. She was glad Toli had waited until they were in the privacy of their hotel suite before beating her. They had been seated in the public dining room when their son, Arlesen McLean, stated his intention, quite a bold step for him, she thought.

Now Arlie stood as though fastened to the closed door and watched his father strike a second blow. Selma, a sturdy, obedient woman, accepted the blow without tears. She felt more deeply about the emotional hurt Toli was visiting upon their son than she felt for her own marked face. She disregarded, too, the blood that trickled from a nostril.

Abruptly, Toli turned and disappeared into the bathroom. He had performed a manly duty and Selma had submitted as women of her culture had been taught. The beating was almost ritual.

Turning to the door, Selma waved her hand at her son. "Go," she whispered.

Arlie McLean silently slipped out into the hall.

Up on the hill, the hospital was deserted except for the night staff and patients.

"I want to see my wife," Arlie McLean said. His face was drawn to a taut mask. Insecurity seemed to be Arlie's constant companion. He had expected his father to follow him up the hill. The nurse at the desk first asked for identification, then directed Arlie to the reception area while she summoned Dr. Erickson.

The physician handed some records to the receptionist, then came over to introduce himself to the husband of his patient. He had a forceful air of competency about him, a presence born of self-assurance and certitude. There was no one else in the waiting area. Dr. Erickson set a straight chair beside the man.

"Is Kristen going to live?"

"I think so," answered the doctor, "but it's too soon to know yet. Her pulse rate has come back up and her body temperature has stabilized now that we've given her several units of blood. She must have swallowed a lot of water. I can't tell how long she was without oxygen, but if it was very long there may be brain damage. That may be the reason she's still unconscious. We'll just have to wait."

"Has she said anything about our kids?" Arlie asked. The question was a stab in his heart.

"She hasn't said a word, period. Not even in delirium. She just lies there the way she was when the helicopter crew brought her in."

"How long will she . . . ?" the husband asked, groping for words.

"If she doesn't regain consciousness in the next twenty-four hours, then I would expect that there has been serious damage to the brain. In that event I would anticipate she could remain in a coma for days, perhaps even weeks. All we can do is keep her blood count up and continue the IV's so she doesn't become dehydrated, and we can control her nutrients."

Arlie looked out the window into the parking lot and chewed on his thumbnail. "Do you think she could have killed our children?" His words were husky with fear.

Dr. Erickson spoke in a gentle, low voice reserved for dreadful matters. "I have no way of knowing."

CHAPTER 17

ALMA SAT IN THE MIDDLE OF THE BOAT. When she spoke she could see her breath, bromos in the cold morning air. Max kept the motor at trolling speed as he worked away from the dock and around the rock shoal at the entrance to the bay. Once they cleared the shoal, he revved up the motor and with a grin headed the boat out onto the lake. "You all right?"

Alma smiled. "Better than I've been in weeks."

The couple had spent the night in Thor Elmgren's tent. The boat passed close to the shore below high bluffs covered with lichen, moss and pine. In the east, the rising sun struggled to burn its way through early morning fog and haze. Over her layers of sweaters and stocking cap, Alma wore the old World War II poncho that Max had brought home from Europe. The olive drab she wore matched a second poncho Max bought for himself at an army surplus store. Alma faced her husband, her hood drawn tight to protect her neck from wind as the boat picked up speed.

The wife of their outfitter, Olga Elmgren, had packed them a shore lunch back at the Sag Store. She had used a five-gallon canister to protect the food from the spray of the water.

Several canoe parties were preparing to launch from the public landing when they passed. Lake traffic from the end of the Gunflint Trail was required to go north on the lake to the narrows before entering the main body of water which was twenty miles long and dotted with dozens of islands. The couple passed two inbound canoe parties. They all exchanged waves.

Max knew that everyone leaving from the United States side was required to go first to the Canadian Customs Island to register and obtain permits for Canadian waters.

Canadian nationals leaving their country were not required to stop at the station. They checked in at the United States customs office in Grand Marais.

"Do you know how far we have to go, Max?"

"Six or seven miles, maybe."

Alma relaxed, stunned by the view, by the majesty of the lake and its wooded sections of high bluffs intersected by coves. They passed through the long slender corridor for five miles, gliding past rocks and palisades that rose up on either side of the channel.

At the narrows, the bluffs folded together leaving only a shallow passage. Once their boat negotiated the narrows, the lake again opened into a wide expanse and the couple saw dozens of perfect little tree- and rock-studded islets spread out on the clean blue water that stretched to a distant, hazy shoreline. It was like floating inside a lovely painting, Alma thought. Everywhere she looked, it was beautiful and perfect.

Max opened the yellow and blue map Elmgren had given him. The storekeeper had drawn a line on the chart which led from Sag Store up through the narrows and threaded its way through the islands until it pinpointed Customs Island. From there the line bent easterly into Red Sucker Bay and finally Saganaga Falls. Elmgren had made a large mark at the falls to indicate where the fishermen had been catching walleye.

Max looked behind him, sighting on the mouth of the narrows he had just left, and placed his finger on the map. Turning, he self-consciously grinned at Alma while he sighted on the island ahead of the boat.

Alma smiled back. "Old fearless leader."

Max nodded confidently, and settled back as the boat made its way across the lake.

After an hour they passed through the islands and out into open waters where they could see the Canadian Maple Leaf banner waving over the docks at Customs Island. Max abruptly throttled back his motor and brought the boat around full circle to give right-of-way to a float plane that was leaving the dock. Except during an emergency, the portion of Lake Saganaga that touched the Gunflint Trail was the only place aircraft could fly below forty-five hundred feet or make a landing. Bush pilots took advantage of the exception to fly fishing parties out of Saganaga to other primitive lakes to the north.

Max Kadunce cut his engine. As their boat rocked in powerless inertia, he and Alma watched the airplane laboriously turn and slowly pick up speed. Despite the drag of the canoe lashed to one of its pontoons, its powerful engine brought the aircraft up on the step of its pontoon and slowly pulled it free of the water. The seaplane rose above the tree line and disappeared to the north, still struggling for altitude.

Max fired up the boat's engine and raced across the open water toward the Canadian flag.

The customs building was a small cabin constructed by the government for its agents to live in during the summer season. Its living room served as an office and, when needed, a place to organize searches. Spread across the water in front of the cabin was an expanse of wooden docks where boats, canoes, and airplanes moored for inspection.

A young couple prepared to leave the dock in their canoe as Max eased the boat alongside and tied up behind them. The man grinned. "Hello."

"Where are you headed?" Max asked, returning the greeting.

The girl pointed. "West. Down in the Quetico. Where are you going?"

"We're going up to Saganaga Falls to do some fishing."

"And search for the wild rice beds," Alma reminded him.

The young man looked over at their gear. "I take it you're not going to stay overnight."

Max shook his head. "No, we're going back down to the end of the trail this evening."

"Have a good trip." The man pushed away from the dock, the young couple pointed the small craft to the west and began a rhythm of matching strokes with their paddles.

Max and Alma watched with a twinge of envy as the pair set off on their own adventure.

The agent for Canadian customs had a homely face that easily rearranged itself into a grin. He was short and quick, able to take three steps in one movement. His dog followed him out on the dock and immediately became concerned with protecting his master from a flock of mallard ducks that were swimming beneath the bridge walk.

"Shut up," the man shouted. The dog quit barking but didn't leave his place on the dock above the flotilla of ducks.

"I told that couple to keep an eye on the weather," the customs agent said. He gestured toward the canoe out on the open water. "If you folks plan to return to the end of the trail tonight, you better watch out for weather, too, else you might find yourselves wind-bound overnight without camp gear."

"We will," Max said as he and Alma stepped onto the dock and followed the agent and his dog to the cabin. The couple sat on the steps as the agent filled out forms in his notebook.

"There's a cold front moving in from north of Winnipeg," the agent said. "When it hits this warm front we have hanging over the lake, we'll have one hell of a blow."

"You need rain to put out these fires," Alma said. "The government should have done something to stop the burning a long time ago. There isn't going to be any forest left up here if the government doesn't do something."

The agent stopped writing. "Some believe that fires set by nature do a number of important jobs in tending forests and making meadows," he said.

"Such as what?" Alma challenged. She hated the burning.

"Random burn patterns are supposed to promote regrowth of all kinds of vegetation at different ages, and these patterns are said to support the life of different kinds of animals. Some say the fires clean out areas of deadfall—old kindling—and other forest fuels that can burn easily. Fires do create fire break corridors and reduce the risk of catastrophic fire spread," the agent added. "That's why, under the policy of natural fires, they are monitored, but not routinely put out."

"It doesn't make sense to me."

The agent started writing again. "I was over in the Quetico checking on the big fire. So far it has burned three thousand acres. Winds were about fifty miles per hour over there. The wind blows from all directions of the compass to replace the column of hot air rising from the fire. Shifts in the wind lob sparks and firebrands into untouched areas and ignite them. Sometimes the wind shift lasts only five minutes but it's enough to start a new fire line. When this happens, cumulus clouds build vertically very rapidly for thousands of feet. They don't signify rain necessarily, but in minutes they create a gale force wind that can swamp a boat. That's another way you can find yourself wind-bound."

The man finished writing and tore the traveler's copy out of the notebook and handed it to Max.

"But you think we've got some rain coming?"

"We have, according to radio reports."

"Well, if it rains, nature will do the government's fire fighting for it," Alma said.

"Lady, forest fires are like spring, summer, fall and winter, though on a much larger scale. They're nature's way of managing these wild lands."

Later, out on the water Alma said, "He never did tell us if he approved of the service's policy of natural burning."

"Maybe he doesn't know which is best."

They spoke no more, rapt as they were in the majestic grandeur of the lake and the blue trees casting stately reflections in the water.

An hour later, Max let the boat work its way up the sandy channel to the portage below the roaring falls. When they reached the fishing waters at the end of the Granite River, a scud of clouds began to form overhead. A dead, unhealthy calm settled over the Boundary Water Canoe Area.

CHAPTER 18

THE STORM WAS FOUL AND OUT-OF-SEASON.

Its savage wind came swooping down from the Arctic, knifing into northern Canada, slashing and shoving against a warm front that pushed up from Winnipeg. Like a syrup, the air stuck to the skin and was wild and cold and viscid. The storm winds conjured up a strangling wall of water and flesh-cutting ice. After being stalled for days, it broke through the thermal barrier and rushed fiercely across eastern Manitoba into the province of Ontario. As the storm moved, it gathered strength enough for a force-ten gale.

Two hundred miles west of the Granite River the storm approached the Kenora airstrip. Dark phalanxes of clouds muscled into the air space, stirring up lacy wisps of marsh fog that hovered in the lowlands, crept quietly in breathless calm just ahead of the wind. There was no lightning, no thunder, only a wall of water behind the storm's leading edge. The warm, sultry air dissipated in the brute rush of cold water. The storm cells gathered in erratic churns of wind and convection. They moved like quicksilver and dissolved in chaotic confusion, only to form again as they invaded the warm, moist summer atmosphere, roiling the air to an angry boil.

First Officer Shaw directed the ground crew who were preparing to protect the Chinook from the approaching storm. "Back that Wedgewood-Ben up to the cargo doors!" He shouted and waved his arms.

The tractor-trailer unit backed along the grass strip until its rear tires almost touched the loading ramp of the helicopter. As soon as the truck stopped, the crew started scrambling to transfer the truck's heavy cargo into the belly of the aircraft.

Shaw wanted the helicopter anchored to the ground securely by the weight of the truck's cargo. After the crew transferred the ballast, Shaw directed two more W-B tractor-trailer units into position alongside the Chinook. He had the drivers jack-knife the trailers so there was a cab at the front and rear of the aircraft with the attached trailers along the sides. The rigs formed a crude, protective wall around the Chinook.

Strange-looking clouds writhed like angry dragons overhead.

Shaw shouted to Lacrosse. "Are those trailers weighted down?" He pointed to the units that were fencing the helicopter.

Lacrosse nodded. He did not try to shout above the screaming wind.

Taking one last look around, Shaw waved to his men and all of them started running for the shelter of a block building. The rain surged across the field in sheets, turned quickly to hail, spewing ice pellets that spread and scattered like buckshot, hammering everything in their path.

Inside the doorway, Shaw paused and looked back at the aircraft. "I hope that we got far enough away from the buildings. I don't want any blowing metal to slice through the fuselage."

Lacrosse nodded. He looked out at the tumultuous sky and the slashing wind. "It's a bad one!"

For an hour the rain fell and the wind blew as the men huddled at the open door and watched the aircraft and vehicles parked on the field. When the rain and hail stopped, a short, fat tornado materialized in the brief lull. Then in a sliver of a second, a smaller funnel appeared alongside and the big one sucked it up. Debris, dredged up by the swollen behemoth, began to swirl like orbiting chunks of matter around a magnetic field. Pieces of metal struck power lines like scimitars hurled by unseen forces. Scraps of glass insulation and dust filled the air.

The men crouched low to protect themselves from flying objects hurtling through a window. The tornado tore off the roof of the building and sucked out a pile of stored fire hoses. The men rolled on the floor between crates of equipment, suddenly addled with shock. The windspout severed utility lines, knocked down a radio tower, broke water pipes and blocked the road with trees ripped out of the earth and slammed down with splintering impact.

The strong tornadic winds had developed on the rain-free side of the severe thunderstorm, descending from a cloud wall which hung like a great horizontal wheel from its flat base, a huge rotating cylinder of air, the source of its powerful energy.

With explosive force the tornado blasted through the airpark, propelling deadly debris outward at turnpike speeds. The wind spurted away from the roofless block building and away from the vehicles protecting the helicopter, then abruptly shifted course. The twister sliced a narrow path back across the airfield. It stripped the roofs from the tractor-trailer units, plunging timbers into the hull of the Chinook. The funneled winds pushed the vehicles and the aircraft together, despite the weight of their cargoes, twisting off the helicopter's rotors like a giant, invisible hand tearing off a dragonfly's wings. Then carrying with it some of the materials torn from the vehicles, the funnel left its complex pattern of destruction and rose again into the clouds. In its wake, a drenching downpour of rain began, less violent than before.

The two pilots and their ground crew survived the flying glass, pipe and lumber, but not without property damage. The Chinook lay crushed and broken out on the field, a tattered, skeletal hulk of its former self, smashed to rubble.

Television station KYD-3, Duluth, Minnesota, hangered its tiny Bell Helicopter at the Duluth International Airport. Its news gathering team consisted of a pilot-cameraman and a co-pilot reporter who had the good sense to know when not to fly.

"Call up to Grand Marais," the reporter said to his cameraman, "and get word to the sheriff that we won't be able to get up there to help him search for those two missing kids until the weather front passes through."

At Kerfoot's Lodge on Gunflint Lake the sheriff's radio operator called each searching canoe party up on the river and warned them of the approaching storm. Radio traffic that he overheard between his calls told him that the bush pilot, who was flying fishermen north from the Customs Island on Lake Saganaga, had elected to take his aircraft to the large airport in Thunder Bay to wait out the storm.

Wedgewood-Ben tractor-trailer units up and down U.S. Highway 61 relayed the weather forecast on their citizen-band radios and raced for their terminals.

Jan Kiel's mechanic who was flying in from Ely to inspect her damaged pontoon also elected to over-fly the town and go on to the larger airport in Thunder Bay, rather than risk letting his Cessna 170 sit out the storm on floats in the Grand Marais Harbor alongside Kiel's De Havilland.

However, those who lived on the north shore of Lake Superior, for the most part, went about preparing for the storm as they would any other inconvenience. The Indians up at Grand Portage storm-proofed their hotel with plywood shutters. Dr. Jens Erickson had the janitor check to be certain that Grand Marais Hospital's emergency generator was gassed and ready for use. Employees at the Cook County Courthouse were permitted to go home for the rest of the day if they chose to do so.

At their destination, up on the iron range below Saganaga Falls, Max and Alma looked at the breathtaking view. Water cascaded over the sheer drop with tremendous force, yet seemed to hang there, defying gravity until it hit the rocks below.

"Well, here we are," Max said. "We have a whole day to fish or hunt for the rice beds before we have to go back."

"Let's walk to the top of the falls, Max. There must be a beautiful view from there."

"I'll pull over to the shore. There's a pathway going up."

"I see it."

Max steered the boat toward shore, cut the engine and drifted to a point where he could tie up. Alma climbed over the bow. He crawled over the picnic canister as she held the boat in. When he was ashore, he tied the boat to a stunted tree on the rocky outcropping.

"It doesn't look too far," she said, looking up.

"No, just don't go too fast. It's still a climb."

They reached the top, panting. When they had caught their breath, they walked out on a shelf of rock and stood. From their vantage point on a high rock they saw rolling, whitecapped waters in Red Sucker Bay.

The couple looked across the broad, blue reaches to the north with its fleet of rocky islands and hazy blue hills. Max thought he saw reflected in the disappearing sunlight the flash of a canoe paddle, but with the high winds he reasoned that he was mistaken. In the solitude he saw no other sign of life.

Below, in the valley of the river that flowed from the foot of the falls, there was a rim of pointed spruce and beyond that, a great wall of towering pines. The stream itself was a churning surface for a short distance until it spread out smooth in Lake Saganaga where it reflected the quivering images of protective timber.

Water spilling over the edge of the falls plunged against boulders and broke into sprays and foam, making an exciting crashing sound that Max and Alma could clearly hear on their rock pinnacle.

Unknown to the couple, behind them, past the shallow pool that separated the roaring falls from the outlet of Horsetail Rapids, beyond the upper end of the portage carved centuries before by voyageurs who never lined their supply canoes through the dangerous waters, an ailing and disfigured stranger abandoned the tent and camp gear, and taking two small girls in the canoe with him, guided it with a pole into the mouth of the river. The current caught them and the three clung to the sides of their fragile craft as it plunged out of Lake Marabeuf into white waters that flowed toward the waterfall that emptied the Granite River into Lake Saganaga.

CHAPTER 19

ERROL JOYCE AND PETER HAUCK SAT IN JUDGE CLEMENS' OFFICE and waited for her to finish making her docket entry.

Both men could see, outside the third floor window of her chambers, the waters of the dead calm harbor. The bay was deserted. All craft, except Jan Kiel's De Havilland Beaver, had been moved into the protected wharf area or taken out of the water and stored on dry land. Errol could see the tilted wing of the float plane sticking out from behind the corner of his office building. The punctured flotation was completely filled with water and rested on the shallow rock bottom. Except for securing it with more rope, there was nothing Jan could do.

It was not yet noon. The courthouse was mostly empty, and the streets of Grand Marais were deserted. It was a day of gray unrest. The sky was leaden, the town pulsing quietly with an eerie stillness. Occasionally, a vehicle sped through and disappeared down the coastal highway, but the tourist traffic had heeded the warnings. The season's most serious storm was approaching from the northwest and there were reports that it was leaving a swath of destruction in its path.

Judge Clemens stopped writing, beamed a friendly smile toward the two counselors. She was petite, middle-aged, with red hair becomingly styled. There was a serious cast to her finely chiseled features, banished temporarily by her warm smile. Her soft hazel eyes shone with intelligence and compassion, but they could also flash anger and annoyance from their depths of gold and amber. Both lawyers knew from experience that in the courtroom, Clemens was a no-nonsense judge; and that in the years before she went on the bench she had been a skilled trial lawyer. Members of the Bar believed her to be fair and usually in good humor.

"Sorry about that," Judge Clemens apologized, raising her eyebrows a trifle. "I let my clerk go on home. They've let the children out of school and she has two of her own waiting for her at the house."

Hauck looked around at the high-ceilinged office. "There's no safer place on the north shore than here," he said in his deep-timbered voice.

Judge Clemens nodded. The large building, a structure without elegance, was constructed of gray granite blocks that sat on bedrock halfway up the side of the Iron Range, where it overlooked the harbor.

"She's worried about her home and children," the judge said. "As for me, I would just as soon wait out the storm here as in my apartment. Our court reporter is also going to stay over rather than drive home."

Errol looked back down the hill at his own waterfront office. He had told Jan he would come back and help secure the airplane.

Judge Clemens picked up the sheet of paper on which she was writing and read aloud, in a crisp Minnesota accent, her docket entry.

"Comes now Peter Hauck, Attorney for and on behalf of Petitioner, Arlesen McLean, and also comes Errol Joyce, Attorney for and on behalf of Respondent, Kristen McLean, and stipulate and agree that this cause may be continued thirty days; that temporary custody of the two minor children shall remain with the father during such period of time, with the right of visitation by the mother at reasonable times and places." At that point Judge Clemens turned to Errol. "I'm not going to make any entry specifying the precise time and place. But if that becomes an issue I expect both of you to immediately inform me so I can amend this order in that regard.

"Unless those kids are found to be safe, and the mother regains consciousness," she added soberly, "it's probably not going to become an issue anyway."

"Kristen McLean has not harmed her children."

"I hope you're right," Judge Clemens replied in a quiet voice.

Hauck nodded in agreement.

Judge Clemens repeated, "I expect both of you to call me if there's a problem."

She then returned to her paper and continued reading. "It is further ordered that during the thirty-day period, the father shall provide a home for his children separate from the household of the grandparents, Toli and Selma McLean; and shall permit the grandparents to visit such minor children only in the presence of the father or mother, Arlesen or Kristen McLean."

"Now, Your Honor, that's not what the agreement was," Hauck protested. "The agreement was that the father would provide a separate home for the children during this thirty-day period. But I didn't agree that the grandparents couldn't visit their grandchildren."

"I understand that," Judge Clemens said, "but the sense of the order is that the children will be with their grandparents only in the presence of one of their own parents. The order might as well permit the children to live in the grandparents' household, if either grandparent is given a private visitation with them in the household provided by the father."

"Respondent will not agree to any order that permits the grandparents to be alone with those children until after the court hears evidence on the custody issue," Errol said.

Hauck argued, "I didn't understand that we had agreed to an order that was restrictive."

"As I said," Judge Clemens interjected, "if the children aren't returned unharmed, it's not going to make any difference."

"Those children have not been harmed by Kristen McLean," Errol insisted. He wished the storm had not prevented the landing of the aircraft from Ely. In his own mind, he was sure that the children were being cared for by some tribe member in an encampment up near Devil's Elbow. However, the storm warnings had delayed Jan's plan to take him on an air search.

"Well," Hauck said, "they certainly haven't been harmed by their grandfather."

Judge Clemens sat back in her chair. She made a small steeple of her index fingers, touched the tips to her lower lip. "In this hearing Errol argues that the grandfather is guilty of impropriety."

"The mother didn't testify to any impropriety by Toli McLean in the last hearing," Hauck said.

"I know," she said, "and because she didn't I granted the father's request that he be given temporary custody and the children be permitted to live in the grandparent's household. But, this new complaint Errol has made on behalf of the mother changes the situation. The law requires me to be sure the children are properly safeguarded until this new issue is resolved."

Judge Clemens turned to Errol. "Why didn't you raise this issue in our first hearing?"

"I didn't know about it until my client wrote and told me."

Judge Clemens shook her head thoughtfully. "I don't understand why the mother didn't speak out if she had a complaint."

"I would guess," Errol said, "that the mother thought she couldn't prove it, and didn't want to put her children through the trauma that kind of accusation would produce if she couldn't."

"If you couldn't prove it then, you sure can't prove it now," Hauck said.

"I would have tried to, back then, if Kristen had told me what she suspected and I assure you I'm going to try to do so in this next hearing."

"Well," the judge said, "I must assume that the children will be found and that they are safe at the moment. If we have an issue of misconduct raised on the part of the grandparent, then until that issue is resolved, the children should not be permitted to stay with the grandparents, except in the presence of someone approved by this court."

"All of this is a waste of time," Hauck protested. "Joyce isn't going to have any more evidence at this hearing than he had at the last one."

Errol started to speak, but Judge Clemens held up her hand to silence him.

"The overriding factor in any decision I make in these hearings is 'what is best for the minor children.' Peter, you've told me the father has rented an apartment in Duluth and that the children would live in the apartment with their father during the thirty days that the father has requested there be a delay. I'm agreeable to that. I think that would be in the best interest of the children, but as long as Errol, on behalf of the mother, contends that the conduct of the grandparents may be improper, then it is to the best interest of the children that they visit with the grandparents only in the presence of their own parents."

Peter Hauck stiffened in his chair and shook his head. "It's all going to be a waste of time, but I'll talk to my client." Looking over at Errol, the older lawyer said, "The results are going to be the same as the last time."

Errol did not reply.

"All right, then," Judge Clemens said. "Let's move on. Is there any way you two lawyers can settle this custody question without our having another hearing?"

"Not according to the McLeans."

"Which McLean?" Errol asked. "Arlesen or his father and mother?"

"I represent Arlesen," Hauck said evenly, "and he wants permanent custody of his children. The family regards Kristen McLean as being a dangerous, unbalanced woman. We think her conduct has demonstrated that. Otherwise, she wouldn't be lying over there in the hospital right now. Her accusations are a fabrication."

A breeze gusted through the open window and for a moment stirred the dead air.

Judge Clemens finished reading her dictum. "It is also ordered that the costs of these proceedings shall be taxed against the petitioner." She laid the piece of paper on her desk. "It's my feeling that the storm has delayed these proceedings without anyone's fault, but the father is the moving party. I'm going to charge the court costs for the delay to him."

"Judge," Hauck said, "I cannot go on record as agreeing to a stipulation in that form. I don't have authority from my client to consent to such a restrictive custody order."

"Is your client still in town?"

"Yes. We're all going to stay down at the Harbor Inn tonight to wait out the storm."

Turning to Errol, she asked, "Did you say Jan is up here from Duluth?"

Errol nodded. "That's her airplane sitting down there in the harbor. I promised her I would get back and help her tie it down so it won't blow away."

The judge turned again to Hauck. "Your client asked for a hearing today on the permanent custody issue. I'm prepared to continue the hearing for thirty days under the terms of the stipulation I read to you. But if my court reporter and I are going to sit out the storm in the courthouse, and if your clients are still in town, there's no reason why we can't get Jan up here and appoint her Guardian Ad Litem for the children and all of us pass our time during the storm hearing the evidence on your client's motion for permanent custody."

"But, Judge, my witnesses won't be available," Errol protested.

"Who will you use?" Judge Clemens asked. "I couldn't hear testimony from the children. They're too young. If the mother were conscious, she couldn't testify as to what the children said; that would be hearsay. Are there any other witnesses available on the issue of the grandparents' conduct, other than those three?"

"No. But I don't agree that a seven-year-old can't be qualified as a witness. There is a precedent for taking testimony from young children in special circumstances."

"I've never heard of a seven-year-old testifying in a Minnesota court.

In any event, it is a discretionary matter for the court to determine if a minor is qualified to testify. I don't want to do that. I don't want to put a young child through the trauma of testifying against a grandparent in my courtroom."

"What about the trauma of putting a child back into an improper home situation?"

"I did not say I would do that," replied Judge Clemens. "I just said I'm not going to require a seven-year-old to testify in my court." She turned again to Hauck. "But the burden is on the McLean family to show that the grandparents' household is a proper place for the children to live. I agree with Errol that by asking for permanent custody the father has again opened up the entire issue of custody. We're going to start over on the question of who shall have custody of the children and where they shall live."

"But the mother is in the hospital unconscious," Hauck protested. "Kristen McLean couldn't care for the two kids, even if she was awarded custody."

"I don't know that. As Judge, I can only act on the record put before me, and up until now, there is nothing in the record about the mother's inability to care for her children. We will hear evidence on the mother's ability to provide care for her children after we get this question about the grandparents straightened out."

"And if my client agrees to your stipulation?" Hauck asked.

Judge Clemens started straightening up the papers on her desk. "If your client agrees to the form of stipulation, I will delay the custody hearing for thirty days on the terms stated in the order. But if we go ahead with a hearing, I propose to allow the mother's lawyer a wide latitude in his cross-examination of the McLeans." The judge held her papers and spoke directly to Peter Hauck. "I want to be completely satisfied that it is proper for those children to be returned to the home of the grandparents before I will let them go back there."

"I'll talk to my client."

Judge Clemens looked at her watch. "If your client has not agreed to the stipulation by three o'clock this afternoon, I will expect you to have him here with his witnesses so we can start rehearing on the custody issue." She turned to Errol Joyce. "Regardless, I will want the lawyers back here at three o'clock, and I will appreciate it if you will tell Jan to call me. I'll be here in my office."

Errol nodded.

The two lawyers rose. "I'll have an answer for you from my client by three o'clock," Hauck said.

Toli McLean paced the hotel room in front of the bed where Peter Hauck was seated. Selma was out of sight in the bathroom and their son sat in a chair by the bathroom door. Arlesen had said nothing in response to Judge Clemens' message. However, the father was livid. "Damn woman judge!" He spat the words bitterly.

"We came up here to have a hearing to get permanent custody. Let's have the hearing," the lawyer advised.

"We expected her to sign the court order when she learned Kristen stole the kids." Toli stopped and made sweeping gestures with both hands. "I didn't expect that my family would be questioned as if we were criminals!" The older man turned to his son, his arms still spread wide. "And now the judge says she might even take away temporary custody of your children, that we have to show our home is a decent home in which to raise the children. The children have lived in our home since the day they were born, and this woman judge says we have to show her our home is a decent home!"

"Damn it, Toli," Hauck said, "when Kristen and Arlie asked for a divorce, they submitted their rights of custody to the jurisdiction of the Minnesota courts. The judge now gets to make the decision as to where the kids will live and who they will live with, and we've got to come up with evidence to support our custody request when the judge tells us to."

"Woman judge!" repeated Toli.

"Man or woman, it doesn't make any difference. The law is the law, so let's have the hearing and get on with it."

"I don't think my family should have to testify."

"Then let's consent to the judge's proposed stipulation."

"Not when I'm accused of not having a home good enough for my own grandchildren!" Toli shouted. He stood, radiating his righteous indignation like an ancient patriarch. His nostrils were distended as if he were about to spew fire and brimstone on the attorney. His eyes, dark beneath tight-knit brows, flashed sparks from their depths.

"You can't have it both ways," Hauck said. "Either your family agrees to the stipulation, or you testify starting at 3:00. Otherwise, you give up custody of the children. You've got to decide now, one way or another."

Toli snorted his displeasure, walked to the bathroom door and shouted in to his wife. "You hear that? Same as the last time. Lies, all lies!"

Hauck' eyes squinched in puzzlement. "What do you mean, same as last time?"

"Just what I said." Toli threw his hands up toward the ceiling. "Like in Vermont. We had a neighbor lady when we lived back in Vermont who claimed we maintained an improper home. I've been through this before and I don't have to stand for this kind of treatment by that lady judge!"

"Wait a minute," Hauck said. "What was that again?"

"A neighbor lady we had in Vermont called the police because I sunbathed in the nude in my back yard. She claimed I was exposing myself to the neighbors. It was a lie. They couldn't prove their lies."

"Were any charges filed over the incident in Vermont?"

"No, no," Toli said. "A man is entitled to sunbathe in his own back yard. She called the police, but no charges were filed. I'm just saying Kristen is telling lies about our home like that other woman did."

The lawyer was silent for a moment. "Do you want me to sign the stipulation or not?" He put the question to Arlesen McLean.

His father answered for him. "No. If we agree to the stipulation it will sound like it's not proper for us to be with our grandchildren. I'll never admit that!"

Hauck rose. "Then the three of you will have to testify, and each of you will have to undergo cross-examination by Kristen's lawyer."

"We'll testify," Toli said.

Hauck nodded. "I'll tell the judge we'll be ready to start the hearing at three o'clock this afternoon."

Outside, a breeze began to agitate the air again. The gust blew, lightly at first, off the range. Halfway up the hill, the flag at the top of the pole on the courthouse lawn began to flutter.

CHAPTER 20

IT WAS CUBBY WHO PREPARED BREAKFAST, granola bars and Kool-Aid. By a series of complicated signs and mouthing of words, the disfigured stranger told Cubby and Niki he had set their squirrel free. And they were glad. The telling took much effort, and the sick man sat on a log and began to retch. Despite the wracking effort, he could bring up nothing from his stomach. When his spasms stopped, he hung his head for a long time before looking up at the girls again with rheumy, pain-shattered eye.

"Are you sick, Mister?" Niki asked.

The man nodded.

"Do you want some of my Kool-Aid?"

He shook his head.

The two girls stood in front of the man seated on the log. "We're sorry you're sick," Cubby offered.

He lifted his scarred face up to them. Salty tears from the one good eye set fire to the burnt tissue they touched. But that didn't seem to matter to the man, for the misshapen corners of his mouth twisted as if trying to bring forth a grin.

With effort, as if drawing on some hidden reservoir of strength, the stranger pushed himself off the log. He made gestures to show the girls that they all must leave. He couldn't tell them he hadn't the stamina to take them across the portage, and he couldn't leave them alone in the woods. He knew he had to chance a running of Horsetail Rapids in the canoe, and he had to take the girls with him.

"He wants us to go with him," Cubby said.

"Okay," Niki said, with an eager lilt to her voice.

After the girls climbed into the canoe and settled in the bow, the stranger pushed off and climbed in as it floated free of the shore, aimed for the river.

Granite River from Gunflint to Saganaga was the route of the ancients. Trappers, Indians, explorers, and voyageurs all had carried canoes on its eight portages of varying lengths, the longest, a quarter of a mile. Sometimes they navigated the dangerous waters to avoid seven of the eight carries. However, few of the skilled canoeists ever attempted to ride the water of Horsetail Rapids. Horsetail was a series of treacherous whirlpools set in motion by the peculiar alignment of granite slabs that flaked off from the Laurentian palisades and scattered along the length of the river. At its very end, the white waters flowed into a swift, shallow pool before plunging over Saganaga Falls into Red Sucker Bay. Eventually, the water spilled out of big Saganaga Lake at Silver Falls, flowed north and northwest through Quetico Provincial Park, and finally, by way of the English River, into Hudson Bay.

The canoe entered the Granite River with a jolt. The front end under Cubby and Niki rode up out of the water and pitched down, throwing the stranger forward and to one side, almost knocking him out of the canoe. He used his pole to hold his balance.

As the boat began rocking and pitching Cubby tightened her legs with a scissors lock around her sister's life preserver. She held to the sides as they gained speed. Their rain gear turned aside the spray of the water that splashed over the bow.

No sooner had the craft entered the river than the current threw the canoe into the broken face of a palisade that turned the stream at a sharp right angle. The canoe twisted in a whirlpool and careened backwards. The stranger at the other end thrust out the pole to keep them from crashing into the wall of rock. The canoe quivered as he shoved against the wall, and the craft stopped for an instant. He knelt, bracing the end of the pole against his chest and, straining with the effort, pushed and swung the front end to align them again with the tongue of the river.

In turning, the pole's shaft bent and splintered. Like a wooden spear, the pole impaled the man's armpit with its jagged point, and tore the muscle as the shattered shaft twisted away and fell into the water.

He pitched forward and fell into the bottom of the canoe. He shuddered in pain. His chest heaved and his throat quivered to release a scream of agony that he could not force through his scorched throat.

The girls did not see the man as he was struck, wounded, and went down. They rolled about the bottom of the canoe and fought to regain their balance, oblivious to his torment.

The craft held to the center of the stream until it struck an obstacle. There was a spine-tearing screech of metal and rock. The canoe swung sideways, its front end hung on a granite slab. Water pressure tore the boat free and it careened out of control until it struck a felled tree trunk that stuck out from the shore. The canoe spun in a tight turn until it was parallel to the current. The water seized the craft in its powerful grip. Riding high on the surface, the canoe twisted, dipped, and turned in the relentless current.

Without paddles or paddlers to interfere with the rushing stream, the canoe somehow held to the narrow slipstream of water, sliding across sinister granite slabs, avoiding the grabbing branches from the trees that stuck out into the stream.

Overhead, drab pillow-shaped clouds bunched in a thick line and advanced from the northwest. Dark indigo sky with twisted gray streamers spread to the horizon behind the line. The valley of the rapids began to fill with black shadows.

The dancing canoe bounced and ducked and darted through the rocks. Sometimes the craft was athwart the river current. Most of the time it traveled straight in the channel. Once they were caught in an eddy; a dirty, frothy whirlpool that spun them in a complete circle before thrusting them out again into the main stream.

Cubby and Niki clung to the sides, caught up in the exhilaration and excitement of their ride. They couldn't understand why the stranger slept through it all. Cubby and Niki liked him. During one extraordinary dip of the craft, Niki let out a squeal, followed by a high-pitched laugh. Cubby scissored her tightly with her legs.

At the very end of the run, a fallen giant pine completely lay across the stream, but the canoe sat low enough in the water so that the girls, heads pulled down, slid under it. The canoe shot out into a shallow pool, suddenly free of turbulence. It bobbed, for a moment, in tranquil waters.

A gentle undertow tugged the craft slowly away from its landing point. Beyond, the water imperceptibly gained speed where it spilled over a ledge. Once the canoe floated to the edge of the pool, where it was inexorably bound, it and its cargo would plunge over Saganaga Falls into Red Sucker Bay.

CHAPTER 21

THE WIND PICKED UP AND THE WATERS of the harbor began to roll and heave. The wing of the De Havilland shuddered, shook as it rose and fell in the pull of the tide. Jan balanced herself on the undamaged float and passed the nylon cord over the single strut that braced the wing on her side of the cabin. After securely tying it, she tossed the rope to Errol, who made a second tie to the wooden pillar that supported his office building. The submerged pontoon continued to rock as Jan worked her way along the back side and jumped to the shore.

She watched as the sunken float shifted on the gravel. She shook her head sadly. "This blow is going to grind the bottom out of that pontoon. The only thing I can hope for is that I lose only a $6,000 float and not the whole airplane."

"You've got it insured, haven't you?"

"This is my baby. I've got insurance, but money could never replace my baby. She's the only airplane I ever owned, the one I've always wanted—one of a kind." With affection, Jan looked back at the aircraft sitting at the water's edge. It was tilted at an awkward angle like a wounded seabird.

The winds were now steady and the surface of Lake Superior beyond the mouth of the harbor sprayed a frothy foam from the top of each wave. Under the protection of the overhanging office building, Jan and Errol inspected the tie-down.

"That's the best we can do," she said and turned her attention to Judge Clemens' message.

"What does the judge want?"

"I think she's going to make you a mother. She's going to appoint you Guardian Ad Litem of the two McLean children so that we can have a hearing this afternoon on the motion of the McLean family to get permanent custody."

Jan knew that under Minnesota law the court could designate a Guardian Ad Litem for certain persons to protect their rights in the courtroom. If Judge Dorothy Clemens made the appointment and Jan consented, the McLean children would become her wards until the court ordered her to be relieved of that responsibility.

"She's going to hold court this afternoon?" Jan looked about at the gathering storm. "Doesn't the judge know about the warnings?"

Errol nodded. "Her court reporter is staying over. She has decided that she is about as happy sitting out the storm in the courthouse as she would be over at her apartment. The McLeans are still in town so she's going to have a hearing while they're here, storm or no storm."

Jan laughed. "That sounds like Judge Clemens."

"If the McLean family will agree to the stipulation we won't have a hearing, but that's what Judge Clemens wants to talk to you about."

"Has anyone heard how Kristen is getting along?"

Errol shook his head. "Not good. She's still unconscious."

"How about her kids?"

"No one has found them."

"I wish we could have flown up there today."

Errol nodded. "I'll bet those kids are camped not too far from Devil's Elbow."

"What do you think about the grandfather? If I'm going to serve as guardian for those two kids, I want to make sure they are safe in whatever home the judge puts them."

"All I know is what Kristen wrote me before she went down to Duluth and picked up her kids. She said Grandpa's a pervert. Kristen genuinely was worried. If what she wrote is true, she had reason to worry about her children being in that household."

"How do you propose to get custody of them for Kristen? She's lying over in the hospital unconscious, and you have no witnesses."

Errol's face was masked with concern. "The only thing I've got going for Kristen is that the burden of proof is upon the McLeans to show that their home is an acceptable home for the kids; and the judge says she is going to permit me to have wide running room when I question the family."

Jan picked up the rain gear she had taken from the airplane. "I'd better get up the hill before this storm gets really bad. I'll see you up at the courthouse."

On Hunter's Island in the Quetico, thirty miles west of Granite River, the fierce, steady wind fanned alive the embers along the fire line and set them flaring. Flames lashed through the brush, setting fire to the smaller pines and making them glow like fat holiday candles. As the heat began to recharge the air, cold blue arms of rain reached down from the clouds. The hot coals and burning wood sputtered and spewed steam when touched by the first drops of water, but quickly the flames were smothered by a continuous deluge. The fires that had burned for weeks, in minutes turned into a gray bleak pudding of mud. Small rivulets and larger streams of the forest ash began to flow down the rocks into the lake, fouling its shoreline and causing the fish to scatter from their feeding grounds.

Max and Alma Kadunce stood on the ledge beside the top of the waterfall and watched the approaching storm and waves on big Saganaga that held them wind-bound.

They heard a shrill scream, then laughter. The old couple turned and saw the canoe shooting into the shallow lagoon above the falls. As they watched, dumbstruck, the craft straightened and bounced swiftly along the edge of the rocks, gliding toward the waterfall and certain destruction. Judging from the happy sounds coming from the craft, the couple realized the occupants were children, oblivious to their danger.

"Oh, my God!" Alma exclaimed under her breath.

CHAPTER 22

MAX KADUNCE BOLTED INTO ACTION.

He leaped from the rock to the water and splashed along the flat stone shelf that extended below the surface to the lip of the falls. Despite the tug of the stream, his movements were precise, calculated to intercept the vessel as it came down the channel. He braced himself, knowing he had only one chance.

At first the craft appeared to be moving with glacial slowness, but the speed increased and it began to turn away from him. Max stood up to his waist in ice water, and yet he was sweating. Moving with the energy of someone much younger, he lunged for the edge of the craft as it shot by.

He had miscalculated.

The weight of the canoe dragged him off-balance. The end swung crossways into the channel away from the shore, twisting him, making him lose his footing. As he was pulled forward, a pair of hands grasped him by his poncho. Alma braced her feet on the submerged rocks and clung to her husband as he strained under the full weight of the canoe and its occupants. His muscles were hardened by a life of work in the warehouse, but it took both of them to hold on to the boat as he shifted to find solid footing.

Alma Kadunce gritted her teeth and closed her eyes and hung on. She arched her spine as she leaned backwards in the numbing cold water.

The old couple fought the waterfall for possession of the craft. Slowly it pivoted, and Max reached hand over hand along its side, letting it turn while hauling it back to him. Again, he almost lost his footing, but Alma steadied him.

The craft swung slowly around and, step by step, they dragged it back to the shore.

Two surprised and excited faces beamed at them from inside the canoe. A man lay sprawled on the bottom for half its length, face down, both arms tight against his body. The man's head was wedged under the metal seat, and his knees were drawn up in a fetal position.

Slowly, very slowly, Alma and Max pulled the canoe onto the sloping rock shelf. There, Max finally was able to wedge one end of it between two boulders. For the moment, there was no danger of the canoe going over the treacherous falls.

"Thank God!" Alma said. She arched her neck and laid her face against the back of her husband's wet rain coat. Both were seated on the ledge, holding onto the canoe. Max slumped over, rested his head on his knees. He was too drained from the exertion to speak.

Niki raised her bright face and smiled. "Hi."

Cubby also grinned at the old couple. A big drop of water splashed on her face. She echoed her sister's greeting.

The children looked up at the darkening sky with its ominous, bulging clouds.

The oncoming storm's first rains began to fall. Droplets pelted their faces and they heard the first muffled tattoo of warning, a sound like sand peppering the dry spruce branches and pine needles, spattering on the rocks and the scaly bark of trees.

Max tied the canoe to the shore with a rope he found attached to its bow. Alma, like a mother hen, sat on the ledge with a child under each arm. She bent over, protecting them from the peppering downfall of rain. The stranger's inert body remained in the bottom of the craft.

The canoe tipped, rolled under his feet, as Max stepped into it and straddled the body. Kneeling, he strained to reach under the thwart and touch the man's chest to find a heartbeat.

The stranger was alive.

Max carefully pulled the man's uninjured arm above his head so he could turn him on his back. He flipped the man over, saw the swollen face, smelled rotted, burnt flesh. He gagged and rocked back on his haunches. He closed his eyes tight.

He leaned over the side of the canoe and retched.

Alma shuddered and held the girls' faces down.

Max began to slowly pull off his poncho. Spreading it, he laid it over the still form to hold the rain off the man's body. He draped one end over the thwart to keep the rain gear from pressing down on the injured man's burnt face. He carefully tucked the sides under the injured man so the wind would not blow the covering away. Then he pushed himself to his feet and stepped onto the shore.

An involuntary shudder coursed through his body as he sat down beside his wife.

"I'm so very sorry," Alma whispered.

"That's all I can do for him now," Max muttered.

"I know," she said tenderly.

"We're going to have to get these kids under shelter somewhere," Max said, after he composed himself.

She clutched the children, held them tightly to her.

"We can take them down to our boat at the bottom of the falls, but that isn't going to be any better than staying up here. I wish we had a tent."

Cubby pulled her head out from under Alma's arm. "We've got a tent."

Niki looked up and echoed the words of her sister. "We've got a tent!"

"Where?" Alma asked.

"Back up there." Cubby pointed in the direction the canoe had come from. "That's where Niki and I slept last night."

Max spoke to Alma. "There isn't any gear in the canoe. They must have come down the river with gear." Turning to the girls he asked, "Where were you last night?"

Cubby pointed again. "Up there."

Max and Alma looked to the portage pathway built into the rock along the ledge beside the foaming rapids.

"How far up there?"

Cubby shrugged.

"A long way," Niki said.

Max rose. The rain was beginning to make the rocks slippery. "You watch the kids. I'll walk up to the other end of the portage to see what I can find."

Alma shook her head. "We'll all go. I don't want us to be separated."

"What about him?" Max asked, gesturing toward the unconscious man in the bottom of the canoe.

"The canoe is tied down," she said.

As the girls stood up, Alma adjusted their rain gear and straightened their life preservers. "You haven't told us your names."

"I'm Cubby."

"I'm Niki."

She smiled. "And I'm Alma and he is Max."

"Do you know where Grandpa Mike lives?" Niki asked.

"No. Who is Grandpa Mike?"

"He's our grandfather," Cubby said.

"We're going to his house," Niki added earnestly.

"Our mother is already there," Cubby said, using her important tone of voice. "But we've been lost," she added matter-of-factly.

"Who is the man in the canoe?" Alma gently asked. "Is he your father?"

"No, he's just a man," Cubby said.

"How did he burn his face?" Alma thought she needed to ask the question.

"I don't know."

"I don't know," Niki repeated.

Max listened while his wife questioned the children. But the rain had begun to fall harder and the wind was turning cold. He motioned to his wife that they should leave.

The two children scrambled ahead of the old couple like sure-footed forest animals and quickly took the lead.

"Be careful," Alma called to them.

"You be careful," Max ordered as he led his wife along a narrow ledge above the roaring waters. The pathway was only a bed of slippery tree roots in places, and round sloping boulders as large as houses. The trail was worn and steep. They carefully picked their footing to keep from slipping on the slick surface.

"I'm worried that one of the children will slip and fall."

"Alma, I'm beginning to think that those two kids are indestructible. All they're worried about is where their Grandpa Mike lives."

Alma stopped, and holding her husband's hand, slid down the side of a slippery rock. "Life is so simple when you're a child."

Max grunted and turned to take the lead again. Behind him Alma watched where she stepped as she spoke. "Do you think that if we forgot about death and just lived for the moment and concerned ourselves with only important things like where our Grandpa Mike lives, we could be happy like them?"

"Death can't be ignored." Max couldn't shake the foreboding feeling when he spoke the word. "Death is back there with the canoe right now."

"Do you really think the man's going to die?"

"Yes," Max said slowly. "I could smell him dying. He's going to die."

The two struggled along in silence.

Cubby and Niki called back for their new friends to hurry. "We see it! We see it!" they chorused.

Max supported Alma's arm as she stepped down from the last ledge. They found themselves looking out on the wide expanse of Marabeuf Lake. On the shore they saw a sturdy tent. Off to one side stood the cook fly the stranger had abandoned when he put the children in the canoe and launched it with his remaining strength into the mouth of the rapids.

The children ran ahead and stood inside the tent, out of the rain. They held the canvas flap open and called for their new friends to hurry and join them.

Inside, Max and Alma found a jumble of sleeping bags, opened packs, and cooking utensils. The woman's first thought, on seeing the open food pack, was of marauding bears, but the camp appeared undisturbed.

While the children rummaged through the packs, searching for candy bars, Max leaned over and whispered to Alma.

"I can't carry the injured man up here."

"I know. I thought of that when we were coming up that awful trail."

"Well, I can't leave him there in the canoe alone. He may regain consciousness and try to get out of it."

"There's not much else you can do."

Max paused, listening to the sounds of the approaching storm. Gusts of wind had begun to lash at the tent. "You're going to have to stay here with the children. I'll take that canvas tarp and go back down to the canoe. I'll make some sort of shelter for the two of us until this storm is over."

"Max, you can't go."

"I have to."

He lowered his head, his stomach churning with waves of nausea. Alma barely heard him when he spoke.

"He's going to die. I don't want to watch him die." A shiver passed through him.

"I'm sorry, Max."

"I don't want him to be alone when he dies."

"I understand." She reached over and touched her husband's face with gentle fingers.

Max kissed his wife. "I love you, Alma," he said hoarsely. She met his lips halfway.

"I love you, too, Max." Alma blinked back the tears that suddenly welled up in her eyes.

Max lifted the tent flap and stepped out into the storm.

CHAPTER 23

E RROL JOYCE MADE A CHURCH OF HIS HANDS. He pulled the steeples of his fingers away from his lips.

"Will you state your full name?" he asked.

"Arlesen Ozard McLean."

"Where do you live?"

"One twenty-two University Terrace, Duluth, Minnesota."

"Are you the owner of the home at that address?"

"No."

"Who is?"

"My father, Toli McLean."

Errol stood with his back to the empty jury box in the almost empty courtroom. The lights were on, even though it was the middle of the afternoon. But the darkness of the overcast sky filtered through the window panes, heaped shadows in the corners. Rising winds rattled the tall windows.

Seated on the first row of benches, beyond the railing that divided litigants from spectators, were the parents of the witness, Toli and Selma McLean. The clerk's desk was empty. The judge, the deputy sheriff and the court reporter were the only officers of the court present.

Peter Hauck sat at the counsel table opposite Errol's empty chair. He had offered his witness to Errol without conducting any direct examination.

Jan Kiel, Guardian Ad Litem to the minor children, sat beside Hauck with a yellow legal pad in her lap.

Errol made a note on the pad he was holding and spoke again to the witness.

"For the record, may we agree that your home is in the same household as your father and mother, Toli and Selma McLean, who are seated in this courtroom in the first row?"

Arlie McLean nodded. "But I have rented an apartment."

"In Duluth?"

"Yes."

"How far from your parents' home?"

The witness looked out at his mother and father. "About a mile, I guess."

"But you haven't moved into the apartment yet?"

"No."

"Have you ever lived away from the home of your parents since the day you were born?"

The witness' eyes again darted to his father. "No." He spoke in a small voice.

"So, if you move to the apartment you just told Judge Clemens you have leased, then that will be the first time you ever lived away from your parents' home. Is that correct?"

"Yes, sir."

"How old are you?"

"Thirty-one."

Errol went back to the list of questions he'd written on his yellow pad. "What is your occupation?"

"School administrator."

"Where do you work?"

"I am assistant principal at the Greenwood Laboratory School on the university campus."

"You mean the campus of the University of Minnesota at Duluth?"

"Yes, sir."

"You are referring to the Laboratory School for kindergarten through grade seven that is operated by its School of Education?"

"Yes, sir."

"How long have you been assistant principal at the Greenwood School?"

"Eight years."

"Is that the only job you have held since you graduated from college?"

"Yes, sir."

"What training have you had to prepare yourself for the work that you do?"

The witness thought for a moment. "I attended grade school and high school in Lyndonville, Vermont. I attended Lyndon State College in Lyndonville during my freshman year in college. Then I transferred to the University of Minnesota at Duluth where I got my bachelor's and master's degrees in education. After I graduated from the university I was employed in my present position as assistant principal of the Greenwood Laboratory School."

"Do you teach any courses there?"

"No."

"Your work is administrative?"

"Yes, my major was in Educational Administration."

"When did you marry Kristen?"

"We've been married seven years."

"And for the record, will you tell us the names and ages of your children?"

"Cubby McLean, age seven, and Niki McLean, age five—both are girls."

Judge Clemens interrupted Errol's examination. "Mr. Joyce, I'm going to ask that both you and the witness keep your voices up. With that wind blowing outside and the windows rattling, I think our court reporter is having some difficulty catching your words."

Turning to the parents sitting on the bench beyond the railing, the judge asked, "Can you hear the witness out there?"

Toli and Selma McLean nodded.

"Can you hear him, Miss Kiel?"

"Most of the time."

The judge settled back in her chair. "This is a difficult courtroom for sound to travel in. The wind outside doesn't help. Please try to keep your voices up. You may continue." She nodded to Errol.

The court reporter raised his hand and signaled the lawyer to wait. He moved his chair and stenotype machine so he could directly face the witness. "This is better," he said.

"Are you ready?"

The reporter nodded.

"Mr. McLean, I was asking you about your children and their mother Kristen."

The witness nodded.

"Have your wife and children also lived in the home of your mother and father the entire period of your marriage?"

"Yes."

"Where did you meet your children's mother?"

"We were classmates at the university. She was a graduate assistant in my father's department."

"Your father teaches at the university?"

"He is the head of the Biology Department."

"A tenured professor at the university?"

"Yes, sir."

"Kristen was one of his students and also worked for him as laboratory assistant on a scholarship. Is that correct?"

"Yes, sir."

"Was your father also a college professor in Vermont when you lived there?"

"He was the head of the Biology Department of Lyndon State College in Lyndonville before he was offered his present position on the Duluth campus."

"Has your father been on the faculty of any other college or university?"

"Yes. But that was when I was a child and I don't remember the names. You'll have to ask him."

"Does your mother have a college degree?"

"No."

"What is the extent of your mother's schooling?"

Arlesen looked out at his mother. "She attended a school for girls on the Island of Cyprus. Their education system is different from ours, but the school was equivalent to our secondary schools here in the states."

"You're saying then that your mother's education was essentially a high school education?"

"Yes, sir."

"Has your mother ever worked away from home?"

"No, sir, not that I know of."

"Your mother is a housewife, is that correct?"

"My mother," the witness said carefully, "is the senior woman in our household. We have servants who take care of the house. My mother is first among the women and has always been in charge of the women in our household for as long as I can remember."

Judge Clemens, who had been taking notes on her own yellow pad, interrupted. "What do you mean by your mother being first among the women in the household?"

The witness turned to her. "In the home, the man is in charge of all of the members of the household including the servants, but the woman has her place with the women of the household, and my mother is the first among them. She manages the women servants and the other women."

"Who manages the men servants, if you have any?" Judge Clemens asked.

"A man!" the witness replied.

Judge Clemens leaned over to talk directly to the witness. "I understand that your family came from an eastern Mediterranean culture, and your father has maintained those ways in your household. Is that correct?"

The witness nodded.

"If, for example, your father hired a man to mow the lawn, would your mother give him his directions? Or would she deal with him? Or hire him or fire him?"

The witness shook his head. "No, she would only deal with the other women in the household and the women servants."

"Who would deal with the man cutting the lawn?"

"Father would or I would."

Judge Clemens thought for a moment and then sat back again in her chair. She nodded to Errol to continue with his examination.

"You also used the phrase that your mother was in charge of the other women in the household. Who would those other women be in the McLean household?"

Arlesen looked directly at the man standing beside the jury box. "Kristen, Cubby, Niki and the women servants."

Errol leaned back against the rail and made another check mark on his yellow tablet. "Did you and your wife have any discussions about the man-woman arrangement in the home of your father?"

The witness nodded.

The court reporter interrupted. "Please speak up. I can't put your nods in the record."

"Yes."

"Did you talk about it often?"

"We did."

"Would it be a fair statement to say you argued about it?"

"Yes."

"Let's turn to another subject," Errol said. "I want to talk with you about the home itself. Will you describe the house your family lived in with your parents and tell the judge the living arrangements you had for your family in that house?"

The witness turned and spoke to the judge. "Our family home is a three-story house. It has six bedrooms. My parents live on the first floor. I live with my family on the second floor, and the servants live on the third floor. Some of the third floor is also used for storage. We have garages for the cars."

"How many cars?"

"Four."

"Does your father have a source of income other than from his salary as a tenured professor?"

"Yes."

"Can you tell us what the source of that income is?"

"Rental properties."

"Where does your father have rental properties?"

"In New Jersey. When my father came to this country from Cyprus with my mother before I was born, he invested his money in commercial properties in New Brunswick, New Jersey. He has had them ever since."

"That is why your family can afford the lifestyle you have described on a college professor's salary, is that correct?"

"I suppose."

"You were telling us about the living arrangements you had in your parents' home. Did you cook together? Did you eat together?"

"The servants do the cooking and we all eat in the downstairs dining room."

"What sort of arrangement did you have with your father and mother to pay your family's share of the household costs?"

"When I was still in college and after Kristen and I married, we didn't pay anything. My father paid all of the bills. Then after I got out of college and went to work at Greenwood Laboratory School we arranged for my check to be deposited directly into my father's bank account to help pay the bills."

"Well, where did you get money to do the things you wanted to do?"

"I wrote a check on my father's bank account."

"And where did Kristen get the money that she wanted for other things?"

"She would ask me or my father, and we would give her money."

"Was the same true with your mother?"

"Yes. Whenever she had something she needed money for, she knew she could come to my father or me, and we would give it to her."

"Now, let me understand what you're saying. If Kristen or either of your two children needed clothes or vitamins or to pay a doctor bill, Kristen would have to ask you for the money because she did not have access to the bank account to write a check. Is that correct?"

"Or she could ask my father."

"And your father would give her the money?"

"Yes, if he thought she needed it."

"This has been true all the time you and Kristen have been married. Is that correct?"

"Yes."

"During your marriage, did your wife have employment?"

"Yes."

"Where?"

"When we were first married she taught science classes in the Greenwood Laboratory School."

"Where you were the assistant principal?"

"Yes."

"And on the campus where your father was the head of the Biology Department?"

"Yes."

"Did she receive a salary for the work that she did?"

"Yes."

"What happened to her salary check?"

"Both of our checks were deposited directly into the household account."

"That's the account you told me you and your father could write checks on, but your mother and Kristen could not. Is that correct?"

"Yes."

"How long did that arrangement exist?"

"Until Kristen quit her job and left home."

"And filed for a divorce?"

"Yes."

Errol changed his tactics. "Did you ever see your father mistreat any member of your family? By family, I am including servants as well as those of you who were related by blood or marriage."

"No."

"Did you ever see your father strike any member of your family?"

"Yes."

"Who?"

The witness looked around the courtroom. "My mother," he replied.

"You saw your father strike your mother. Is that correct?"

"Yes."

"More than once?"

"Yes."

"Often?"

"More than once," the witness hedged.

"And yet you told me that your father didn't mistreat your mother."

"I didn't say my father mistreated my mother. I said my father struck my mother."

"You don't call that mistreatment?"

"No."

"What do you call it?"

"That's the way a man keeps harmony in the family."

Jan Kiel looked up at the judge. Their eyes met but neither woman changed her expression.

"Are there locks on the doors in the house?"

Peter Hauck rose to his feet. "I object to the question, Your Honor. It's irrelevant." Then in his powerful voice, the older lawyer spoke so he could be heard above the sound of the wind blowing outside. "I realize, Your Honor, that we do not have a jury and that you told us you would give Mr. Joyce a wide latitude in his examination of the McLean family regarding the home environment, but we are now going far afield. Mr. Joyce is asking about the architecture of the lock system in my client's home and that has absolutely no relevance to the issues before us in this hearing."

Judge Clemens looked down at Hauck over the top of her glasses. "Overruled," she said dryly. She turned to Errol, "You may continue."

"Are there locks on the doors to the rooms in the McLean home?" Errol repeated.

"I think some, but I don't know where the keys are."

"As a practical matter, the doors inside your home are unlocked all of the time, and it's possible for anyone in the house to walk into any room, unannounced. Isn't that true?"

"Yes."

"Did you and Kristen have any discussion about her taking the children to her former home up on Thunder Bay Reservation?"

"Some."

"Did you argue about it?"

"Yes."

"What was the essence of your argument?"

"I didn't want her to take Cubby and Niki up there."

"Why not?"

"I didn't want them to grow up like wild animals. Whenever she took the girls up on the lakes or to the reservation, they were unmanageable when they came back."

"What do you mean by unmanageable?"

"They would talk back to me, or talk back to their grandparents. They'd forget the things they'd been taught."

"Things like a woman's place is in the home?"

"Something like that."

"I have the impression that outside of the McLean home, your wife Kristen was somewhat of an independent woman, and your two girls imitated their mother. Would that be about right?"

"Sometimes."

Errol made a check mark on his yellow pad. "Now, I want to turn to the matter of sex."

Judge Clemens sounded her gavel. "I expect that this is as good a place as any for us to stop."

Errol smiled.

"Is there any reason you can't come back here at eight o'clock tomorrow morning?" Judge Clemens asked those present in the courtroom.

"Only the storm," said Hauck.

"It doesn't appear that the storm is going to be as bad as we thought," the judge remarked, looked out the window.

She pounded her gavel. "There being no objection, I recess this hearing until eight o'clock tomorrow morning."

Toli McLean rose to his feet, scowling at Errol Joyce. The echoes of the fallen gavel faded away. As the McLean family left the courtroom, the wind sniffed at the windows like some prowling wolf and the light outside seemed to dwindle into a deeper, more ominous darkness.

Errol made one more check mark on his note pad. Like the others remaining in the courtroom, he wore a pensive, noncommittal look on his face when he put his pen away.

CHAPTER 24

ALMA KADUNCE PREPARED A GRAND DINNER for the McLean children: stove-top biscuits, beef stroganoff, and pudding—all done inside the tent in a downpour of rain while the darkness descended on their campsite. Niki begged Alma to stir up a second pan of the biscuit mix after the first smelled and tasted so good. The tiny propane camp stove put out a surprising amount of heat as she cooked the pot of freeze-dried beef stroganoff that she found in a foil packet. Alma and the girls removed their sweaters, despite the cold wind and rain blowing outside.

Cubby located the package of Kool-Aid, and with a four-quart kettle from the cook gear, she and her sister stirred the mixture, spilling only a part of it on the ground cloth. The battery lantern hanging from the tent pole cast a pale orange light inside the tent. While the girls ate their pudding, Alma entertained with hand-shadows on the canvas wall, creating clever images of animals.

And when they were finished, Alma delighted them further by showing them how to weight down the cooking utensils with rocks, and let the rain wash them clean.

By zipping two large sleeping bags together, Alma made a pouch that all three of them could sleep in. After they had settled inside the bag, and each girl kissed her goodnight, Alma Kadunce realized she felt better than she had in years, despite her aching muscles.

Cubby and Niki quickly fell asleep in Alma's arms. She lay awake listening to the storm's shrill wind and slashing rain and thought about what Max must do. She blinked back tears.

In the Maple Hill apartment complex beside the Gunflint Trail where it rose out of the town of Grand Marais, Dorothy Lee Clemens lay awake and stared up at her bedroom ceiling. The intensity of the storm was increasing, but it wasn't the storm that was keeping her awake. It was the child custody case and the puzzle of the McLean household.

This was an educated, well-to-do family who had transplanted their culture to the Midwest, and she was called upon to apply to this alien culture the American understanding of justice and fair play.

Unfolding in the courtroom, from Arlesen McLean's testimony, was the picture of a native American mother and her two children who were in conflict with a culture, as much as with the people involved.

Like Arab and Jew, thought Dorothy. Like Moslem and Christian. A conflict of age-old social values that the American court system was never designed to resolve.

The conduct of Toli McLean and his son; the abject subservience of Selma McLean—the first among women of her household—was entirely proper and acceptable in the Mediterranean culture. There was no law that prohibited immigrants from bringing their culture and values to this country. Scandinavians, Poles, and many who came from the eastern bloc of European nations, had done so when they settled in the mining and fishing communities on Minnesota's north shore.

Dorothy Clemens had strong feelings about the role the law should play in individual family life, in the lives of those for whom the law is enacted; and she felt the law should interfere as little as possible with the lifestyle the McLeans had brought with them to this country. But how to balance the values of an old culture with the freedom to learn, to express, that should be made available to all children in their formative years?

She felt the walls shudder from a particularly strong gust of wind.

When, she wondered, does discipline become abuse in a family? When does education become exploitation of a child? And when we teach about sex, when do art and eroticism become pornography? When is freedom of expression a trespass upon sensibilities? When does a father—a head of a household—who has been reared in a different culture become so adamant in his intent to preserve that culture, that he creates an oppressive environment which is unfit for children?

The violence of the storm outside matched the turbulence of thoughts that swarmed in Dorothy's mind and kept her starkly awake, staring at her bedroom ceiling.

Max gently laid the unconscious stranger on the high ground. Still, the slight jarring caused the clotting of blood in the man's armpit to break open and seep. He had found no first aid kit at the campsite where he'd left Alma and the girls on the other end of the trail, so he did the best he could. He pressed the injured arm against the man's own body and prayed that the bleeding would stop.

Then Max overturned the canoe and leaned it against a standing rock to make a shelter over the man's body. He crawled out of the rain and huddled under the canoe beside the injured man. He tried not to think about the hideous, scarred face and he fought to ignore the foul smell.

Once, during the long night, the man stirred. He seemed in pain and Max felt the man's feeble grip on his leg where his hand lay. After that, the man did not move. There was only the sound of the dying man's shallow breathing, a faint undertone beneath the incessant tattoo of rain.

Max could not sleep as the rain pounded on the metal canoe and water poured down around them. Fatigue seeped through him. He felt the weight of his years. Sleeplessness ragged at his mind, twisted his thoughts into grotesque shapes. He should just put the stranger out of his misery. It would be a merciful act, he thought. In the black recess of the Indian's mind, he knew he could kill swiftly, painlessly. And as badly as the man was injured, he thought, no one would ever know. Time melted away, flowed back and forth, compressed, and warped the present into a maze of passages and dark tunnels. It was only an illusion, borne of weariness and the hollow rattle of rain on the aluminum hull. Max's mind played tricks on him, bent time into a circle. He followed one of the maze's eerie corridors, one leading backward to the past.

In his dream, the ghost grandfather appeared and accused him. "The justice of the Ojibwa, the Amika, the Missiseanga, and the Nippissings demands that you lie under the scaffold.

"When I was a young boy," said the ghost, "I learned the death gift ritual of our ancient people. The old ones placed the body of the dead on a scaffold as high as a man could reach and covered it with a coffin of bark. It was not the criminal who was punished, it was the crime. Your entire family and village are responsible for your crime. You, who struck the burned stranger down, are required to lie on the ground under the body as it rots. Your family can bring you food, but you cannot cover your bowl to prevent the droppings from falling in it. You will be punished in great humiliation, a punishment that will go on until the burnt man's family allows your family to redeem you from under the scaffold by performing the death gift ritual."

In his dream, Max recoiled.

The old-man illusion stared past him as he recalled the instructions. "One gift each is given for the four corner posts that support the burial scaffold. Four gifts are given for the four platform staves that the body lies upon. One gift is given for the support that serves as a pillow for the head. Eleven gifts are given for the eleven principal bones of the body. Fifty principal gifts are placed on a platform in the center of the village where all can see. When the family of the burnt man perceives that justice has been done, they will accept the gifts and you will be redeemed. Thereafter the life of the tribe will go on as before."

"And the murderer goes free?" Max asked of the ghost.

The spectral old man of the dream sighed. "Nothing can bring back the life. From the death gifts, the victim's family receives some satisfaction, and reprisals that would have interrupted our trade, or incited tribal wars, are avoided by the ritual."

Max shrank from the ghost. "Our old ways of justice permit the wrongdoer to go free."

The ghost nodded. "True, he does go free, but for the rest of his life he must deal with his own family, his own tribe, which has to share in his punishment by redeeming him. His humiliation continues long after he crawls out from beneath the burial scaffold. And, because each tribesman knows his family or tribe has to share in the punishment for his wrongdoing, the death gift ritual is a deterrent, the like of which is not found in the white man's law—in the white man's concept of justice."

"And you want me to lie beneath the scaffold until I am redeemed?"

The ghost nodded.

Cold water seeping across the rock where Max Kadunce laid his head awakened him and the ghostly shape of his grandfather vanished. Max reached out and touched the body of the stranger. To his relief, he felt movement. The stranger was not dead. Max tried to shake free of the ghostly dream.

Errol Joyce was neither fully awake nor fully asleep. He was just comfortable lying in bed with Jan Kiel in his arms. He could hear the thunder of pounding waves out in the harbor and the staccato rain lancing the roof. In her sleep Jan murmured and pushed closer, her legs and arms gripping him. Her head was buried in the alcove of his neck.

Errol held her tight. When a man and a woman find they can sleep together comfortably without sex, he thought, that had to be the ultimate in a relationship.

He floated in the calm eye of the storm, that netherworld between sleep and wakefulness, soothed by the rain drone and the wind's breathy whispers, comfortable with himself, totally at peace.

The rogue bear reached the west shore of Marabeuf Lake and found that its passage was blocked by the swift flowing waters of the Granite River where it boiled and plunged into Horsetail Rapids.

The bear stood up on its hind legs and sifted the night air with its quivering black nose. The hair on its shoulders stood up. Fur sleeked by the rain, it towered tall against the backdrop of a lightning-lit stormy sky, a startling image of brute strength and beauty. Then the bear dropped on all fours and paced along the bank. The brute was three hundred pounds of bone and muscle. Its head was slung low, ears pinned back, eyes red, teeth constantly grinding. As the animal paced the shore and tried to see through the darkness across the water, its muscles rippled under its shaggy coat.

The gaunt beast was hungry, and it smelled food.

CHAPTER 25

THE COURTROOM SEEMED TO CRACKLE WITH STATIC ELECTRICITY, as if the air inside had been charged by the storm raging outside. Watching Errol Joyce, Jan felt that his energy might shock anyone who touched him. The feeling was so palpable she shivered involuntarily.

She wondered if the witness felt the same way. She glanced at Judge Clemens, who sat at her bench, one delicate hand anchored thoughtfully to her chin. Peter Hauck had a pencil stuck crosswise in his mouth. Body language, she thought. Hauck looked as if he was intentionally gagging himself during the intensive interrogation of his client.

"Do you know what the phrase 'sexually inappropriate conduct' means?" Errol asked.

Arlesen McLean sat in the witness chair and stared back at the lawyer for a long time. "While in college I took a course in Abnormal Psychology and I'll tell you what I was taught that it means."

"And what was that?"

" 'Sexually inappropriate conduct' or 'sexually inappropriate behavior' are code phrases psychologists use when they think someone is guilty of sexual deviation and can't prove it."

"Is that something you learned in a college class or is that a definition that Arlesen McLean made up?"

"You asked me what the phrase meant. That's what I think it means."

The witness' response was followed by a long silence. The lawyer was not certain the witness was finished answering. The courtroom was deadly still except for the storm lashing the windows outside.

Errol left the empty jury box and moved across to the witness chair. He spoke to Arlesen as if they were the only two persons in the room.

"Kristen McLean overheard your children say they did not want to be alone with your father." Errol paused. "My question to you, sir, is: Did your children ever express a similar reluctance to you?"

Arlesen sat back in his chair. "Yes."

"Did you say 'yes'?"

"Yes. Cubby and Niki have told me that they do not like to be alone with my father."

Errol stared at the witness.

"Weren't you the least bit concerned when your children told you that?"

"Of course I was concerned. I want my children to love their grandfather and to get along with him."

"That's all that their complaint indicated to you?"

"Mr. Joyce, you know my father. He is a difficult man to be around if you don't understand him. He is sometimes loud and blunt in the way he says things. He believes in the ways of the old country and he is sometimes a stubborn man, but he is not a perverse man."

"Have your children ever told you that your father touched them on their bottoms?"

"He has spanked Cubby. It is his home. It is his right."

"How about coming into the bathrooms and bedrooms unannounced? Have you ever known your father to do that?"

"It is his home," repeated the witness. "He is entitled to go wherever and whenever he pleases in his own home."

"Including your bedroom?"

"Yes."

"And you approve of that?"

"When I am the head of the household, then that privilege will be mine."

Errol walked back to the jury box and made a pencilled note on his yellow pad. He looked across the counsel table and saw that both Jan and Hauck were watching him closely. His examination was not going as he had expected.

Turning again to the witness, he said boldly, "Am I to understand,

Arlesen, that you want Judge Clemens to believe that your father, Toli McLean, is a paragon of virtue?"

"I didn't say that. I said my father acts properly around my children. He is simply exercising his rights as the head of our household."

"How about adults? What is the relationship between him and your mother and your friends?"

"Are you asking if my father has had affairs with women other than my mother?" Arlesen asked levelly.

"Yes, I'll ask that, now that you've raised that point." The lawyer turned to look at the elder McLeans beyond the rail. Both sat expressionless, apparently unperturbed by the line of questioning he was using.

"Mr. Joyce, if you lived in the eastern Mediterranean where my parents come from, you would know that it is entirely proper for a man to have four wives."

"You're not implying that your father has four wives, are you?"

"No, not at all. I'm just trying to make you understand that in my family, situations that for you may be an affair or be considered immoral are not regarded in that light by my family. It is not at all unusual for the head of the household in the Mideastern culture to have more than one wife or more than one girl friend. So, yes, I do regard my father as a paragon of virtue, as you so aptly put it in your question."

Shit, Errol thought. His cross examination of the witness wasn't working at all. He looked again out in the courtroom expecting to see Toli McLean showing some visible signs of agitation. Instead, the man's face was devoid of expression. But his dark eyes watched Errol Joyce's every move.

"Would you say that your children are happy in the home provided by their grandfather?"

"I believe they are happy. The two girls are different, like everybody's children. Niki is the live wire of the two. She's outgoing and gets along with everybody in the household. Cubby is more quiet. Cubby is shy, especially when she's around men. There were probably too many women in our family when she was small. So when she got older she was shy. That's one of the reasons that my father did special teaching. He felt that if he took the time to teach her basic learning skills in our home, rather than in public school where there are mostly women teachers, it would help Cubby overcome her shyness."

"Did it?"

"I think so, but we're talking about a seven-year-old girl, still in her formative years. We'll have to wait and see."

"You have credentials from the State of Minnesota to teach, do you not?"

"Yes."

"And the children's mother Kristen also has her teaching certificate?"

"Yes."

"If you were going to teach early learning skills to your daughter Cubby in your home, why didn't you teach her? Or why didn't their mother teach her, rather than your father Toli?"

"I think my father was better qualified."

"Did Kristen think that?"

Arlesen shook his head. "No."

"I take it she must have argued with you and your father about that?"

"Yes."

"But you agreed with your father?"

"Yes."

"Your mother agreed with your father?"

"Yes."

"Despite the fact that your father never taught an elementary school class in his life, and all of his teaching career has been in administration at the head of the department, or teaching college level courses, you and your mother sided against Kristen, both on the question of whether or not Cubby should be taught in public school and who should do the teaching in the home. Is that correct?"

Arlesen McLean spoke carefully. "All four of us talked about it, and we agreed that my father was correct."

"Kristen didn't agree to that," Errol asserted.

"No," the witness admitted, "but that was the family decision."

"The one who had the final say was the head of the household, your father. Is that correct?"

"Yes."

Errol paused and glanced through his notes.

"Do you have any more questions for this witness, Mr. Joyce?" Judge Clemens asked.

"I wonder if I might have a short recess?" Errol asked. "I would like to have an opportunity to go over my notes before I excuse the witness."

"All right." Judge Clemens sounded her gavel. "This court will be in recess for ten minutes." Leaning over to her court reporter, she said, "Let's see if we can get an updated weather report. Our deputy sheriff didn't show up this morning. I understand that there are some trees down and some of the roads are blocked."

Jan Kiel followed the judge into her chambers.

Errol took his chair at the counsel table and started leafing through his file. Hauck waited until the witness and his parents went out in the hall and he and Errol were alone in the empty courtroom before speaking. "You'll never make it stick," he said. "You'll never prove that Toli McLean acts inappropriately around his grandchildren."

"Damn it, Peter. Kristen told me that Toli is a pervert and she wouldn't lie to me about something like that."

"Probably not, but what you don't understand, Errol, is that the family believes it is perfectly proper for the head of the household to run his home like his own little fiefdom. And all Toli McLean is doing is treating and raising the women in his household exactly the same way women are treated and raised in millions of households in the Mideast. And, there is no law in the State of Minnesota that says he can't do that."

"Unless he is abusing them."

"Unless he's abusing them," Hauck admitted. "But, Errol, you're not going to be able to prove that he is because the facts are, he's not. The law does not require Toli to run his home the same way everybody else does in St. Louis County, Minnesota."

"I know," Errol said, his brow furrowing.

Peter Hauck sat back in his chair. "Kristen McLean may have thought she was doing the right thing when she ran off to the wilderness country with her children, but the facts indicate the reason her children did not like the old man is because he is an obnoxious, overbearing bastard. Not because he's a pervert."

Errol's jaw hardened, but he said nothing. He was beginning to think he'd taken on the toughest job in his law career by submitting Kristen McLean to a hearing without her being present to defend herself. A muscle along his cheekbone quivered as his eyes turned to flint.

CHAPTER 26

ARE YOU READY TO CONTINUE, MR. JOYCE?"

"Yes, Your Honor."

Turning to the witness, Judge Clemens said, "Mr. McLean, for the record, I will remind you that you are still under oath."

"Yes, ma'am," Arlesen McLean said and sat in the witness chair.

"Proceed, Mr. Joyce."

"Mr. McLean, in your earlier testimony you told us that you and your wife Kristen had been married approximately seven years. Is that correct?"

"Yes, sir."

"And you lived together as husband and wife during that entire period of time. Is that correct?"

"Yes, sir."

"In your opinion, was Kristen McLean a good mother to her children?"

"Except for one incident, I would say yes."

"And what is that incident?"

The witness hesitated for a moment and looked out into the courtroom at the first bench. Then he looked down at his lap before lifting his head and speaking directly to the lawyer.

"I do not believe Kristen was being a good mother when she took Cubby and Niki from our home in Duluth and then abandoned them up on the Granite River." He swallowed hard after he spoke.

"Mr. McLean. You do not know for a fact that Kristen abandoned your children up on the Granite River, do you?"

Arlesen pressed his lips together, then spoke in a low voice. "She took the kids with her, and when they found Kristen, the girls weren't with her."

Errol waited. But the witness didn't say anything more.

"And that's the only basis for your statement that she was not a good mother? Because you think she abandoned her children on the Granite River?"

The witness nodded. "She shouldn't have done that."

"Aside from whatever has happened with your wife and children up on the Granite River, would you say that Kristen has been a good mother to your children?"

"Yes. I didn't like it when she would take the kids up to the woods on the Indian reservation or out on the lakes, but I understand why she did that."

"And why did she do that?"

"Because that was her home where she grew up, and she wanted the girls to see it."

Errol pressed his point. "But you agree that Kristen has always been a good mother to your children, the possible exception being the incident that took place up on the Granite River where she was found and which is still being investigated. Is that a correct statement?"

The witness nodded. "Yes."

Errol walked over to the counsel table and laid down his yellow pad. "That's all I have for this witness, Your Honor," he said and sat down.

Judge Clemens turned to Hauck. "Any further questions, Mr. Hauck?"

"No, Your Honor."

She looked over at Jan Kiel. "On behalf of the Guardian Ad Litem, are there any questions of this witness?"

Judge Clemens had appointed Jan Kiel as the Guardian at Law. It was her obligation to speak for the minors in the courtroom. It was her duty to insure that the children received unbiased consideration by the court. Only Jan knew how difficult it was for her to do so. The drinking habits of her own father before and after her mother's death had taken him out of her life for months at a time and periodically had returned him to her doorstep with pledges of abstinence. Ingrained in Jan was a deep-rooted personal wish. If at all possible, she wanted Cubby and Niki to have the loving home she never had. She was obliged to keep an open mind as she heard the evidence, but she desperately wanted Errol to be wrong about the grandfather.

Jan shook her head. "The Guardian Ad Litem has no cross examination at this time, Your Honor. I'll wait until we have further evidence from the Petitioner and the Respondent."

Arlesen McLean started to rise from the witness chair.

"Just a moment, Mr. McLean," Judge Clemens said. "I want you to clear up one thing for me that was referred to in the questions put to you by Mr. Joyce."

The witness slumped back in the chair.

Judge Clemens riffled through her notes. "You have told us that on more than one occasion your father has struck or beaten your mother in your presence. Wasn't that your testimony?"

"Yes, ma'am."

"And I think you used the phrase, 'that was the way the head of the household would keep harmony in that home.' Do you remember that?"

"Yes, ma'am."

"Was 'harmony' the word you used?"

"Yes, ma'am."

"Am I to understand that in your home both the male and female members of the family unit believe it to be acceptable conduct for a man to punish a woman by beating her to get her to do his bidding. Is that what you're telling this court?"

The witness twisted in the chair. "I'm not certain what you mean when you say, 'do his bidding.' But the head of the household is always a father or oldest brother or uncle, and he is responsible for keeping harmony in the household. And if it is necessary to resort to beating the wife or daughter or sister or aunt, then it is not only proper, it is his duty to do so."

Judge Clemens toyed with her pencil for a moment. "Does the man in the household ever discipline other men? For example, when you were growing up, did your father ever beat you?"

He thought for a moment. "No."

"Never?"

Arlesen looked out at his father, then turned back to the judge and tried to explain. "If a man or a boy in our household needed to be corrected, my father would talk to him and explain this need to him. My father would be obeyed because," he said with a shrug, "that's the way we do things. Men understand."

"And women do not?"

"Usually, yes, but sometimes not. That's the only time the head of the household would beat them."

Judge Clemens looked down at the lawyers at the counsel table and then past them at the parents of the witness while she gathered her thoughts. She turned again to the witness. "Is it the sense of your testimony that in your home a male member of the family may punish a female member of the family by beating her, and this is a common and accepted practice?"

"Yes, when necessary," Arlesen answered.

The judge carefully phrased her next question. "To your knowledge, did your father ever strike or beat your mother in the presence of your children?"

McLean thought for a long moment. "No, not that I know of."

Judge Clemens sat for a moment and stared at the witness. Then she started to make additions to her notes. There was a hush in the courtroom except for the undertones of wind and rain yammering sporadically at the windows.

Looking up, the judge said, "If there are no other questions, this witness is excused."

Jan scrawled a question with large letters across the face of her yellow pad and showed it to Peter Hauck. She wrote: "What kind of family is this?"

Hauck reached over and in small letters pencilled an answer, "A harmonious family!"

Jan gave him a dark look and tore up the sheet of paper.

The ill-tempered black bear lay in the wet brush and raised its nose to the smells that came from across the channel. Early morning light penetrated the trees. The rain continued to come down in sheets. The near-sighted animal could not discern the thing that was on the other bank of the Granite River.

Lurching stiffly to its feet, the animal worked its way along the west bank of Horsetail Rapids, searching downstream for a crossing point. The animal moved slowly and cautiously, seeking to pounce upon an unsuspecting rodent or to find a fish stranded in the backwater along the shore. The driving rain swept across its oiled fur and streamed down its sides. Sometimes water got in its eyes and it shook its head violently, throwing a wide spray in a ragged half-arc.

Suddenly its nose caught a new scent—the rotted scent of a kill, the unmistakable smell of the dying and the dead. The animal stood up on its hind legs and spread its front paws as it threw back its head to locate the source of the rotted flesh. Squinting through porcine eyes, it spotted the log that lay across the narrow river at the foot of the rapids.

The Black dropped back down on all fours and investigated the fallen tree that formed a primitive bridge to the other side of the stream. Lolling its head from side to side, the black bear tried to discern whether the smell that attracted it was coming from its own side of the river or the other side.

Max Kadunce sat in the early morning light on a rock by the over-turned canoe, wrapped in the canvas cook fly. Both he and the dying stranger were soaked. Sometimes the driving rain seemed to come from all directions at once. The wind chilled him to the marrow.

Huddled in the canvas with his back against the rock, Max found some protection.

More than once during the night he had thought that the stranger was dead. And once, in the grip of his own hallucination, Max thought he was the one who was dead. For one horrifying instant, when he turned on the flashlight and the surreal shadows danced around the inside of the over-turned canoe, he thought he was staring at his own body.

After long intervals, because Max knew that it was his duty, he forced himself to roll over and look under the canoe to determine if the injured stranger was still breathing. When the wind blew toward him and brought with it the stench of the dying man, Max could feel his stomach constrict into a painful knot.

God, he thought, I wish this storm would stop. I wish the man would die. I wish Alma and I could go home.

Then Max, horrified by his own thinking, said aloud in a whisper, "Dear God, I didn't mean that. I don't want him to die."

He lowered his head to his knees and felt the storm's rain pour down on his covering and shuddered in the chill of its gelid wind.

"What's the matter, Alma?" Cubby asked.

"What's the matter?" Niki repeated. "Why don't you get up?"

Alma had pulled herself halfway out of the sleeping bag when the sharp pain went through her back. She put her hands on the ground cloth behind her and leaned back, tipping her head and stretching her neck to straighten her spine down to her hips.

She grimaced.

She knew the pain was not really in her back, but closer to the kidney.

Sufficient daylight filtered through the wet walls of the tent to permit them to see without the lantern. Both girls stood by the tent pole and watched as Alma made another attempt to disentangle herself from the two sleeping bags.

The children were startled by her outcry of pain. Alma sat on the floor of the tent and put her hands in her lap. She looked up at the two concerned faces and gave a short laugh.

"Don't worry about Alma," she said. "Alma is getting old and some of her parts are wearing out."

Niki threw back her head and giggled. She thought that was one of the funniest things she'd ever heard. "Alma's parts are wearing out," she repeated.

Alma and Cubby laughed with her.

KYD-3 TV's news team stood in the cavernous hanger beside their small Bell helicopter and looked through the open door at the dark clouds moving across the end of the airfield. The Duluth International Airport sat up on the iron range between lakes that were surrounded by suburban homes.

Airport weather conditions didn't always match the weather below in the Duluth-Superior twin harbors. The dark clouds that the two men were watching had appeared to curl up out of the bay and spread across the airfield just when the news crew thought it was clearing enough for them to attempt a flight.

The pilot spoke to his companion. "There's no use trying it now. The back side of the storm is starting to move through. We're not going to get off the ground today."

"I hate to think about those kids out there all alone in that stuff."

"If they're still alive," the pilot said.

"Don't even think it."

As the pilot and his friend watched, a thin funnel dropped down from the cloud like a dangling piece of yarn, and then pulled back up again out of sight. It looked like a snake coiling back into a dark hiding place.

CHAPTER 27

S OMETIMES PETER HAUCK CAN BE A COMPLETE ASSHOLE," Jan said. She glanced at her friend's reflection in the lavatory mirror and saw Dorothy Clemens smile at her. The two women were alone in the courthouse restroom.

"What did Peter do to you?" Dorothy asked.

"One of his smartass answers," Jan said, without explaining further. She still rankled at the words Peter had written on her yellow tablet. "He was the same way when you and I worked in his law office. Do you remember?"

"Yes, I remember."

Both women had begun their careers as trial lawyers with the Duluth law firm of Hauck and Figg, a law group that was the training ground for several of Minnesota's top-ranked trial counsel.

Dorothy applied her lipstick while she listened in amusement to her friend. In the mirror she could see Jan's vexation as the younger woman spoke.

"One time, when I was your law clerk, the summer before I took the bar exam, Peter gave me a patronizing lecture about the role of a woman in the practice of law. He did it in front of four other lawyers in a court-room with a bunch of spectators present, while we were waiting for a judge to start a pre-trial conference." Jan leaned over and put her face in front of Dorothy's. "And do you know what he said?"

Dorothy shook her head.

"He told me in front of all those people, that female lawyers'—get this, 'female lawyers' legal careers are only temporary excursions from the home. I was the only women in the courtroom, and that's what the condescending ass said."

"And what did you say?"

"I said he could take his law clerk job and shove it."

"You didn't say that."

"No," Jan confessed, "I didn't say that, but I wanted to."

Dorothy put her makeup away. "You did like the rest of us," she said. "You smiled and said, 'Yes, Professor Hauck,' and you put up with it because he was the best teacher of trial tactics that any of us ever had."

"Yes, but why does Hauck have to be like that? At other times he can be as gracious as any man I ever met. Once we had lunch together when I was working for him, and he told me fascinating stories about the time he was on the law school faculty at the University of Michigan. He was polite, he didn't put me down; it was a great lunch—just the opposite of the way he treated me in the courtroom."

Dorothy laughed. She genuinely like the younger lawyer who had been her associate at the Duluth law firm before she became a judge and before Jan left to accept her appointment as Assistant Attorney General.

"The difference," she said, "is that Peter thought you were misplaced in the courtroom. But as a luncheon companion you were in your proper place."

The judge patted her friend on the shoulder. "I know Peter Hauck believes you are a good lawyer, and I know he is proud of the fact that you are an alumna of his law firm, but he just honestly believes that the place for the little woman is in the home."

"Men! Sometimes I just hate them."

"Don't we all," Dorothy said with a smile.

During her second year in law school, Jan had been one of five undergraduates hired by the Duluth law firm of Hauck & Figg. She was the only woman law clerk and was assigned to work with Dorothy, its only woman lawyer. Dorothy was then married, but used her maiden name, Clemens, as her professional name.

Hauck & Figg permitted Jan to juggle her schedule so she could fly charters that earned her more money than the law firm paid. Dorothy was concerned with substance, not form. So the two worked well together: Jan, a superb research assistant and apt pupil; Dorothy, a talented trial lawyer and unselfish teacher.

While in college, Jan had assumed a stern, almost martial look except for her hair. It was Dorothy who told the law student her blonde, waist-length hair tended to drag her face down, aging her. She showed Jan how to change her wardrobe from the plain style of an aircraft pilot to that of a sophisticated professional woman. She taught her to rearrange her hair and wear vibrant colors, circle skirts with classic silk blouses or elegant sweaters.

"And let me give you some advice about men," Dorothy had said, "and I am speaking from experience. Don't let any man swallow you up in his world so that you lose your own physical and emotional space. The most important person in your life is you—now and always."

"But," Jan had asked, "did you ever think that you might want to have another important person in your life—a baby, a child of your own?"

Dorothy had nodded her head slowly. "Yes—I have."

"I would like to have a baby," Jan confided, "but after what happened with the marriage of my own parents, I'm afraid to get too close to any man in a serious relationship."

Jan recalled Dorothy's words of advice as they stood there in the restroom.

"Ready?" Dorothy asked, snapping her purse shut.

Jan broke from her reverie and smiled. She took one last glance at her image in the mirror. "Sure."

Jan stepped aside and let Dorothy go through the door first. Outside the courtroom, they were Dorothy and Jan, friends and confidantes. But in the courtroom, they were Judge Clemens and Assistant District Attorney General Kiel. Members of the Judiciary and the Bar, particularly those in urban communities on the east coast, had difficulty understanding the rapport that existed among the smaller legal fraternity in the rural Midwest. Some viewed it as a split personality trait when lawyers and judges battled in the courtroom and enjoyed each other's company afterwards. The urban bar tended to hold grudges. The rural bar was more pragmatic and, as a consequence, its members usually enjoyed a friendship and intellectual exchange with colleagues outside the law's arena that their peers in the city did not.

Jan Kiel followed the judge out into the hallway. "I still think he's a condescending ass," she grumbled.

"Point noted," the judge said, with a spirited laugh.

The death of the stranger came quietly. At the last, Max Kadunce gently held the man's head in his lap and protected it from the slackening rain. During those final moments the smell didn't seem so bad, nor the face so grotesque. The injured man looked at him with his one good eye and Max Kadunce saw in it the gratification that every man has when he knows he will not be alone at the time of his passing. Max didn't cry; he didn't hallucinate. He was bone weary and wet and cold, but, at the last, none of that mattered. He had helped, at least Max thought he had helped, the stranger and himself deal with their mortality.

The hooked shape of the bear's knife-like claws were perfect for climbing trees, as black bears were wont to do. So the animal had no difficulty maintaining its balance as it walked the fallen tree trunk lying across the frothing rapids of the Granite River. When it reached the other side, the animal let out a roar and rushed the figure sitting on the rock in the rain, holding a bundle wrapped in old World War II rain gear.

Max Kadunce saw the animal, like death itself, coming across the rocks at an incredible speed. Before Max could move, the Black overran him, knocking him off the ledge and sending the dead body of the stranger rolling out of the wet poncho, smearing Max with the man's stench and bile.

Whether the bear slipped on the wet rocks or whether it delayed a second rush while it adjusted its near-sighted eyes, Max never knew.

For at that instant the tornado struck. It scattered rock and debris through the basin of the lagoon. Its ferocious winds held the water back from the falls. It uprooted trees and sent the aluminum canoe spinning through the air, the poncho and cook fly still attached to its hull.

Max became wedged between two blocks of granite, and the stranger's body lay like a broken doll in the lagoon.

CHAPTER 28

ETER HAUCK PREFERRED TO EXAMINE WITNESSES while standing behind his chair at the counsel table where he had his case file at his fingertips. Before a trial, he always outlined the examination of all witnesses in a small black notebook. During the course of the trial he made copious and meticulous notes in that same notebook.

The tall, aging lawyer addressed Judge Clemens, speaking in his deep, sonorous voice. "May it please the Court."

No one in the courtroom had difficulty hearing him over the sound of the wind and rain that continued to drive against the courthouse windows.

"Mr. Hauck." Judge Clemens nodded.

"At this time, Your Honor, the Petitioner calls to the witness stand Selma McLean."

Selma, after a nod of assent from her husband, rose and slouched heavily toward the witness stand. Her weight caused her to walk with an odd shuffling gait. When she sat, she curled her feet under her. She raised her hand and Judge Clemens delivered the oath.

"Do you solemnly swear that the testimony you are about to give in the cause is the truth and the whole truth, so help you God?"

"Yes," the woman said in a quiet voice.

He smiled at the witness and commenced his examination. "Will you state your name please?"

"Selma Itbitissam McLean."

"You are the mother of Arlesen McLean who just finished testifying in this hearing?"

"I am."

"And you are the wife of Toli McLean who is seated on the bench in the front row of the courtroom, isn't that correct?"

The woman looked at her husband, then spoke carefully. "I am the wife of Dr. Toli Ozard McLean."

"I believe that Ozard is also the middle name of your son. Is that correct?"

"It is."

"As a matter of curiosity, will you tell us why your son and your husband have the same middle name?"

"All of the men of our family have the same middle name, Ozard," Selma McLean said.

"Why? What is the significance?"

"I don't know."

"As I understand, both you and Dr. McLean are naturalized citizens of this country. Is that correct?"

"We are."

"And your son was born in this country and is a citizen of this country. Is that correct?"

"He is."

"Where were you born, Mrs. McLean?"

"In Baghdad, Iraq. Shortly after I was born, because of Turks fighting with the Kurds, my father took his family to the Republic of Cyprus where we lived on the Greek side of the island. That is where I spent most of my life as a child and where I went to school."

"When did you leave Cyprus?"

"When I married."

"How old were you at that time?"

"Sixteen."

"Did you leave the island after you married Dr. McLean?"

"Yes."

"Where did you live after you left Cyprus?"

"In Cambridge, a town in England. We lived there for four years until my husband received his degrees. Then we moved to the United States."

"Where was your husband born?"

"Athens, Greece."

"Was he a Greek national before he came to the United States?"

"No."

"What was his nationality?"

"English. My husband had never lived in England before we married and moved there, but his father was a Scotsman and even though he was born and reared in Greece, my husband has dual citizenship because he retained his English nationality."

At the counsel table, Errol Joyce looked out into the courtroom at the impassive face of Toli McLean. Without expression Toli sat straight-backed against the bench, arms folded, staring directly at his wife, as if carefully judging each of her answers. Something caught his eye, a movement beyond where the McLeans were sitting. Errol nearly lost his composure at that moment. For in the back row, his face hidden in shadow, sat P.M. Gregory, silent as a wraith, listening to the proceedings.

Errol wondered if P.M. had come to watch him fail.

Hauck's lengthy inquiry into the background of the children's grandparents was probably irrelevant thought Errol, but he made no objection. Jan, at the opposite side of the counsel table, was writing notes on her yellow tablet.

"Since you have been in the United States, where have you lived?"

Selma looked at her husband. "Atlanta, Georgia, where my husband worked for a short time for the National Health Service when we first came to this country. We lived one year in the Bronx, New York, when my husband had a teaching position at Columbia University. We lived in Vermont, and we lived in Duluth."

Hauck reached down and turned a page in his notebook. "Do you have other children?"

"No. Arlesen is our only child."

"You have been present in the courtroom during the testimony of your son, Arlesen, isn't that correct?"

"Yes, I have."

"Did your son correctly describe your home and the relationship of his wife Kristen and his two children, Niki and Cubby, in the home?"

"What do you mean, relationship?" she asked.

"In his testimony, your son described the size and kind of home you have, the rooms in the house, where he lived, where you lived, and where your servants lived. My question is, in your opinion, did he describe them correctly to Judge Clemens?"

"Yes."

"During the period your daughter-in-law and your two grandchildren lived in your home, did you have the opportunity to observe them?"

"Yes, of course."

"What kind of home was provided for your daughter-in-law and for your grandchildren?"

"A good home."

"Was it clean? Were they provided proper food? Did your grandchildren go to school?"

"Our home is a good, clean home," the woman said emphatically.

"Were the grandchildren and their mother properly given an opportunity to be educated?"

Errol observed that Toli McLean, who sat on the first bench, was becoming agitated at the witness' confusion.

Selma McLean said to the lawyer, "My home was always a good, clean home. The food was good, the clothes were clean."

"How about schooling? Were the children given the opportunity to receive an education?"

Selma McLean sat for a moment and looked out at her husband and didn't reply.

Hauck repeated. "Did the children receive schooling?"

"No. Not in a school."

"Were they too young?"

"No. Niki was not old enough to go to kindergarten, but Kristen wanted Cubby to go to public school when she was six. As my son said, she wasn't permitted to go."

Hauck turned to another subject. "Mrs. McLean, were you in the household at the time Kristen came and took the children?"

"Yes."

"Tell Judge Clemens in your own words just how that happened. What did Kristen do, and what did you do?"

Selma McLean twisted in her seat and looked over at Judge Clemens. "Kristen came to the house. She had left several days before. She came to the house while my husband and my son were gone. She didn't come in. She came around the side yard to the back where Cubby and Niki were playing. I went out and asked her what she wanted, and she said she wanted the children. She took them and drove off with them."

"Did you try to stop her?"

"I told her not to do that because Toli said the children could not leave the yard."

"And what did your daughter-in-law say in response to that?"

"She called my husband a very bad name and left with the children."

"What was the name she called your husband?"

"I don't want to repeat it."

"What did you do?"

"My husband had told me that if Kristen ever came back to the house, I was to call him and tell him and that's what I did."

"Did you ever see your daughter-in-law or your grandchildren after that time?"

"No, I did not."

"Were the children taken from the home without your permission?"

"Yes, they were."

"Would it be a fair characterization to say that your daughter-in-law forcibly took the children from the back yard of your home, put them in her car, and drove away?"

"Yes."

Hauck then turned to Errol. "You may inquire."

Errol rose, took his yellow pad and walked over to stand by the empty jury box.

He faced the witness. "Mrs. McLean, if I speak from here, can you hear me all right with the storm going on outside?"

"Yes, I can hear you."

"Mrs. McLean, in your testimony a few moments ago, Mr. Hauck asked you if the children received school instruction and your answer was that although Cubby was old enough to go to kindergarten, she was not permitted to go. Was that your answer?"

"Yes."

"Who didn't permit her to go—her father or her grandfather?"

"Her grandfather."

"Was Cubby's father or mother consulted about that?"

"I don't know."

"I believe you said your daughter-in-law wanted Cubby to go to kindergarten. Isn't that correct?"

"Yes."

"Did you hear the testimony of your son Arlesen to the effect that the family, including you, helped make the decision that Cubby would be taught at home by her grandfather?"

"I heard him say that."

"Did that happen?"

"I don't recall."

"Did your husband, Toli McLean, ever give you a reason why Cubby was not permitted to go to public school?"

"He said he would teach her."

Errol turned and looked out at the man on the front bench and then back at the witness. "Is it your testimony that your husband refused to let your granddaughter start into public school because he proposed to teach her himself?"

"Yes."

"Did he?"

"Yes."

"Were you ever present when he was teaching Cubby?"

"No."

"Was Kristen, your daughter-in-law, present?"

"No, because she argued with Toli."

"How about your son Arlesen? Was he present?"

"He was at work."

"Do you know of anyone who was ever with your husband when he was teaching Cubby whatever it was that he taught her?"

"No."

"Where did this little private school take place?"

"In the library of our home."

"Do you know what he taught her?"

"No."

"Did you ever ask to be present during those teaching sessions?"

"No."

"Did your husband ever ask you to be present during those teaching sessions?"

"No."

"I assume," Errol said, "that he never asked your daughter-in-law Kristen to be present during those teaching sessions?"

"Not that I know of."

"Or your son?"

"Not that I know of."

Errol looked down at his note pad and back again at the witness. "Mrs. McLean, you also testified that when Kristen came to your home and took Cubby and Niki away, you called your husband Toli. Is that correct?"

"Yes."

"You didn't call your son Arlesen, who is the father of the children?"

"No. Toli told me to call him if Kristen came to the house."

"Were you concerned about the safety of the children when their mother picked them up?"

"She wasn't supposed to do that."

"How do you know she wasn't supposed to do that?"

"Because my husband told me she wasn't supposed to do that."

"Mrs. McLean, wasn't it rather strange that it was your husband rather than the father of the children whom you called at the time their mother took them away?"

"No."

"You do not regard that as unusual?"

"No." Selma looked out into the courtroom. "My husband is the head of our family."

"And I take it, that within the family, whatever your husband says is the law. Is that right?"

"I don't know what you mean."

"When you said your husband was the head of the household, I assume that what you were saying was that it's your view that, if your husband said the children were or were not to go to public school; if your husband said the children were to be taught by him or someone else; if your husband said Kristen was not to be permitted on your property; if your husband said to call him rather than your son—all of those things you would do because your husband had the right to order you to do those things because he is the head of the household. Is that what you're telling us?"

The woman stared at her husband, a blank expression on her face. With only the slightest movement of his head, Toli nodded to her.

"Yes."

Errol paused, made two check marks on his note pad. He drew a breath, looked at the woman in the witness box. He was beginning to form a picture of her in his mind.

Selma McLean was chattel that belonged to the men of her family. Despite her years on college campuses, she had not rid herself of her childhood teaching. Then she was the property of her father and uncles; and now she was the property of her husband and son. But sometimes the woman in Selma surfaced, and Errol could feel her inner doubts, perhaps the slightest of defiant tremors against her lot in life.

There was a strong woman here, he thought, but mostly she was only chattel, a position that she must not always find intolerable, because she was allowed to be the first among the women of the household. That was the proverbial carrot. But Toli still held the stick.

"Did you ever observe what you would regard to be misconduct or an improper relationship between your husband and your granddaughter?"

Selma McLean sat up straight in the witness chair and raised her chin. "Absolutely not!"

"Never?"

"Never. My husband loves our grandchildren. They are the jewels of our family. Cubby has always been his favorite, but he cares for and loves both of them."

"Were the children afraid of your husband?"

"I wouldn't say they were afraid of him."

"Did you ever observe him punish the children when their parents were not around?"

"There have been occasions when he has disciplined the children or sent them to their room when they misbehaved. But he was always fair and sensitive about their feelings," the witness insisted. "He never punished them in the presence of other members of the household."

"What would he do?"

"Usually he would take them to their room or to the library or to the kitchen and have a talk with them."

"Your son has testified that on occasions your husband has spanked the children. Were you aware of that?"

"There was one time that he had to take Cubby into the library and spank her, but he's never spanked Niki that I know of. My husband loves his grandchildren very much. He has worked as hard as anyone else in our household to raise them properly."

"It sounds as if what you are saying is that your husband was playing the role of father to Cubby and Niki, rather than grandfather."

"My husband is the head of our household," the woman repeated. "It is his duty."

"The duty to run everybody's lives?"

"No. My husband doesn't run everybody's lives. Cubby was his favorite. He tried to help her. He devoted hours to her schooling that she could never have gotten in public school."

"How frequently did your husband have these sessions with your granddaughter?"

"Sometimes in the morning, sometimes in the evening."

"Every day?"

"The professor is a busy man. Sometimes he locks himself up in the library for hours working on the department's budget or preparing his lessons or grading examination papers. He is a busy man. He did not teach Cubby every day, but as I say, he usually tried to find time with her in the mornings or in the evenings."

"Did Cubby think her grandfather was a good teacher?"

Selma McLean settled against the back of her chair. "You know how children are. No child wants to go to school. The truth of the matter is my husband probably at times forgot he wasn't teaching a college student. He made her work hard on her reading and writing and her numbers. And of course he's a biologist. He thought it was important for children to learn about science. I think Cubby thought he was asking a lot of her. But that's why he wanted to teach her."

"What I don't understand," Errol said, "is why didn't Cubby's mother teach her those subjects rather than her grandfather? Wouldn't it have made more sense to you?"

"My husband pointed out to Kristen that a mother is too easy on her children to be both teacher and mother."

"I assume your husband said the same thing about Cubby's father?"

"Yes. Parents tend to spare the rod and spoil the child."

"I see."

"You understand, Mr. Joyce, I do not claim to be an educated woman. Education is the profession of my husband and my son. I'm just telling you what I have observed from the work that they do. I'm just saying I feel my husband was right."

She closed her eyes, pressed her lips together, and leaned back, resting her head against the chair, as if just remembering that her granddaughters were missing. She opened her eyes and looked down at her hands. "If Cubby were here right now you would find that she is a very bright girl who has learned to read at a level superior to most children her age. I'm sorry she's not here so you can see her!" Selma choked as she fought to control her emotions.

Judge Clemens leaned over to the witness. "Mrs. McLean, would you like a short recess?"

The woman looked at her gratefully and shook her head. "No."

"Any more questions, Mr. Joyce?" Judge Clemens asked.

"No, I have no more questions for this witness. Thank you, Mrs. McLean."

Judge Clemens turned to Jan. "Do you have any questions on behalf of the Guardian Ad Litem?"

"Just one," said Jan, rising to her feet.

"Mrs. McLean, how many years of public schooling did Cubby miss because she was being taught by her grandfather?"

"One."

"She was not old enough to be in first grade this year?" Jan asked.

"Her birthday is in November. She would have to wait almost a full year before she could enroll."

"The year of public schooling that Cubby missed then was kindergarten. Is that correct?"

"Yes, it is next fall when she will be eligible to enter the first grade."

"I have no further questions."

Judge Clemens looked down at her notes and spoke to Peter Hauck. "Does the Petitioner intend to call the grandfather to the witness stand?"

Hauck rose. "Yes, Your Honor, we do."

Judge Clemens turned to the woman sitting beside her. "I had one or two points that I wanted clarified but perhaps your husband's testimony will clarify them for me. You may be excused for now."

Jan Kiel sensed that everyone in the courtroom breathed a sigh of relief, including Judge Clemens. Jan still felt the ripple of electricity in the room, an undercurrent of energy that could spark an explosion at any moment.

CHAPTER 29

WITH HORROR, MAX WATCHED AS THE BEAR SCRAMBLED down to the pool. The huge beast sank a claw in the dead man's groin and pulled the corpse to shore. As lightning crashed with a sound like thousands of iron hammers striking brass cymbals, illuminating the scene with an eerie phosphorescence, the bear grabbed up the carcass in its jaws and shambled off into the woods. There was something almost grotesquely human about the animal as it lumbered off with the body, the stranger's legs and arms dangling, hands and feet scraping the ground.

Like a rag doll, Max thought, and the image of the body floating in the pool filled his thoughts again.

Max shuddered to think what the bear would do with the dead man. He turned away as a gust of wind dashed rain into his face, stung his eyes with sharp needles. He ran to find shelter from the whipping wind, the lancing rain.

When the storm subsided, Max jerked off his reeking shirt. He threw the foul-smelling garment away as if it were cursed. Then he stood half-naked in the rain and shivered. There was nothing more he could do, he decided, and so he set out on the portage for Marabeuf Lake to find Alma and the girls.

Max stumbled on the treacherous ledge. Twice he dropped to his knees and crawled along the slick path. Finally, in the downpour, he sat on the rocks above the river and lowered his head in weariness. His soiled pants, like the shirt, smelled of death; his nostrils filled with the acrid stench of mortified and decomposing flesh.

Max tore at the laces of his boots and laid them aside. He pulled at his wet trousers, shoved them down his legs. Naked, he put his boots back on. He pushed himself into a standing position. He wadded the foul-smelling trousers into a bundle and with a mindless scream, threw it into the water.

In the downpour, he lifted his face and spread his arms. The rain splashed over him and washed him clean, washed the stench from his nostrils, washed the horror from his mind. He was left with a pervasive feeling of absolution that brought him a deep spiritual solace, a metaphysical peace, that passed all human understanding.

CHAPTER 30

TOLI MCLEAN SETTLED HIS HEAVY FRAME into the witness chair. His face was impassive as he raised his hand and took the oath. He didn't change expression as he surveyed the lawyers at the counsel table.

He can be as cold as a January pickerel, thought Errol.

Jan Kiel was perturbed that she found Toli's steel gray hair and olive, classic features attractive. For she was prepared to dislike the man.

Judge Clemens turned a fresh page on her yellow pad. Peter Hauck rose and stood behind his chair in preparation for his examination of the witness. Selma McLean sat beside Arlesen in the courtroom.

The storm outside seemed to draw a breath and abate momentarily, leaving only a breezy susurrance in its wake. The windows stopped rattling and an ominous silence seeped through the nearly empty building.

Toli McLean answered a series of questions Hauck asked him about his birth, his education, and his arrival in this country.

Hauck flipped a page in his notebook and wrote a notation on the margin. Putting down his pen, he turned again to the witness. "Mr. McLean, I now want to turn to the issue of the adequacy of the home provided your grandchildren, Cubby and Niki McLean."

The witness nodded.

"Now, the first question I want to put to you in that regard has to do with the home itself. Will you describe to Judge Clemens the physical arrangement of the McLean home?"

Professor McLean turned in his chair so he could speak directly to Judge Clemens. "My home is a three-story house, six blocks off the university campus in Duluth. It is situated on a half-acre of land. We have a total of six bedrooms and a living or sitting room on each floor. There are two baths on each floor and a full bath off the recreation room in the basement." Toli spoke as if he were listing his home with a real estate broker. "After the original home was built, an additional room was added at the opposite end from the garages to house the kitchen and the dining area. I had that installed after my family and I moved there."

"Are there any recreational facilities at the home?"

"Yes, there is a tennis court and a small, very small, enclosed swimming pool that I had converted into a large sauna so we could use it in winter as well as summer."

"Describe the neighborhood for us."

"It's a nice neighborhood. There are several other blocks of homes similar to ours. Most of them are occupied by families whose provider is a professional man."

"What are the living arrangements for your family in that home?"

"We have three servants who live on the third floor, a cook and a maid and a lady who helps them. They are Korean ladies who are in this country with work permits. We contract with a lawn and garden company for the caretaking of the grounds and with another company to take care of the sauna."

"I understand you have several cars."

"Four."

"Do you employ a chauffeur?"

"No. My wife and my daughter-in-law, when she lived with us, preferred to drive themselves, so I have not employed a chauffeur since I have lived in the United States."

Hauck gestured with his yellow tablet. "Mr. McLean, the answers you have made to the questions I put to you indicate that you are a man of greater means than one would expect living on the salary of a university professor. Do you have other income?"

"I am not a man of affluence. However, I am fortunate enough to have made investments which yield me an income with which I supplement my salary as a member of the university faculty."

"Your son has stated in his testimony that your income is from rental property. Is that correct?"

"Yes. And I also have some other income from stock dividends."

"Would it be a fair statement to say that your income is adequate to continue to maintain your present lifestyle in the foreseeable future while your grandchildren and their parents are living in your home?"

"Yes."

"Do you believe then that if Judge Clemens awards custody of your grandchildren to your son, and the three of them continue to live in your home, they will live in the same manner as they have in the past?"

The witness' eyes focused on the judge. "I have every expectation that my income will continue at its present level or higher and shall provide to my household a standard of living which is equal to, or superior to, that which we have enjoyed these past seven years during my son's marriage."

Judge Clemens wrote what the witness said on her yellow tablet.

"Let me turn to another subject," Hauck said. "During the past seven years that your grandchildren have lived in your home, have they been provided with proper food and clothing and the social amenities other children of their age receive in the Duluth community?"

"They have."

"If Judge Clemens awards custody of the children to their father and they live in your home, are you willing to state under oath that you will continue to provide food, shelter and clothing in cooperation with their father, during the time of their minority, as you have done in the past?"

"I am, and I so state under oath."

"An issue has been raised concerning the education of the older girl, Cubby. As I understand, last year she did not attend public school, but instead she was taught in the home by you. Is that correct?"

"That is correct."

"Do you have qualifications to teach the child?"

"Objection," Errol said. "Respondent objects to the conclusion of the witness concerning his qualifications."

"Sustained."

Hauck rephrased the question. "Mr. McLean, will you please state to the court the credentials you have in the field of education?"

"I have the degrees of Bachelor of Science, Master of Science, and Doctor of Philosophy. My graduate work was in the area of molecular and Mendelian genetics and the basic processes of evolution. However, my thesis was based upon research and studies I did in England on Reproductive Physiology. I have taught college level courses most of my adult life in several colleges and universities, including during my present position as Chairman of the Department of Biology on the Duluth

Campus of the University of Minnesota."

"Based upon your experience and training, do you have an opinion as to whether or not you are qualified to teach kindergarten level courses to your granddaughter, Cubby McLean?"

"I do."

"What is that opinion?"

"I am qualified to teach kindergarten classes to my granddaughter, Cubby McLean."

"Now, let's turn to another subject. I'll try to dispose of it with a single question. Mr. McLean, have you ever at any time, any place, in the presence of either or both of your grandchildren, conducted yourself in a sexually inappropriate manner?"

"No, sir, I have not!" The witness spat the words while looking darkly at Errol Joyce.

Hauck closed his trial notebook and held it in his folded arms. "Were you present at your home when Kristen McLean came and took away your granddaughters?"

"I was not."

"I assume then, that you have no independent knowledge concerning what transpired at that time."

Toli shook his head. "You'll have to ask my wife. She was there."

Hauck looked up at Judge Clemens. "I have no further questions for this witness," he said and sat down.

Judge Clemens looked over her glasses at Errol Joyce. "You may inquire."

Errol picked up his tablet and walked over to the railing of the empty jury box. For a moment it appeared as if the witness and the lawyer were in a staring match.

"Your name is Toli Ozard McLean?"

"It is."

"Your wife has said that all of the male members of your family have the same middle name, 'Ozard.' Is that correct?"

"It is."

"Does the name 'Ozard' have a particular significance to your family?"

"It does."

"Would you mind sharing it with us?"

"Not at all." Toli raised his chin. "My mother's ancestry originated on the steppes of the Kush Mountains in what is known as Afghanistan. All male members of the family who were the head of the household, or someday would become the head of the household, were given the name 'Ozard,' which means 'man strength' or 'strength to man.' A more precise translation into English does not come to my mind right now. But that is the sense of the meaning of Ozard."

"Your father was a Scot. Is that correct?"

"I never knew my father," evaded the witness.

"I had understood that you were reared by your father and mother in Greece."

Toli shook his head. "No, I never knew my father. I was reared by my mother's family, who were merchants who had come to Greece from the old country. However, my mother continued to keep my English citizenship instead of exclusively taking the Greek nationality as she and other members of her family had done after they came there from the old country."

"And you went from Greece to the Island of Cyprus where you met and married your sixteen-year-old bride; and from there you went to England where you received your education and then came to the United States. Isn't that correct?"

"Essentially so."

"When you lived in Greece and were growing up, did your mother's family maintain in your home the traditions of their old country?"

"Yes."

"And after you married and made your home in England, did you continue to maintain those traditions?"

"As closely as I could."

"Was that also true when you lived in Georgia and Vermont before you moved to Minnesota?"

"Yes."

"And is that true today?"

"Yes."

"So there will be no misunderstanding," Errol said, "the home environment into which you propose to raise your grandchildren is an environment, a culture, that is different from the American culture?"

"Objection," Peter Hauck rose to his feet. "I object because the question is vague and ambiguous; for the reason that there is no such thing as an American culture. If there was, there is no law in the State of Minnesota that requires a child to be reared in a home dominated by any certain culture."

Judge Clemens looked down at the two lawyers. "I'm going to sustain the objection, Mr. Joyce. I know of no law in this country that defines the kind of culture that a child must be raised in. The American people are made up of such diverse nationalities that I'm not certain myself that there is such a thing as a definable American culture. Our laws have limitations as to what must be done in raising a child, but I know of no cultural bias that our laws approve. So I'm going to sustain the objection."

Errol wrote on his yellow pad a reminder to make exception to the court's ruling. "Why did you instruct your wife to call you instead of your son in the event Kristen returned to your home after she left and filed suit for divorce?"

"I am the head of the household. I am the one who is required to deal with that situation."

"Why didn't you leave it up to your son? This was a domestic matter between parents. Why, as grandparent, did you interfere?"

"I did not interfere, Mr. Joyce. When I take an action or give an instruction in my home, that is not interference, that is my duty. Just as in the classroom I am given the responsibility to teach my students at the university so they will learn to decipher the mysteries of biology. It is my duty to instruct them in my classroom and it is their duty to obey. In the household it is the duty of the members of the household to obey. Otherwise, there can be no harmony in the classroom; no harmony in the household. Each would have only chaos."

"I take it," Errol said, "in your home and in your classrooms you're the boss."

The witness nodded. "I'm the boss."

Judge Clemens sat up straight in her chair. "Mr. Joyce, if you have reached a point where it is convenient for us to take a break without interfering with your thoughts, I think it would be well for us to take a short recess."

Errol nodded. He turned to look toward the back of the courtroom. P.M. was still sitting there, as Joyce knew he would be. Watching, waiting. Judging.

Judge Clemens rapped the gavel. "Court will be in recess."

"Draw," Jan whispered to herself. She felt a distinct release of tension in the entire courtroom when the judge stood up and smiled at her reassuringly.

But Jan knew it was not over. Something in Errol's manner warned her that Errol was already in trouble. Something was missing from Toli's testimony. Something important. And her woman's intuition told her that he knew he was losing the case for his client.

CHAPTER 31

U P ON THE IRON RANGE THE STORM PAUSED as if gathering its strength for another onslaught. By instinct, the woods creatures remained in their shelters. They waited for the back side of the storm to arrive. The calm eye of the turbulence moved across the camp clearing at the end of Marabeuf Lake.

Max, naked except for unlaced boots and socks, picked his way slowly across the clearing. Then calling hoarsely, he scratched on the closed tent flap.

There was a squeal and flurry of movement inside the tent. Max held on to its side to keep his balance and waited as Alma opened the tent flap.

"Max, what happened?" Alma reached behind her for her rain gear.

Alma quickly adjusted the poncho she pulled over Max's head and tied the cord at his waist. Then she led him inside the tent.

"My God, what happened to you?"

Max shook his head. "It's all right now. He's dead."

"Where are your clothes?"

"I don't want to talk about it."

Alma's face froze.

Max reached over and put his hand on her shoulder. "Please, Alma," he said hoarsely, "not now. We'll talk about it later."

Her face softened. She bit her lower lip and nodded. Then she reached out and took him into her arms, and he shivered against her warmth.

The canvas covering at the entrance of the tent began flapping as the wind picked up. Alma worked with the zipper until she got it closed. Max sat on the ground cloth. He eyed the food on the plates.

"Eat this." Alma handed him her plate. "I'll make some hot chocolate."

She lit the tiny propane stove. The heat brought warmth to Max's shaking body.

Niki knelt close beside Alma and tried to help her prepare the hot chocolate.

On the far side, Cubby sat and scooted back until she settled snug against the tent wall. She stared at Max in rapt fascination.

CHAPTER 32

I T WAS AFTERNOON. JUDGE CLEMENS SOUNDED HER GAVEL and pointed to the counsel table. "I want to see you three lawyers in my chambers right away. The court will be in recess for twenty minutes."

In chambers, Peter Hauck, Errol Joyce and Jan Kiel took chairs opposite the judge and waited while she poured herself a cup of coffee, then sat down behind her desk and began flipping through her notes. She glanced at Hauck when she came upon one notation and sighed audibly. There was more talent in this room, she thought, than in many a law school.

Hauck was a graduate of the University of Michigan School of Law and for a time had served as the youngest instructor on its faculty. The Duluth law firm of Hauck & Figg, of which he was the senior partner, had been organized forty years earlier, after he left the tedium of his faculty duties. Hauck, even though he was 70, continued to be propelled by nervous energy and had no thought of retirement. He remained an active member of the Minnesota trial bar and a force in state politics. He was privy to the loose network of men in both political parties who manipulated candidates. He backed winners because they would be winners and concerned himself with issues and principles only after they won. He was single-minded in his quest for clients, and he was not above asking, sometimes demanding, reciprocity from politicians he had helped put into office.

Errol Joyce and Peter Hauck had known and respected each other for years. Their battles in the courtrooms across Minnesota were legend to members of the bar who had witnessed them. When Errol started practicing law, Hauck was the man the young lawyers had to beat in the courtroom to gain reputation and status. Errol won his cases enough times and lost enough times that both men developed genuine respect, if not affection, for each other.

Judge Clemens looked at Errol, clenching her lips tightly. He was not so fathomable as Hauck. Errol ran cool and hot and there was just no way to figure him out. The trick was, she'd found, to stay just one jump ahead of him. Even then, he might overtake the unwary. He was smooth and clever, but he had none of the arrogance of many trial lawyers. His strength and charisma came from his enormous self-confidence. He wasn't cocky about it. He just had it and knew he had it.

Judge Clemens relaxed her mouth, leaned back in her chair and pushed her notes slightly forward so she could refer to them at any time.

"Where are you going with this line of questioning?" she asked Errol Joyce.

"I'm going to prove that the McLean home is not a proper home in which to raise those two children."

"I understand that, but specifically, why is it relevant to the issues we have here, to examine this witness regarding his philosophy about how public school is conducted?"

Hauck interrupted. "I agree with you, Judge. I've not made any objections in light of the court's ruling on the wide latitude you are allowing on cross examination. But I see absolutely no relevancy at all to any further examination of this witness as to the type of education the McLean family is providing their seven-year-old granddaughter."

Jan sat silent.

"Errol?" the judge ignored Hauck's interjection.

"If I can establish that there is reasonable doubt as to Toli McLean's actions; if I can show in any degree that his actions around the children have been sexually inappropriate, then it is incumbent upon the court to deny custody of the two children to the father who would take them to live in that home."

"I understand what you're saying, but the term 'sexual inappropriateness' is a psychologist's term. It isn't a legal term. Are you contending that you're going to be able to show there was some overt act of misconduct on the part of the grandfather toward the granddaughter during those sessions?"

"I don't have to prove that. All I have to prove is that he conducted himself in such a manner that his behavior was sexually inappropriate in the presence of a seven-year-old girl."

Jan was sitting where she could watch. "Errol, I'm Guardian Ad Litem of those children and if you have any evidence that points to misconduct I want to know."

"Well," Errol said, "the first thing I set out to prove, and I have proven, is that Toli McLean had the opportunity to be alone with the girl on a regular basis. And the second thing I've been able to establish by everyone except Toli McLean himself is that the girl did not want to attend—"

Judge Clemens interrupted. "There is no use in going through a litany of classic examples that identify child abuse. All I want to know is the purpose of your examination. I want to know how your questions are relevant. I'll decide later what your examination shows, if it is admissible."

"The relevancy is that I'm entitled to show this witness' conduct is such that it would reasonably cause any seven-year-old girl to be apprehensive and create an unhealthy atmosphere for her in the household. It doesn't make any difference if he is guilty of misconduct or not. And it doesn't make any difference how well-intentioned his actions were in dealing with the girl. If, in fact, he has created an environment that in the eyes of a seven-year-old child was inappropriate sexual conduct, this court should not put that child back into that environment. That's all I'm saying."

Judge Clemens turned to Jan. "Are you going to make objection to this line of questioning?"

Jan shook her head. "No."

"And you?" The judge turned to Hauck.

"I object to this entire line of questioning on the grounds that it is irrelevant. And I ask that the previous testimony of the witness in this regard be stricken from the record."

Judge Clemens shook her head. "No. I'm going to overrule your objection. I want to hear what the witness has to say." She turned to Errol. "I assume this is the only witness you're going to have on this subject?"

He shrugged. "What other witness is there? There were only two of them in that library, McLean and Cubby. Cubby is missing somewhere up on the Granite River and you say you wouldn't let a seven-year-old testify even if she were here."

Judge Clemens nodded. "That's the reason I'm leaning over backwards to let you ask whatever you want in that regard from this witness. But I'm afraid we are going very far afield and there may be merit in Petitioner's objections on the grounds of relevancy."

Judge Clemens glanced at her watch. "We'll get started again in five minutes."

After the others left her chambers, the judge let out another sigh.

It didn't help. Peter Hauck and Errol Joyce would be at each other's throats if she didn't hold the reins tight in her judicial hands. So far, the questioning had been reasonably bloodless. But Errol Joyce was venturing into unknown and dangerous territory. And, on the sidelines, Jan Kiel was watching both combatants like a hawk.

Back in the courtroom, Judge Clemens reminded the witness that he was still under oath. Errol continued his cross examination.

"Mr. McLean, did you tell Cubby that the work she was doing in her class, including her drawings, was to remain a secret?"

Toli McLean laughed. "Yes. That was a game we played. You must remember, Mr. Joyce, that I was taking the mind of a seven-year-old which is in its most formative stage, and I was applying the same techniques that I apply in college classes to make the student stretch. Because one's potential is always greater than one thinks it is."

"Please explain to the court what you mean."

"In college we often engage in role-playing or have the students make certain assumptions or make a strategy game out of the problem we're giving them. This teaches them to reason and deal with it as if it were a real life problem. You can't be that complicated in dealing with the mind of a seven-year-old; so I made a game out of it as if the numbers she was learning, the science she was learning, and the drawings she was doing, were part of a great secret project, like she was a spy for her country. It was a game. So, to that extent, yes, I told Cubby it was a secret. But there was nothing sinister in that. All of her life she will remember the skills she first learned by associating them with the game."

"I see." Errol remained standing. He fixed Toli with a cold stare.

In the icy silence, the witness felt compelled to speak again. "I do that with my college students all the time. It's just a teaching tool."

Errol stood beside the jury box and said nothing.

"That's all it was," said McLean shrugging.

Errol made a notation on his yellow pad. "Did you ever tell their mother Kristen about your games?"

"No. Kristen and I never discussed the school work Cubby was doing."

"Because Kristen always insisted that Cubby be in public school, isn't that correct?"

"Yes."

"Did you ever discuss this game with their father?"

"No."

"With your wife Selma?"

"No."

"Niki. How about little Niki? Did you ever discuss it with her?"

"Of course not."

"Why do you say 'of course not'?"

"Niki was too young to understand."

"The facts are you never discussed this secret game or this way of teaching with anyone except your granddaughter Cubby. Is that correct?"

"That's correct. She was the student and I was the teacher," said the witness.

"Tell us what subjects you taught Cubby."

"Her numbers, reading, art, and science."

"Including your specialty, biology?"

"Yes, some," Toli said.

"That sounds quite adult for a seven-year-old."

"I taught her these subjects utilizing only the most elementary terms. Just the basic elements of science."

"Including the creation of life?" Errol asked innocently.

"Yes, of course. And I taught her about death also."

"That is a rather morbid subject for a seven-year-old, isn't it?"

The witness smiled. "The creation and the extinction of life forms are the most basic lessons we all must learn if we are to understand the world we live in."

"Why didn't you let Niki attend these sessions when she asked to?"

Toli smiled tolerantly. "I thought Niki would be a disturbing influence."

"Why didn't you let her mother or her father attend these sessions?"

"Parents are notoriously poor teachers of their own."

"Why didn't you let Cubby's grandmother attend these sessions?"

"My wife had her own duties to perform in our home," the witness said crisply.

"Was there any other reason that you insisted Cubby stay home rather than go to public school?"

"Yes. Mr. Joyce, people in Duluth resent the fact that my family is different. They think of us as foreigners. They don't agree with our close-knit lifestyle. I knew those prejudices would inhibit my granddaughter's education."

"Are you saying that your family is alienated from the rest of the community?"

" 'Alienated' is too strong a word. 'Misunderstood' would be a better word."

Joyce took a pace to one side, as if entering another arena. He stopped, took a different stance. He appeared casual in his movements as a cat stalking a bird.

"Mr. McLean, I want to turn to another subject now. Earlier in your testimony you referred to your own youth when you were about Cubby's age and lived in Greece. Do you remember that testimony?"

"I do."

"You testified that your father was an Englishman, your mother was Iraqi, and the teachers in the Greek school you attended regarded you as a foreigner and, in any event, didn't understand you. I believe that was your testimony. Is that correct?"

"Approximately so."

"Was your father living in the home at that time?"

"No. I told you I never actually knew my father."

"Your father had left your mother before you were old enough to know him? Is that correct?"

"That's correct."

"Tell me about this school you went to in Greece when you were seven years old."

"It was a boys' school. We did not live in a very affluent neighborhood in the city. It was an average school by Greek standards at that time."

"Girls didn't attend the school?"

"No."

"Did you have men teachers or women teachers?"

"Men teachers."

"The sense of your testimony is that you were mistreated by your teachers when you were a young student. Is that correct?"

"Mr. Joyce, I would say that if you had experienced what I experienced, you would have described the treatment as being cruel."

"I see. So the sense of your testimony is that when you were a young man, in school in Greece, you felt you were discriminated against, and the teachers were cruel to you."

"That's what I said."

"Were they verbally abusive to you?"

"Yes."

"Did they ever strike you?"

"Yes."

"Would you say they beat you?"

"Yes."

"Was this with reason or, in your opinion, without provocation?"

"I didn't do anything to deserve being beaten, if that's what you're asking."

"Mr. McLean," Errol spoke the words very carefully, "were you ever sexually abused while you were in school in Greece?"

"I don't remember."

"By that I mean, by anyone in school. Students or teachers or anyone else?"

"I don't remember," the witness repeated.

"I would assume that even at the age of seven, if you had been, you would have remembered, wouldn't you?"

"I suppose."

Peter Hauck rose to his feet. "Your Honor, I'm going to object to any further questions to the witness along this line on the ground that it is repetitious. The witness has answered that question several times and has said that he doesn't remember."

"Objection sustained," Judge Clemens said. "Move along, Mr. Joyce."

Hauck sat down.

"Mr. McLean, when was the last time you had sexual relations with your wife?"

Hauck bolted to his feet. "I object to that question. It has absolutely no relevance to this litigation!"

Errol turned to the judge. "Your Honor, my question is highly relevant to the issues in this court concerning the advisability of requiring these minor children to live in this home."

Judge Clemens said, "I'm not sure where the question is going to lead us, but I will permit the witness to answer."

Hauck sank slowly to his seat once again. But he hunched over the table on full alert. Unconsciously, he began to grind his teeth. Jan noticed the slight sound and tapped her pencil's eraser softly on the table. There was a definite change in Errol's attitude, she noticed. He appeared cool and unflappable. But she sensed that his muscles were bunched under his clothing. There was something almost feral about his manner. But it was nothing she could detect with her eyes. It was just something she sensed as she watched Errol masterfully lead Toli through a minefield of delicately-phrased questions.

Toli McLean appeared to be completely undisturbed by the question. He turned and spoke directly to Judge Clemens. "Your Honor, I have no hesitancy in answering that question." He then turned and faced Errol Joyce. "My wife and I make no secret of the fact that we have not had intimate relations, haven't slept together for at least four years."

"And what is the reason for that?"

Again Hauck was on his feet. "Objection!"

"Sustained," the judge said before Hauck assigned a reason.

"May I assume that during these past four years, you have not been celibate?"

"You may not assume that."

"Well," Errol said, "tell me. In the past four years, have you been celibate?"

"I have."

"Is it a fair statement to say that in these past four years you have abstained from sexual activity with your wife, and you have abstained from sexual activity outside your home?"

"That's correct."

Errol walked back to his chair at the counsel table. "Your Honor, I have no more questions for this witness right now. However, I do not want the witness excused, for I may want to recall him at a later time."

"The witness plans to remain in town until the conclusion of the hearing," Hauck said.

"You have no objection to Mr. Joyce reserving the right to recall the witness?"

"None."

"All right." Judge Clemens gestured toward the window. "It appears that our storm is picking up again. Before it gets much worse, I'm going to adjourn these proceedings and ask that all of you be back here tomorrow morning. Perhaps we will have some improvement in the weather by then."

With taps of the gavel, she announced, "Court is in recess."

Errol Joyce did not move. He continued to stare at Toli as the man left the witness chair and rejoined his family. As the McLeans were going out the door, the professor looked back. Errol still stood there, his eyes fixed on Toli.

Jan saw the subtle exchange and felt a ripple of excitement. It was like watching two gladiators in a Roman arena as they stopped fighting for a moment to pick up a different set of weapons.

After Toli left, she looked back at Errol. Their eyes met. Her eyebrows arched in a silent question. Was he losing it? Their eyes locked, but she saw no visible sign that he was a defeated man. She increased the intensity of her gaze, hoping to penetrate beyond the mask he wore.

Errol never blinked.

CHAPTER 33

D R. JENS ERICKSON WAVED A HAND toward the chair. "Sit down, Errol," he said. The rain had brought early evening shadows to the slopes of the iron range.

The lawyer took the seat and waited until the doctor closed the door to the hospital corridor and settled behind his desk.

"How can I help you?"

"Doc, I need a witness."

"For what?"

"I need a witness who can explain to Judge Dorothy Clemens the guidelines you medical people use when you suspect a child is exposed to sexual abuse. I think the phrase is 'sexually inappropriate behavior.' "

"I'm a general practitioner, Errol. For that, you need somebody out of the psychiatry department of the University Hospital down in Minneapolis."

"I must have my expert by tomorrow morning."

"I don't specialize in psychiatry. Judge Clemens knows that."

"You have an M.D. degree; you have done psychiatric studies. You're familiar with the basic scientific literature in the field."

"What do you need from an expert?"

"Two things. First, I need a statement of the guidelines that are used in cases of suspected child abuse which are recognized by the medical profession; and I need an explanation so the judge will understand those guidelines."

Dr. Erickson looked behind him at the rows of medical texts on the bookshelf that covered the back of his wall. "Errol, I wouldn't have any trouble testifying as to the guidelines. They're pretty standard in medical literature. And I wouldn't have any trouble explaining them to Judge Clemens. But if you ask me a hypothetical question, based on a set of facts and you ask if they fall within those guidelines, I'm going to have to tell you I don't know because that is not a specialty I have practiced since I got out of medical school."

Errol thought for a moment. "Well, Doc, what if I pose this question to you tomorrow on the witness stand: 'Assuming an adult arranged to meet at regular intervals several times a week with a seven-year-old child for the stated purpose of educating that child, do you have an opinion based upon reasonable medical certainty whether or not that circumstance would fit within the guidelines you have described?'"

Dr. Erickson shook his head. "I couldn't give you an affirmative answer to a question like that."

"Why not? It's obvious from the way I worded the question that the adult would be alone with the child at regular intervals."

"Millions and millions of adults, every day in the United States, are alone with minor children. The fact that they are is not indicative that they have the psychological profile of a pedophile. You've got to have more than that."

"I don't have more than that. There are going to be only two people present in the room, the adult and the child. And the child either can't testify or won't be permitted to do so. The adult's going to deny it."

"That's what I'm saying. You've asked me to give an opinion based upon 'reasonable medical certainty,' and—"

Errol interrupted, "That's the test under the law which we have to use."

"I know. I'm telling you we can't meet the test with that question unless we have more information about the adult and the child and their activities when they are alone."

"It's a catch-22 situation."

"I don't know what you call it, I'm just saying to you that I cannot testify to that opinion as a matter of reasonable certainty."

Errol shook his head.

"For that matter, I think if you went down to the University Hospital and got an expert out of the psychiatry department, he couldn't tell you either." He leaned across the desk toward the lawyer. "The facts are, Errol, when you're dealing with the question of 'sexually inappropriate conduct,' that term in itself indicates you do not have the evidence to establish that any perversion has taken place."

"That's what Arlesen said."

"That was what?"

Errol waved his hand. "I was just saying I've already had a witness on the stand, the father of the child, and he said about the same thing you just said."

"Well, that is so," the doctor said, "but on the other hand, just because we cannot establish that an overt act of misconduct has or has not taken place doesn't keep the adult's actions from creating a climate of inappropriate conduct that a minor should avoid. It isn't so much what happened or what could happen as it is what the child thinks happens or the child fears could happen, that will psychologically scar the child."

"Would you say that on the witness stand tomorrow?"

"Who's the opposing attorney?"

"Peter Hauck."

Jens Erickson shrugged. "I suppose if the judge would let me. But I'm not sure I'm saying anything more than Judge Clemens would know herself. It doesn't take a great amount of expertise to realize that sometimes the things we say and do in front of small children deliver an entirely different message from what we think we're delivering. If we do that on a continuing basis, it's entirely possible for any adult, without fault on his part, to create an environment that we shouldn't leave children in."

"Exactly. That's the point I'm trying to convince Judge Clemens to understand. In this hearing I'm not trying to prove what happened in the room between the adult and the minor. I'm only trying to prove that there was inappropriate conduct which has created a condition in the home that requires the judge to say that the children will not be forced to live in the home under those conditions."

"Now you lose me, Errol. Those are legal points. I'm just telling you that if you put me on the witness stand tomorrow as an expert on psychiatric matters, Peter Hauck is going to ask about my credentials. I've known Peter for a long time. We're never going to convince the judge over his objections that I'm an expert in that field."

"But at least I can establish that you have the credentials to explain the guidelines that observers look for in trying to determine situations of child abuse. At least that will be helpful. Will you testify?"

Jens Erickson nodded. "If you want me to, I'll come over."

Errol rose. "Thanks, Doc. Has there been any change in Kristen's condition since this morning?"

Dr. Erickson shook his head. "No."

"Do you expect any improvement?"

"It's now been over thirty hours. If she doesn't regain consciousness in the next twenty-four hours, I think that will be indicative of some pretty serious brain damage from loss of oxygen. If this storm moves out of here tomorrow, I'm going to try to get an ambulance helicopter in here from Minneapolis to transfer her down to the University Medical Center."

Errol nodded. He started to leave the room, then paused. "Do you want me to get a subpoena served on you for tomorrow?"

"No, I'll pick it up when I get to the courthouse."

"Thanks, Doc."

The doctor dismissed him with a wave of the hand.

But Errol Joyce's presence lingered, as if the air in the room had been charged by some mysterious force.

CHAPTER 34

RAIN CONTINUED TO FALL ON THE GRAND MARAIS HARBOR, but the downpour had slackened. Wisps of fog gathering in the north shore coves signaled there would be a change in the weather.

The door to the apartment opened and the two lawyers entered arguing.

"Why the hell would you do a thing like that?" exploded Errol Joyce.

Jan's eyes flashed. "Because it's my job. Now that we've heard from all the witnesses, I think it's in the best interest of the girls to stay with their father and have the advantages the McLean family can offer."

The couple stood in the center of Errol's living room. The apartment was dark except for reflections from the harbor lights. Outside the sliding glass door, the tilted wing of Jan's airplane rose and fell with the surf.

"I thought you'd be the one person I could convince as to what's happening to those kids in that home," Errol said angrily.

"Why? Because I went to bed with you!" Jan flushed. "That just pisses me off, Errol, that you think my recommendation would be swayed by a personal relationship. Damn it! I'm the Guardian Ad Litem of those kids. It's my job to make sure the court makes a decision that's in their best interest. I resent the fact that you would believe that what happened between us would make any difference about what I think is best for those kids."

"Good Lord, Jan," he said, turning to the window in frustration. "I never said anything about your going to bed with me."

"Well, that's what you meant."

Errol Joyce turned back to her. "How in the hell do you know what I meant?"

"I heard what you said."

"Jan, I'm just simply saying that as a woman, you of all people ought to realize that those two girls should not be made to live in that household."

"Errol," Jan pointed her finger at him. "Invariably when you men question my professional judgment, you put it on some sort of personal basis."

"No, I don't! I'm just saying you're wrong if you make that recommendation to the judge."

"You said because I'm a woman I should know that."

"Damn it, Jan!" Errol threw up his arms. "When you argue about legal matters, you're so defensive about being a woman that nobody can reason with you."

"Oh, no, don't give me that story. I came here to warn you what my recommendation is going to be tomorrow, and you started putting it on some personal basis. Damn you, Errol! I resent your insinuating that I would make my recommendation on any basis other than my professional judgment."

Errol took a deep breath. He exhaled slowly to control his anger.

"Please sit down." He pointed to the couch.

Jan hesitated.

"Please?" he asked.

Jan sat and kicked off her shoes. Errol pushed a stool over for her feet. He walked to the window and stood beside the gathered drapes, looking out at the lighthouse at the entrance to the bay. He spoke quietly.

"Jan, the hearing is not over yet. All I'm asking you is please do not indicate your views to the judge until we finish with all the witnesses."

"I thought we were finished with all the witnesses."

"No."

"You told the judge you had no other witnesses because Kristen is in the hospital. She wouldn't let the kids testify even if they were here."

Errol stared out of the window.

Jan shook her head slowly. "Those two kids are entitled to the opportunities the McLean family will give them: a great home, money, an education. We can't substitute our judgment for theirs as to how they raise the children unless there is some evidence of abuse. And there's none. None at all. The test of law is, what is best for the children. I can't make my recommendations to the judge just because my sympathy is with the mother."

"I'm not questioning your motives. I'm saying I don't believe things are right in that household. I don't believe that's a place for those kids to be raised."

"Because you think Professor McLean is guilty of some sort of sexual misconduct."

"Yes, that is what I think."

"And you won't give him the benefit of the doubt. You won't say that the man is innocent until proven guilty?"

"Not when you've got two young children involved."

"Errol!" Jan put her feet on the floor and sat up straight on the couch. "Do you hear what you're saying to me? I can't base my recommendation to the court on what you think personally. I must base it on evidence I heard on the witness stand, and when I give the grandfather the benefit of the doubt, I have no other choice. I must recommend that the children have the advantages the McLean family can give them and their mother cannot."

Errol turned back again to the window. Looking out, he saw a star. The rain had stopped.

After Jan's outburst, neither spoke. Errol remained at the window, uncomfortably silent. Jan sat stiffly, facing him, but not looking directly at him. She, too, stared out the window at the lights on the waters of the harbor. A ripple of thoughts ran through her mind. She remembered the first time she let Errol hold her in his arms, and she also remembered why.

Jan's father had made an unexpected appearance at the courthouse. He had been drunk. Embarrassed, Jan had asked Errol to consent to a recess in their trial so she could get her father out of the courtroom and on a bus out of town. Afterwards, when Jan sought out Errol to thank him, she found that he, too, was drunk.

Jan found Errol at the Harbor Inn On-Sales Restaurant and Lounge. "On-Sales, Off-Sales" licenses determined where you drank in Minnesota. According to Errol, "The Liquor Licensing Statute was enacted for the purpose of providing relief to brooding Minnesota lawyers."

Jan walked beside him up to the courthouse. She still carried her soft leather briefcase. He said he'd left his on the counsel table. The damp night air had a sobering effect on him.

Jan opened the courthouse door. Inside, she had asked, "Why the booze?" She admired this lawyer with whom she debated in courthouses on the Masabe Iron Range. But that night he reminded her of her father, for whom she had bitter memories and no respect.

Jan pushed through swinging doors into the quiet, empty courtroom and switched on lights. She watched Errol walk over to the jury box. His movements were like those of an athlete. His head was youthful, alert, but covered with graying hair. His eyes had the fixed hypnotic gaze of an animal tamer, authoritative and violent. He smiled innocently at Jan and ran his hand along the polished wooden rail. His youthful smile softened the steely effect of his eyes and left Jan with feelings she could not clarify. She thought he had this same effect on witnesses when he questioned them. If she were to describe the lawyer in one word she would have chosen "aristocratic."

Errol took a seat in the front row of the jury box and contemplated the rest of the chamber with a look of pure love and joy for all he beheld. "We'll never be chosen to serve on a jury," he observed wistfully.

Jan left her purse on the counsel table and joined him in the empty jury box. "Why the booze tonight?" she repeated, stretching her long legs out on the wooden rail that fenced the jury box.

"I'm celebrating life, the law."

"You can do that without booze."

He looked at the profile of the woman beside him, highlighted in the glow from the ceiling lamps. "God, you're beautiful."

Jan smiled sadly. "Errol, you're drunk."

"I am that," he admitted, "but you're still a beautiful woman."

"I never think of myself that way. My father said I was plain and ordinary."

"He was wrong."

"My father drinks too much."

"Like me?"

"More. I didn't really have a father," she added resentfully. "I never dated. My father was always an alcoholic, and my mother constantly found fault with him. Because of her scolding and his drunken babbling, I wouldn't bring a boy into our home. I wanted my father to be proud of me, but I could never please him. He always said I could do better. Both of my parents wanted a perfect child."

"Surely he was proud of you when you graduated from school."

"My father left home when I was fifteen and went to Duluth to live with a woman who didn't nag him about his drinking. Once I went to Duluth to see him, and she was there. Her blouse was open, and she was barefoot. She wasn't much older than me. I was valedictorian of my high school graduation class, which I worked hard for, and I had gone to ask my father to come to my graduation so he could hear my speech. I imagined how it would be when he came and sat down in front with my graduation gift in his lap—a gift wrapped in white tissue paper and tied with ribbon."

"Did he come?"

"He came to the graduation, but he wouldn't come into the auditorium," she said bitterly. Tears stung her eyes. "He stood out in the hall, drunk. He didn't bring any gift. He just stood there until I saw him, and then he left. He didn't even wait until it was my turn at the podium. I wrote him a letter after that. I told my father I never wanted to see or hear from him again."

"You do though."

Jan nodded. "After my mother died, he started coming around and bringing his trouble with him."

She got up and took a tissue out of her purse, which lay on the counsel table.

Errol looked across at her. "Did you cry when your father didn't come into the auditorium to hear your valedictory speech?" he asked gently.

"No." She shook her head. "I didn't cry, but I got angry, and that anger stayed with me all through those difficult years while I was working my way through law school. Crying would not have gotten me my law degree, but the anger did."

"So he did give you a gift the night of your graduation."

"What gift?"

"Determination."

Jan stared out the window of the courthouse at the harbor lights winking on the breakwater. Errol got out of his chair and walked up behind her. Gently he put his arms around her and held her close.

The sound of Errol's voice shook Jan from her memories.

"I'm sorry," she said. "I was thinking of something else."

"I said, I do have one more witness."

"Who?"

"I'm going to put Dr. Erickson on the witness stand, first thing tomorrow morning."

"Will he testify that the McLean household is not a fit place to raise those kids?"

"Not exactly."

"Is he going to give an opinion that the grandfather is guilty of sexual misconduct?"

"No, I won't tell you that he's going to say that, Jan. I don't suppose we can find any witness who can give us direct evidence on that. In these kinds of situations the minor and adult are alone. The adult denies it, and the kid either can't or won't testify as to what happened when the two were alone. But the doctor can tell us of those things the medical profession looks for in signs of child abuse."

Errol continued, "I don't want you to make your recommendation to the judge until she hears what Dr. Erickson has to say. And I don't want you to jump to any final conclusions until after you hear what the doctor has to say."

He walked over and sat on the couch beside her. He put his feet up on the stool next to hers.

Jan closed her eyes and leaned back. "I want so very much for you to be wrong on this one. I'm doing all I can to remain objective, but I have to admit that when I was a little girl and my father abandoned our family, I used to dream of how wonderful it would be to have rich grandparents who would love me." She looked sideways at him. "You haven't presented a damned shred of evidence in the courtroom to indicate that the grandfather is guilty of sexual misconduct."

"Jan, every new baby is born a savage."

She looked at him, puzzled by his statement.

"Really, they are. Every child, each one of us, comes into the world a naked savage. We bring with us our instincts for survival, instincts that if kept and followed when we become adults are called greed, lust, envy, the entire list of seven deadly sins. And we overlay these instincts with a veneer that we call civilization. Without that veneer we are like animals. We fight with one another for food and for our mates and for shelter. And sometimes, just for fun, we destroy so that we can live for the moment instead of laying away for the future. We weave this societal cloth which has to be rewoven by each generation."

Jan looked at Errol intently. She loved him when he spoke of his true love, the law. He was magnificent in his beliefs. He lent a kind of nobility to simple truths when he talked this way. She leaned toward him, eager to hear what he had to say. His tone told her that what he was saying was important to him. And he was not just trying to persuade her to change her mind about the McLean children.

"That courtroom," he said, "is, in microcosm, a clash of cultures. Look what's happened to the Eastern Mediterranean where orderly governments have been destroyed by selfish clans with tribal religious interests.

Fanatic sects have put their interest before any rule of law. The Arab, the Moslem, the Jew, the Christian, the Hindu, the Sikh, the Kurd. A whole army of governments that spread from the Bosphorus, on the Turkish Greek border, east to the Malayan peninsula. Time after time, in bloody conflict, entire nations tear apart the fabric of law and order because they have basely allowed their individual tribal instincts to destroy the concept of equity and fair play and of tolerance and understanding that a rule of law brings with it.

"What has happened to those tribes and families, religious enclaves in the Eastern Mediterranean, southeast Asia, can happen here if we don't have the strong belief in or are not willing to commit ourselves to the sanctity of the law. The wool of civilization that the rule of law has knitted together in the form of our constitutions, our declarations of independence, our statutes, the sanctity of the precedence, is shabby, showing wear at the seams. The law is not perfect. It requires constant weaving to mend the holes and the tears in it which many fall through. And if the cracks get too large or if the holes become too many, then the law becomes replaced by the anarchy and greed of people gone savage. And it's the role of the lawyer to mend these dark holes with their arguments and fights for unpopular causes. The lawyer must insist on justice and fair play, must support the unpopular causes, must take a stand with the defense of the guilty, must insure that everyone has his day in court, must insist that the man be regarded innocent until proven guilty.

"Even the smallest rent in the seam of civilization or justice through which we let someone fall must be mended or it will grow and eventually cast us into the chaos of the Middle East or the bigotry of discrimination or the cruelty of genocide."

"And you're saying that the children of Kristen McLean have fallen through such a crevice," Jan said softly.

"I am. And we cannot simply sit by and say the dog is entitled to his first bite. It's not enough to say that the battered woman must take her blows before she is entitled to protection. It's not enough to say that a child has no lawful rights in its dispute with its parents because the law has failed to create a remedy.

"Those of us who accept the fruits of the practice of law without being faithful to this trust of preserving, repairing, renewing the garment of civilization that the rule of law has woven, are shysters and deserve to be ridiculed and condemned by those from whom they take and those who seek to live in a civil society. Those kinds are not lawyers. They are members of the bar, but they are not lawyers.

"Kristen McLean has done what she has done because the law has failed her," Errol said bitterly. "I failed her. Peter Hauck failed her. Judge Clemens failed her."

"And you think I am failing her, too," Jan said, her voice feeble against the wash of his tide of indignation.

"All of us who have touched her case are in part responsible because we can't figure out a way to resolve the conflict between the presumption of innocence, the right for a man to contend he is innocent until proven guilty, against the gross injustice of a crime going unpunished. The system can fail just simply because the aggrieved party has no witness or aid other than his own word to prove his or her innocence. It's not enough to say that this has been a dilemma of man in his efforts to preserve civilization, to preserve the rule of law, a dilemma of presumption of innocence *vis-à-vis* the unpunished crime.

"That's really what the practice of law is, Jan. It's the filling in and the sealing of these cracks and these holes."

"And law makes the difference."

"The law does make a difference, and the lawyer is the instrument through which the law works to make that difference. It's a never-ending battle of intellects, a battle against disorder and chaos. But the law works only if all parties to a civilization recognize its value and importance."

For several minutes the two lawyers sat and looked at the reflections in the waters of the harbor.

"I won't make any recommendation to the judge until you rest your case," Jan said finally. "But, Errol, if you don't come up with some evidence tomorrow to directly show sexual misconduct by the grandfather, my recommendation will be that the father be given custody and the children live in the McLean home."

Errol nodded and looked over at her. "I'm sorry I shouted at you."

"You should be." She patted him on the knee. "I've got to go. Tomorrow is going to be a long day."

In the quiet of the hospital room, the nurse standing beside Kristen McLean's bed was certain she heard the patient speak. Bending over her, she said, "Kristen! Kristen! Do you hear me? Can you hear me?"

The patient's eyes remained closed but her lips began working and her breathing quickened. The nurse bent closer and distinctly heard the patient's whispered words.

"Drink of water."

The nurse put her hand on Kristen's forehead. "Honey, I've been waiting to hear you say that," she said softly and left to summon the doctor.

Inside, the tent was pitch dark. Alma, Niki and Cubby lay in the two sleeping bags. In a makeshift bed fashioned from the poncho and the large emptied canvas Duluth packs, Max lay beside them.

They could not see the storm's movements, but they could hear, and sometimes feel, the lashing of the canvas shelter as the winds flayed it with surging whips of air. After the late afternoon lull, the winds had commenced again from the opposite direction. The rains diminished but the velocity of the storm created an unstable atmospheric turbulence.

The four of them stared into the dark above them, listening to the storm.

Outside, the trees groaned as the wind bent their tops; branches creaked, needles rustled like whisk brooms shuffling across a floor.

The root system of the great stands of Norway Pines on the Laurentian shield was the most fragile part of the tree. The hard granite forced the growing vegetation to spread only shallow roots that clung to the cracks and crevices and searched for nurturing soil. As a consequence the forest giants stood top-heavy, with only a tentative grip on the forest floor.

The tent which sheltered Cubby and Niki and Max and Alma was pitched beneath one of the magnificent giants.

When the funnels dipped down from unseen clouds and writhed in the darkness of the night, they chose for destruction the large pine that overhung the fragile tent. The freakish currents of wind whipped across the top of the clearing and struck down only that one tree, leaving the others unharmed.

A member of the Ojibwa tribe later said that the forest spirit thought kindly of the children and the old couple, because the other trees caught the giant as it fell, held it, and then gently laid it on the ground. In doing so, they laid its great trunk to one side of the clearing, and let its branches hold it away from the wet canvas walls where Max, Alma and the children lay listening.

Dorothy Clemens stood in her nightgown and looked out the front door of her apartment. She couldn't sleep. It was the same as the night before, she thought. For she knew it wasn't the storm. It was the McLean lawsuit that was keeping her awake.

"I'm going to get out of this office," she resolved. "Running other people's lives is more of a drain than I thought it would be. I'm going to give it up and go back to practicing law."

As she stood in the doorway and looked out at the slackening rain, she said to herself, "This time I mean it."

As if in reply, a sudden gust of wind surged against the apartment, rattling the door on its hinges. Startled, she stepped back from the door, visibly shaken. She had the odd feeling that something supernatural, something malevolent and cruel, had upset the balance of nature, not only in the storm-racked land, but in her courtroom, as well.

The next morning, Alma bundled Cubby and Niki in their rain gear. The rains had stopped. The clouds were breaking up.

"Do we have to wear the life preservers?" Cubby asked.

"Yes, dear," Alma said, fitting it around her. "We have a long way to go on water before we get to the end of the trail."

"I've got mine on," Niki announced.

The wind that followed the storm was sharp and cold. Alma rummaged through the packs to find extra dry clothes for the children, and she found a jacket for herself.

Max stood up. "We ready?" he asked. He still had not laced up his boots. The laces dangled like loose wires, but he didn't notice them.

Alma tied the flap of the tent and turned to him. The two children appeared eager. With the light of day, Cubby had brightened and announced that she was prepared to hike out of the woods.

"Me, too," Niki said.

Alma looked around the campsite, then nodded to her husband. "We're ready."

"Are you sure you feel up to it?"

Alma smiled. "If you only knew how you looked, Max, you would be worrying about yourself, not me. If you can walk out to Lake Saganaga like that, I can."

"I can do it." Cubby smiled tentatively at Max.

"I'll go first," Niki said.

"No," Alma ordered, "we'll all stay together. The trail is wet and slippery, and we don't want anybody to fall in the river."

The four set off from the campsite and climbed the bluff behind the clearing. Max led them around the fallen pine tree up to the voyageurs' portage. They picked their way along the ledge above the white waters of the river. Sometimes they paused to reach out and join hands to keep their balance, and sometimes they sat down and slid on the path where it was wet and smooth. The portage from Marabeuf Lake to the lagoon was mostly downhill, following the winding river as they headed toward the uprooted tree that lay across the lower end of the rapids.

Water dripped from the trees and made each step for the adults slippery and treacherous. The children seemed to flip from handhold to handhold and dance along the rocks as if they were a couple of ground squirrels. But Alma, who continued to be plagued with back and stomach pains, and Max, who carried their backpack with food, maps, and a compass, had trouble with their footing.

"Wait up," Max called.

The hikers were strung along the ledge using the tree roots on the upper slope for hand-holds. Max had snagged one of his boot laces and pulled the boot off. The bulky woolen sock was caught on a broken root.

"Wait," Alma called, and the two children stopped on the ledge and looked back. Then she kneeled down, pulled the woolen sock loose and slipped it back on Max's foot while he balanced his pack. Then she put on his boot. She threaded the laces through the eyelets and tied each at the top with a neat bow. The large bows added a touch of elegance to the homely boots. At the ludicrous sight of her bows, Max started laughing. Alma, squatting on the ledge in front of him, joined him. Their laughter rang out in the bright, clearing day, above the sparkling waters of Horsetail Rapids and brought to the valley an atmosphere of spontaneous joy. The two children clinging to the ledge ahead of them threw back their heads and started shrieking with laughter.

"Let's go again," Max called.

Reaching down, he helped Alma to her feet and they started to follow the children. Beyond, Max remembered from the map, the trail would widen and the fallen pine would mark the end of the rapids and the lagoon above Saganaga Falls where they had left their boat.

In that instant, the joy in Alma's heart turned into shuddering terror.

On the pathway in front of Niki and Cubby there appeared an apparition, a hulking black ghost. The four hikers froze in their tracks. Max, with one hand on Alma's elbow, clung to a root with the other. Alma, one foot suspended in midair, froze. Niki and Cubby, six rods ahead of the old couple, were face to face with the black bear.

The rogue had approached from the opposite direction without a sound except the clicking of its teeth. It swayed from side to side as if ready to lunge and bite. The animal confronted them in a spot where the rock ledge widened and was overhung by broken blocks of granite.

The black hulk filled the width of the trail. Its crinkling nose constantly tested the air. It was close enough that they could see the bloodshot feral eyes, close enough for the near-sighted Black to distinguish the quarry it confronted. The ghost-like animal had brought with it the odious smell of the rotted flesh it had been eating.

Both girls stood stark still. Without hesitation they had remembered and obeyed their mother's admonition. No movement, no fear.

Time also stood still.

Then there arose from the pathway a pure, sweet tremolo sound. With a haunting, pulsating vibrato, not unlike the long piercing wail of a loon, Cubby threw back her head and sang.

"I came from above. I am holy. This is my second life. At another time I, too, was a bear. We are sisters!"

When the enchanting song ended, the bear was transfixed and the figures on the ledge stood unmoving like a life-sized wood carving.

CHAPTER 35

ERROL ASKED THAT THE DOCTOR be given the witness oath. Peter Hauck tried to make eye contact with Judge Clemens, but she ignored him. Jan Kiel sat at the counsel table with a bemused look on her face. P.M. again sat in the back of the courtroom, unobtrusive as the woodwork. But Errol felt his presence, if no one else did. He was careful not to acknowledge the ex-judge's presence, however. Had P.M. wanted to be noticed, he would have sat up front, in plain sight.

Errol put his hands behind his back as if to show that he was carrying no weapons. No one in the courtroom was fooled by his manner. Rather, it made everyone slightly uncomfortable. Hauck sat up straight, his senses at full alert. He could feel Toli's eyes boring into the back of his neck.

"Will you state your name, sir?" the lawyer asked.

"Jens Erickson."

"Where do you live?"

"I have a place over near Hoveland, here in Cook County."

"What is your occupation?"

"I am a medical doctor."

"How long have you practiced your profession?"

"Forty-five years, counting the war years."

"What training have you received to prepare yourself for performing the duties of your profession?"

"I am a graduate of the University of Minnesota, School of Medicine; I did my intern residency at the Soderlund Institute of Medicine in Drystand, Norway, during World War II. Following my release from detention in Norway, I returned to this country and finished my residency in Family Medicine at the Mayo Clinic in Rochester and came to Cook County where I have maintained a practice ever since."

"As a matter of curiosity, Doctor, how did you happen to do your internship in occupied Norway during the war?"

"My family came from Norway. I was the namesake of my grandfather, Jens Erickson. I had gone to visit him right after I got out of medical school and was detained there by the Germans when they occupied the country. Rather than sit out the war in an internment camp, I offered my services and received residency credit for my four years of work at Soderlund Institute."

"Have you had the opportunity to study, and have you studied, as a part of your medical training, the psychology of human beings?"

"I have."

"Have you studied, and are you familiar with the literature on the subject of the psychology of human beings?"

"I am."

Errol paused, as if to let Erickson's answer sink in. Jan looked at him with frank admiration. He had attached the poisoned arrow so deftly. Now, it remained to be seen if it would find a target. She could feel the tension in the courtroom tauten like a drawn bowstring.

"Have your studies included abnormal psychology?"

"Yes."

"Sexual dysfunction?"

"Yes."

Peter Hauck strangled on something in his throat. His neck swelled visibly. But he bit his tongue and gritted his teeth in silence.

Errol looked over at opposing counsel and smiled disarmingly.

"Do you hold yourself out to be a specialist in that area of practice?" Errol asked, turning back to the witness.

Hauck sucked in a breath, the obstruction in his throat apparently dissipated.

"No. As I previously said, my post-graduate work has been in family medicine. However, one cannot practice family medicine without dealing with the psychology of the family. I have tried to stay abreast of the literature and the most recent developments in that area."

"Doctor, are you acquainted with the term, 'sexually inappropriate behavior'?"

"I am."

"Tell Judge Clemens what that term means."

Hauck, no longer able to control his ire, rose to his feet at the counsel table. "Your Honor, I object on the grounds that the witness has not been properly qualified. By his own admission he is not a specialist in the field of diagnosing or treating psychological disorders. He has told us his specialty is in family medicine and in the general practice of medicine. Consequently, the witness is not qualified to offer an expert opinion on psychological matters."

Judge Clemens looked back to Errol. "Do you propose to ask this witness for an opinion based on the hypothesizing of facts to indicate psychological disorders?"

"No, ma'am."

"The objection will be overruled"

Hauck remained standing. "Your Honor, then I move that the witness' testimony be stricken because his testimony could not be relevant to any issue in this cause. There is no substantive evidence that this witness has any independent knowledge of the issues raised in this case, which is the condition of the home environment of the Toli McLean residence, or the question of whether or not the temporary custody order of the court should be made permanent. There is no medical issue before the court that would call for the witness' expertise. Consequently, Petitioner asks that this testimony be stricken and the witness be discharged."

Judge Clemens turned to Errol.

"What do you say to that, counselor?"

"I am entitled to offer in evidence the witness' authentication of medical research and conclusions set forth in the medical literature and explain them so laymen can understand them."

Judge Clemens smiled. "You mean a non-medical lay person like me?"

"And me," Errol said.

"Mr. Joyce, you know in cases where the court is called upon to remove children from the home because of child abuse, there is first an investigation of the home by the Minnesota Department of Family Services, and also there is a psychological evaluation of the children and the adults involved. You have none of that here."

"I agree, Judge, but this is not a case in which you are being asked to remove the children from a home because they have been sexually abused.

In this case, the father has always lived in the home of his parents and has asked for permanent custody of his children so that they can live with him in that house. The burden of proof is upon the father to convince the court that the home of his parents is a proper environment or the preferable environment in which to raise the children. What I am trying to convince the court is not to award permanent custody to him, because in that home the grandfather has conducted himself in a sexually inappropriate manner, and that some other place is a more appropriate or preferable place to raise those children."

Errol added, "The sense of Dr. Erickson's testimony will be that because of his training and his knowledge of medical literature, he knows what it is that the medical profession looks for when they are trying to determine if an adult has behaved in a sexually inappropriate manner. I propose to establish with this witness, that in making that determination, the medical profession views the conduct through the perception of the child, not through the eyes of the adult."

"And you're saying Dr. Erickson has the expertise to testify as to those indicators and as to the way the medical profession believes those indicators should be viewed?"

"Yes, Your Honor. He knows more about that subject than anyone else in this courtroom."

"What do you say to that?" the judge asked Peter Hauck.

"Just because he has an M.D. doesn't make him an expert in matters of psychiatry or qualify him to draw the psychological profile of a sex deviate."

"But," Judge Clemens said with a wry smile, "it does mean he knows more about it than those of us with law degrees."

Hauck sat down, silent as stone.

Jan tried to give him a comforting look, but Hauck would take no solace from her. He looked like a man standing on quicksand. There was no solid footing and he was slowly sinking into a quagmire.

Errol Joyce seemed perfectly poised to use up his entire quiver of arrows. Cool, Jan thought. So irritatingly cool. He looked as if the judge's decision were preordained.

"All right," Judge Clemens said after a moment. "I'm going to let him answer. After I hear the testimony I'll sort out whether or not his opinion is helpful to the court in resolving these issues."

Errol turned back to the witness, without a trace of smugness. Jan suppressed a smile.

"Dr. Erickson, would you please identify for the court the medically accepted indicators that the medical profession looks for to determine the likelihood of sexually inappropriate behavior between an adult and a minor?"

"Mr. Joyce, experience has shown that there are several phases to sexual abuse, which one must understand before one can look for the so-called indicators."

"What are the phases of sexual abuse?"

"First, the adult has the opportunity to be alone with the child. Next, the adult introduces sexual activity as a game. Then there occurs less intimate sexual activity, such as exposure or masturbation or fondling. The next phase is more intimate sexual activity at a greater frequency. Then to prevent exposure, the adult may make threats or demand secrecy. After exposure, there is a phase when the family tries to suppress public knowledge by rejecting help or counseling and trying to get the victim to recant. Now, those are the classic phases that the medical community recognizes in almost every situation of child abuse."

"What does the medical profession look for to discover if, in fact, sexual abuse has, or is likely to occur?"

"Over-secretiveness; over-possessiveness; frequent opportunities for them to be alone; fearfulness on the part of the child. The level of power and knowledge and resource of the adult as compared to the child."

"Pardon me, Doctor," Errol interjected. "I think as laymen we can understand what you're saying, except for that last one. You said, 'the level of power and knowledge and resource of the adult as compared to the child.' What do you mean by that?"

"The difference in the age of the adult and the child, their relative educations, the relative difference in their wealth, their employment. In practically every situation of child abuse, the abuser is superior to the victim in each of these instances," the witness said.

"Like a college professor and a seven-year-old child?" Errol asked, loosing the arrow. Jan could feel the shaft winging through the air straight for its shadowy target.

"Objection!" Hauck said. "That's a hypothetical question. The witness has admitted he is not qualified to answer that question."

"Sustained!"

"Doctor," Errol said, "what would your profession expect to see in the child if that child was abused or likely to be abused?"

"Withdrawal, crying without provocation, fear of others of the same sex as the adult, poor relationships with other children, fear of being alone with the adult. And, sometimes the child will come right out and tell the doctor."

"How about the adult? What are the indicators you look for in an adult child abuser?"

"Probably the single most common trait in all adults guilty of sexually inappropriate behavior is their feeling of isolation. No matter what kind of front they put up, they feel rejected by the outside world. The other two common traits are a chaotic childhood with numerous moves and family marriage problems and being a victim themselves, when they were children."

"Thank you, Dr. Erickson," Errol said. "Those are all the questions I have."

Hauck rose. This time, Jan noticed, he did not stand behind his chair at the counsel table. Instead, he walked to the empty jury box to make his stand as Errol had done. Invading Errol Joyce's territory, she thought. But she knew there was another strategic reason for taking up that position. From there he could watch both the face of the witness and of the judge and their reactions to his cross-examination.

"Doctor," Hauck began, "you are not contending you maintain a specialty, as a part of your practice, in the areas of psychology and psychiatry?"

"That's correct."

"And you agree, do you not, there are others who have specialized in that discipline that are more knowledgeable on the subject than you are?"

"Yes."

"The answers you have given to the questions asked by Mr. Joyce are based entirely upon classes you had in your college years over forty years ago and occasional continuing medical seminars that you have attended since you have been engaged in private practice?"

"And," the witness added, "a lifetime of dealing with the psychology of the family in my own specialty of family medicine. The practice of medicine is an art as well as a science, and in dealing with our patients and their families, none of us finds a fine line of division between any of the disciplines. In the forty-plus years I've practiced medicine, I've been surgeon, pharmacist, obstetrician, gynecologist, you name it. When you practice medicine in rural Minnesota, you do it all and that experience becomes an important part of your education also."

"But this emphasis on child abuse or the sexually dysfunctional family is a relatively new area of practice that has emerged in the past fifteen or twenty years, don't you agree?"

"No, I do not agree. I dealt with abused children when I did my intern work. The sexually dysfunctional family has been around for generations, maybe for as long as we have had families. It's only of late that you lawyers and our court system have addressed the problem, because it has been a taboo that no one wanted to talk about except the medical profession and the priest in the confessional. Over the years, the church hasn't had any better answer to the problem than the medical profession. It's not something new as you lawyers think," concluded the witness.

"Doctor, there have been thousands of relationships in this community alone; millions in the state; an untold number of relationships where adults have been alone with children; have shared secrets with children; have shown favoritism to a particular child in the family; where there have been sibling rivalries within the family; where parents have not been compatible. But statistics show that the number of cases of child abuse is minuscule in comparison to the number of such relationships. Isn't that correct?"

"Nobody knows the proportion of the abnormal relationships to the normal in those situations."

"That's what I'm getting at. Just because Professor McLean rules his household with an iron hand and is also alone with his seven-year-old granddaughter to teach her subjects he believes she should know or because she didn't like him or didn't like to go to his school or because she was the apple of his eye, so to speak, those conditions, in and of themselves, are not indicative of inappropriate sexual conduct, are they?"

"No," the witness admitted, "not alone and of themselves."

"All of us could assume, just as well, that statistically the relationship which I described would fall within the norm rather than the abnormal because the overwhelming number of such relationships are normal. Isn't that true, Doctor?"

"We can draw that assumption, but if we do, we have no more certainty that the family life you have described is normal than we have that it's abnormal in that individual situation. Statistics do not deal with nor reveal the truth about individual situations," the witness said. "Doctors have to deal with individuals, and what you lawyers are finding out, now that you're beginning to talk about it, is that you can't talk in terms of what the statistics show. You've got to deal with individual lives. You're finding, in dealing with them, that you lawyers have the same problems the clergy and the medical profession have had for years. That is, trying to find out how a child perceives its treatment by an adult. You're trying to do that with a specific child and a specific adult. It's a difficult call, and I think you lawyers are going to find out that, as time passes, you're going to have to do exactly what the clergy and the medical profession do, and that is err on the side of the child. The adult is more likely to cope if we make a mistake than the child is."

"Doctor, how do you arrive at that assumption? Isn't it a traumatic experience for a child to be taken out of its home, away from the loving care of its family, if a mistake has been made in diagnosis, or for that matter, if Judge Clemens makes a mistake in a custody decision in her court?"

"There is no question that taking a child out of its accustomed family and home in itself has a traumatic effect on the child. I'm simply saying that when we don't know, when we've got a close call on the decision of whether or not a child is being subjected to inappropriate sexual behavior, then I think we should err on the side of the child."

"Dr. Erickson, do you have any independent knowledge concerning the physical or mental condition of the McLean family?"

"No."

"Have you ever had occasion to examine any member of the McLean family or to treat them?"

"I'm presently treating Kristen McLean."

Hauck rephrased his question. "Prior to this particular incident concerning Kristen McLean, have you ever examined or treated any member of the McLean family?"

"No."

"Have you ever been with them on social occasions, visited in their home or had them visit in your home?"

"No."

"No further questions for this witness," Peter Hauck said. Errol noted that there was just the slightest trace of smugness in Hauck's mien. Unconsciously, he looked toward the back of the courtroom. P.M. leaned on the back of the seat in front of him, as if he had been listening to the testimony with more than idle interest. Errol drew in a deep breath. He looked at Jan, shaking his head slightly.

Judge Clemens waited until Hauck had taken his seat at the counsel table. "Any questions on behalf of the Guardian Ad Litem?"

"Yes," Jan said, rising.

Errol noticed an air of confidence in the way she stood. Perhaps, he thought, Jan could seal the cracks he had missed.

"You may inquire."

"Dr. Erickson, I want you to assume that the following facts are true," Jan said. "Assume that Toli McLean is the grandfather of Cubby McLean;

that Cubby McLean is a girl seven years of age; that as often as three times per week the grandfather was alone with the granddaughter in the library of his home, sometimes with the door locked, sometimes with it unlocked. Further assume there were occasions when other members of the family requested to be present in that room with the grandfather and the child, and their presence was denied by the grandfather. And assume the grandfather, by his action and word, indicated to other members of the family that Cubby McLean held a favored position in his eyes; and assume that the grandfather requested that some of the activities they engaged in while alone in the library not be revealed to anyone else for the reason that the secrets they shared would be helpful in her education; and assume that Cubby McLean, at the grandfather's insistence, was not permitted to obtain a public school education.

"And assume that the child, by word or actions, indicated she did not want to attend the sessions I have described; and assume that part of the discussions between the grandfather and the child while alone concerned biological matters, including the creation of life. Further assume that the grandfather and his wife for several years did not engage in sexual intimacy; and assume during this time the grandfather did not seek sexual companionship outside the family. Assuming all of the facts I have stated to be true, do you have an opinion based upon reasonable medical certainty, whether or not the home environment I have described is a sexually inappropriate environment for a seven-year-old girl?"

"Yes, I have an opinion," the doctor said.

"Wait a minute!" Peter Hauck rose to his feet. "That's the same question the court would not let counsel for the Respondent ask. The witness is not qualified."

Judge Clemens lifted her hands to silence the lawyers. She turned to the witness. "Dr. Erickson, just a few moments ago, you indicated you could not answer a hypothetical question with reasonable medical certainty and, in response to Miss Kiel's inquiry, you say you can. Which answer is correct?"

Dr. Erickson turned to face Judge Clemens. "Judge, the test you lawyers and the courts use asks for an opinion based upon reasonable medical certainty. A test that's really meaningless to anybody in the healing arts. But after Mr. Hauck asked me his questions and made me sit here on the witness stand and think about the experience I've had in dealing with the psychology of family members over the years of my career, I know I have an opinion. And I'm as certain in my opinion as any of you are in yours. So, although I told Errol Joyce last night that I couldn't testify about psychological matters with reasonable certainty, now that I've thought about it, I think I can. I've had more experience in these matters than you have."

Judge Clemens smiled. "I expect you're right, Doctor." She then addressed the lawyers at the counsel table. "I'm going to let the witness answer the question. It's my duty to ascertain the facts in this case and the believability of the witnesses. So, as I said earlier, I'm going to let the witness give his answers and I'll sort out later whether or not I feel the questions and the answers are to be taken into consideration in arriving at my decision." She nodded to Jan. "You may proceed."

"Do you have such an opinion?" the lawyer repeated.

The witness turned back to her. "I do."

"And what is that opinion?"

"In my opinion, the circumstances you described and asked me to assume would constitute inappropriate sexual conduct and raise sufficient doubt as a medical doctor, I would advise that the child be removed from that kind of environment."

Dr. Erickson hunched forward on the witness chair. "In giving my opinion, what I'm trying to do is err on the side of the child. It may be completely unfair to the adult when we infer that the conduct is sexually inappropriate, but we've got to look at it through the eyes of the child."

The doctor paused and rubbed his forehead. "Masturbation is regarded as a completely normal sexual activity. But in the eyes of a seven-year-old child, if this child observed masturbation by an adult, then what is sexually appropriate conduct for the adult is not sexually appropriate conduct for the child. For that matter, the same thing could be said about intercourse or the display of nude art. What I'm trying to get across to you is that a long time ago the clergy and the healing arts learned to look at these situations through the eyes of the child. That's what you people in the legal profession are going to have to do also."

"Thank you," Jan said. "That's all I have for this witness." She sat down.

"Any other questions?" Judge Clemens asked.

Hauck rose and directed only one question to the witness. "The sense of your testimony, Doctor, is that based upon the hypothetical question put to you by Miss Kiel, you don't know, and can't say, one way or the other, whether or not there is any inappropriate sexual activity, or sexual dysfunction in the McLean family, can you?"

"No, I can't. I'm just saying when in doubt, you've got to look at the circumstances through the eyes of the child and if we're going to err, let's err on the side of the child."

Hauck sat down and made a notation in his notebook. "No further questions."

Judge Clemens turned toward the witness. "I have a general question that I would like to ask you, Doctor."

The witness turned in his chair to face her.

"In circumstances like we're talking about here—not just specifically in this case, but in circumstances generally—when somebody questions the conduct between a member of the family and a child in that family, would it be helpful to do a psychological evaluation of that child and talk to the child and do some kind of psychological evaluation of the family to give the courts and the lawyers a more accurate measure upon which they can base a decision?"

The doctor shook his head. "That type of evaluation is helpful to the profession in treating the family and in treating the child, but it's not going to help you lawyers who want a yes or no answer. The history of these things is, the child is scared or frightened or confused or doesn't want to talk or won't talk about it. No matter what the adult has done, the child will most of the time choose to protect the caretaker, the adult, or the child will be fearful that he will be taken from his home. Children don't want to lose their family. At the same time, the family invariably will rally together to try to avoid the stigma by denying the incident occurred or they will try to get the child to change his story. So, no, if you have a psychological evaluation of the child, in my opinion, you are not going to get the yes or no—the black or white—answer you're looking for. You're going to have to make a judgment call like those of us in the clergy and medical professions have done for years."

"Thank you." Judge Clemens pounded her gavel. "Court will be in recess for ten minutes."

Jan looked over at Errol. He was not smiling. He had good cause to worry. He had not only opened a can of worms, he had served each person in the courtroom a generous helping. What had seemed, at first glance, a relatively simple custody case had turned into something dark and evil, with resonances that reached far beyond the courtroom. Her own childhood loomed in the background, just out of sight, but not out of mind.

She looked back at Toli McLean. He was sitting stock-still, staring at Errol Joyce. For him, she thought wryly, the recess would be a long ten minutes.

CHAPTER 36

D URING THE COURT'S RECESS, Jens Erickson asked Jan Kiel to meet him out in the hall. The storm was over and Jan had opened the windows to allow the clean, fresh air to sweep through the building. The doctor walked Jan down to the far end of the corridor away from the McLean family who had also stepped out of the courtroom.

"Before I leave," Dr. Erickson said, "I have one other thing that I meant to tell you, but hadn't gotten around to."

Jan stopped at the open window. "What's that, Doctor?"

"Well, it seems to me that if Toli McLean had the psychological bent of a pedophile then there wouldn't be just this one isolated incident."

The doctor looked at Jan and saw her puzzled expression. "What I'm saying is that the hole in Errol's case against Toli McLean is that there is no evidence of sexual misconduct by the man over the years. If Peter Hauck is right, that all these indicators are nothing more than normal relationships people have with kids, then this isolated incident would not show sexual dysfunction."

"But, still, you don't rule out that the family situation is unusual enough so that such conduct could occur."

"Well," Dr. Erickson said, turning to leave, "if Toli McLean has a sexual hangup around kids, then some place you're going to find that he had other abnormal sexual experiences with small children. The history of these things is, if he did, it will be with someone of approximately the same age. Someone he had an opportunity to be with, someone who either trusted him or someone he had power and control over. So if you and Errol don't find that in the conduct of Toli McLean, then it would be my opinion that Kristen and Errol are wrong, and Peter Hauck is right; that the only reason kids don't like him is because he's an overbearing son-of-a-bitch. But that's not being sexually dysfunctional."

Jan looked over Dr. Erickson's shoulder and saw Arlesen McLean watching them. As their eyes locked, Jan said under her breath, "I just wonder . . ."

Jan turned her attention back to Erickson. "Doctor, you're right. I should have thought of that, too." She touched his coat sleeve. "Thanks for the advice. I'm sure Errol is glad you came over and testified."

The doctor turned and went down the stairs.

Jan walked the length of the hall, not taking her eyes off Arlesen McLean. By the time she reached the three McLeans they turned to face her. Jan ignored the grandparents and spoke directly to Arlesen.

"You're not planning to leave yet, are you?"

Arlesen shook his head.

"Good, because you're going to be my witness."

In the men's room Errol ran cold water over his hands and looked over at the towel rack where P.M. was drying his delicate hands. The sound of water echoed in the tile-floored room with its full length urinals, wooden stalls, cream-painted walls that were peeling from age and humidity. P.M. stood by the window, leaning against the cast-iron steam radiator. The opaque glass window was open.

Errol dried his hands, walked over to the radiator.

"Well?" he asked.

P.M. shook his head. "I hope you have something else, Errol, because you've gone about as far as you can with this line of questioning. It's a dead end. A brick wall."

"I know. Damn it, P.M., I just can't let it go."

"Sometimes, son, you have to walk away from it. The law can't right all wrongs."

"Toli's a pervert. I know it."

"The court doesn't know it. You haven't proven it. You're beating your head against that wall, Errol. Cut your losses and get out gracefully. You did your best."

Errol looked out the window, but his eyes did not fix on any object. Rather, they looked beyond, to an empty void. Something stormed up in him and caught in his throat. He swallowed hard and turned to his friend.

"P.M.," he said, "did you ever cry before a jury? I mean really cry before a jury? I don't mean just put on some show of theatrics or try to pull a sympathetic response for your client out of a third juror on the back row. I mean really cry."

P.M. shook his head. "No." His soft voice echoed in the hollow emptiness of the room.

"Whenever you do, it's because you're really caught up in the wave of technicalities that is washing over your client. The law is either going to carry him into a safe harbor or it's going to drown him."

Errol was so intense, so locked into his inner world that P.M. doubted he heard anything except the sound of his own voice, his own heart.

"You know, P.M., the most emotional reaction I ever had to a case happened down state about eight years ago. It wasn't a big case. It wasn't a sensational case. I wasn't representing some monied corporation or trying to defend a client on some sensational criminal charge. The state was trying to put my client, who was a Korean War veteran, in jail for passing insufficient funds checks. My client went into the Korean War as an innocent young boy and came out an innocent young alcoholic. When I met him, he was in his thirties, living with his widowed mother. He had never married, was unable to hold down a job, living from one drink to another as so many unfortunates do. A liquor store took a check from him for booze. He had written the check on an account that had been closed out. Every time he got drunk he'd write bad checks to get liquor, and merchants of the town knew him and took the checks. But this time when he didn't make good on them, the state prosecuted him.

"I begged that jury to find him not guilty. I was hanging my argument on a technical defense of no criminal intent and writing the checks while he was drunk. But what to do with him? If the jury turned him loose on the streets, he'd get drunk again and write more bad checks. I sent one of my suits to the jail because it fit him. I bought him a white shirt and tie. The sheriff got him a decent-looking pair of shoes from the Salvation Army. I argued to the jury that if they would find him not guilty, I would personally put him in my car and take him to the Veterans Hospital in Fort Snelling where he could get treatment. But the state showed that he'd been in the Veterans Hospital and walked away from their alcoholic program.

"P.M., there we were in the courtroom, twelve jurors, the state's attorney, me, the judge, the court reporter, the clerk, and the deputy sheriff. All of us making a life decision for this man. Would he go to jail for three years, then be turned free to go back to his old habits?

"I cried when I argued that case, P.M. And some of the jury cried. And later, after they convicted him and sent him off to jail, the entire jury panel, all twelve of them, waited for me at the bottom of the stairs at the courthouse and tried to explain to me again that they didn't know what else to do except to lock him up to give him a chance to sober up and dry out for three years because none of the rehabilitation programs at the Veterans Hospital had worked. They knew why I wanted to give him one more chance. The jurors wanted to tell someone they were sorry."

"Jesus, that's a hell of a story."

Errol looked hard at P.M. and tears brimmed up in his eyes. Errol blinked and struggled with his emotions, then his voice broke as he continued.

"I can't help it. I believe the law is different for me than it is for you and those who think of it as a job or a way to make a living. We have this wonderful, unique system of adjusting the conflicts that we have in our lives. It isn't perfect. It doesn't work all the time. It didn't work for Kristen the first time, and it looks like I can't make it work for her now."

Errol paused. Tears coursed down his cheeks. He wept unashamedly, openly. He wept like a man in the grip of something so powerful he was helpless against its force.

"Those kids are going to fall through the cracks, and I can't keep it from happening."

"Sometimes the system breaks down," P.M. said.

"But it's all we have, and I've got to believe in the system and believe that it'll work, because without that kind of belief, I can't be a lawyer. I can't practice law just to make a living. I've got to make the law work for everyone and all the time."

Errol took out his handkerchief, dabbed at his eyes. But the tears still flowed down his cheeks and there was a look of torment on his face.

P.M. put his hand on Errol's shoulder. Errol's voice cracked again and rose in pitch until every word seemed torn from his throat, every word cried out to be heard, to be remembered.

"Practicing law truly is an article of faith with me. God, I love it!"

Then, he broke into a broad smile and triumphant tears shone on his face giving it a radiant glow.

P.M. realized that he was weeping, too, and he smiled at Errol, smiled with the understanding of a father who realizes how much he loves his son and how much his son loves him.

Above Horsetail Rapids, on the ledge, Max loosened his grip on Alma's arm and carefully slipped off his backpack. Alma heard the movement of her husband behind her, but didn't turn her head.

The bear had stopped swinging its head. The animal stood still, staring at the girl standing before it. Cubby again repeated the incantation, this time in a voice that dropped to a croon, almost like the cooing of a dove. The beast and the child stared into each other's eyes, transfixed. Neither blinked. They communicated in a mysterious way that only an untamed beast and an innocent child could understand.

Max froze, unable to move. The trail was so narrow he couldn't put himself between the bear and the girls. Alma stood on the ledge with her eyes clamped shut. Niki and Cubby stood in front of the animal, without guile, totally trusting in their belief that they would come to no harm.

Suddenly, the bear shook its shaggy shoulders and turned its back on the girls. As the girls and the Kadunces watched in disbelief, the huge bear lumbered off in the opposite direction, as docile as a cub with a belly full of mother's milk.

Cubby and Niki squealed with delight and waved as the beast disappeared around the bend.

Alma let out a sigh of relief. Max made them wait fifteen minutes before going on. As they walked, he kept looking around, but didn't see the bear on the trail and knew it must have gone back into the woods.

The girls arrived at the ledge beside the falls before Alma and Max. The falls dropped into a short canyon flanked by a forest of birch and pine. The trees absorbed the roar of the water and muted the sound that rose from the mist.

"Oh, look!" Niki called.

She pointed toward a rainbow in the mist as the sunlight broke through the clouds. The sun touched them. In the sharp wind they savored its warmth.

An expanse of ice blue water spread out from the valley, dotted with islands that seemed to dance on the waves kicked up by the wind. The clean-washed azure sky opened as the clouds drifted to the east, leaving only the warm midday sun.

The fishing boat below Saganaga Falls was completely under water. Max knew that the water-logged motor would never start.

"I'm going to get the boat up," he said. "If I can take the weight of the motor off the rear end, I should be able to pull it up on the rocks and empty the water out of it."

"Shouldn't we wait here?" Alma asked.

"Not with that bear still about. We've still got the oars. I can row out into the open water and maybe someone will see us."

Max waded into the stream and, holding his chin high, he reached down and stretched to grasp the handles on the clamps that held the outboard motor to the back of the boat. Slowly he loosened them from the boat transom. Holding his breath, he squatted completely under the water and grasped the machinery.

Alma and the girls watched anxiously from the shore.

"Shit!" Max exclaimed, surfacing and gasping for breath. The motor had slipped out of his grasp and fallen to the bottom of the pool but remained strapped to the boat by a chain that snaked out and anchored the sunken craft.

He again filled his lungs with air and dove to unsnap the chain. The motor fell free and was lost among the jumble of submerged rocks. Without the weight of the motor, the wooden craft shifted, and he pulled it to the shore.

Alma and the girls helped Max raise one side of the boat and empty the water.

Alma sat in the back of the boat facing her husband who had placed the oars in their locks and was preparing to pull away from the portage. Cubby and Niki sat in the bow, side by side, with the backpack at their feet. Pulling on the oars, Max thrust the craft out into the swift stream below Saganaga Falls. The boat turned and the waters carried them away.

Alma looked back toward the plunging falls. "Beautiful. It's all just so beautiful."

Then, above them at the top of the falls, the bear appeared once again. It reared up on its hind legs, stretched to its full height, ears laid back, its giant claws spread as if to reach all that way to catch them. It stood, hunched slightly forward, its massive shoulder muscles bunched as if to charge. Water dripped from its shaggy hair. Froth oozed from the animal's gaping jaws. Its great chest heaved as it sucked mouthfuls of air and expelled its fetid breath with a guttural roar of defiance. The bear had taken possession of the Granite River.

Max kept the boat to the center of the stream where the river flattened over reed beds as its water spread and its current slowed. Watching the small rocky islands at the mouth of the river, he rowed with sweeping strokes until they had cleared the end of the Granite River and drifted out onto the open expanse of Red Sucker Bay.

In the fresh-scrubbed sky, the clouds were almost gone. Only a few tatters could be seen on the horizon to the east. The wind had laid back and Lake Saganaga had settled into a gentle rolling motion that quietly rocked them.

Looking over his shoulder, Max pointed the bow toward the island, the first point of reference on his map. He began the long trip back to Canadian Customs Island and the end of the Gunflint Trail.

CHAPTER 37

WHAT DID YOU DO WITH YOUR MOTOR?" shouted the big Scandinavian, as he let his boat drift up to the other boat in which Max, Alma and the two girls were seated.

"It's a long story," Max said.

Alma's face lit up. "Are we glad to see you!"

The big man grinned. "I thought you might be needing some help. I would have gotten up here sooner but we couldn't get out on the big water above the narrows until the lake stopped whitecapping. How are you doing?" Thor Elmgren hooked a leg over the edge of Max's boat to keep them from drifting apart.

"Our motor's in the bottom of the lake," Max said. "A lot has happened."

"I see that you've added two more members to your party."

"Yes, it's been a very eventful trip," Alma said.

The girls smiled shyly at the outfitter.

"Girls," Alma said, "this is the man who lives at the end of the lake by the road. He's going to take us home."

"Any of you hurt?" the outfitter asked.

"No," Max and Alma chorused. "Just exhausted."

The outfitter turned to the girls. "I take it you two are the McLean kids?"

"I'm Niki."

"I'm Cubby. How did you know our name?"

"Because everybody on the north shore is looking for you two," the man replied.

"Do you know where our Grandpa Mike lives?" Cubby asked.

"Yes, I know where Mike Dushone lives. He's got a trapper's cabin over on Northern Light Lake. Is your mother's name Kristen?"

Both girls nodded.

The outfitter looked over at Alma Kadunce as if he started to share a secret with her, then said simply, "Well, kids, your mother is down at Grand Marais and I expect she'll be mighty glad to see you."

"Our mother went to Grandpa Mike's," Cubby said softly.

"I think she changed her mind," Elmgren said. "I heard some talk on the radio that your mother got a ride in a helicopter and she's waiting for you down at Grand Marais."

"Oh," Cubby said.

"We've got a lot to talk about," Max said, "but let's talk later." He looked out over the restless waters of Lake Saganaga. "Let's get these kids down to the end of the trail."

The outfitter nodded. He tossed Max a loop of rope. "Tie on to my boat with this, and I'll tow you."

As the two boats began the long, slow trip, they left a wake that rose and folded and spread out until it disappeared. When they went out of sight behind an island, a loon surfaced and looked about. Above, on warming currents of air, an osprey spread its wings and sailed effortlessly on its way to new fishing ground; and the lake returned to its restless solitude, as it had three hundred years before, after the first voyageurs passed that way.

CHAPTER 38

WHEN JUDGE CLEMENS RECONVENED THE HEARING following the recess, she was surprised to hear Jan Kiel recall Arlesen McLean. The judge reminded the witness of his oath and all those present in the courtroom settled in their accustomed places to see why Jan Kiel had chosen to question Toli's son.

"Mr. McLean," Jan said, leaning back against the rail of the jury box, "if you will indulge me just a moment, I want to ask you a couple of preliminary questions before I get to the real reason that I called you back to the witness stand. Is that all right with you, sir?"

The witness looked bewildered. He didn't understand why the lawyer thought she needed the witness' permission to ask him questions. But the others in the courtroom who had seen Jan try lawsuits before, who knew her work as Assistant Attorney General, knew her disarming approach usually signalled the start of vigorous cross-examination.

Jan smiled as if the witness had given her the permission she needed. "Now first off, Mr. McLean, I'll tell you that frankly I couldn't understand how a man with your education, born and reared in the United States, could put up with the conduct of your father and the way he ran your family and your personal home life. I've been thinking about that these last two days, and I've decided you really love your father, don't you?"

Arlesen McLean was surprised at the question. He sat up straight in the witness chair, looking out at his father. "Yes," he said.

"And you respect your father, don't you?"

"Yes."

"And you respect the traditions your father has taught you?"

"Yes."

"And someday you anticipate you will be the head of your household, and you will try to retain these same traditions and values you believe your father and his family before him have preserved?"

The witness thought for a moment. "Yes, I think that's right."

"Do you believe your father to be an honorable man?"

"Sure."

"Do you believe him to be an honest man?"

"Yes."

"As you think back over the relationship with your father, would you say that he is a man whom you and your mother are ashamed of?"

"No, of course not."

Hauck stirred in his chair at the counsel table and started to voice an objection. But Judge Clemens raised her hand to silence him and let Jan continue.

"Do you think your father has raised you properly?"

"Yes, I think so."

"Now, let me ask you another preliminary question. You have told Judge Clemens that you received your college education, one year in Vermont and the balance at the University in Duluth. Is that correct?"

"Yes."

"Did you attend public school when you went to high school?"

"Yes."

"Did you attend public school when you went to grade school?"

The witness looked out at his father and mother. "Yes."

"Did you attend all grades in the public school when you were growing up?"

"Not all of them. No."

"What grades did you miss?"

"I didn't miss any grades, but I didn't start attending public school until I was in the third grade."

Jan made a note on her pad and for a moment said nothing. There was a sudden silence in the courtroom. "Now, Mr. McLean, I want to turn to the reason I recalled you to the witness stand. Will you please tell Judge Clemens who taught you and where you were taught for your first and second grades?"

The witness looked out into the courtroom again. "I was taught my first and second grade classes in our home."

"And who taught you?"

"My father."

"One of the reasons you and your mother Selma McLean sided with your father rather than with your wife Kristen on whether or not Cubby should attend public school was because your family had already been through that experience. That's where you got your first two grades of education—from your father, at home. Isn't that right?"

"Yes."

"Did he teach you your numbers?"

"Yes."

"Art and drawing?"

"Yes."

"Did he teach you to read?"

"Yes."

"Did he teach you about science?"

"Yes."

"Including biology?"

"Yes."

"Including the creation of life?" Jan asked quietly.

"Yes."

"Did he teach you about the conception of life?"

"Yes."

"Human anatomy?"

"Yes."

"How did he teach you?"

Errol looked sharply at Jan. Something about her voice, its tempo and timbre, had alerted him. Jan looked different now. Her manner had changed subtly. She appeared calm, patient as a ministering nurse. Her tone of voice was almost soothing, he thought. Like a snake charmer's sonorous flute, delicate, soporific. She was lulling the witness into a state of serenity with the consummate skill of a born actress. It was a masterly performance, so nearly imperceptible that he almost missed the subtle shift in Jan's skillful attack.

"About what?" asked the witness, totally oblivious to the treacherous ground Jan was laying before him like a cool green carpet of summer grasses.

"About human anatomy—about the conception of life?"

"We examined anatomy. We talked about conception."

"What do you mean, you examined anatomy?"

There were sharp needles in her voice, Errol thought. But, the witness didn't feel them.

"Just that," the witness said.

"You mean you looked at pictures?"

"Yes."

"Did you look at a real human body?"

"Yes."

"Whose?"

"Mine."

"Was anyone present when these classes were conducted by your father?"

"No."

"How did you examine your body?"

"I just took off my clothes."

"Your father had you take off your clothes?"

"Yes."

"Did he take off his clothes?"

"Yes."

"How old were you then?"

"I was in the first grade, second grade."

"Six, seven, eight years old?"

"About that, yes."

"Did you tell your mother about that?"

"She knew about it."

"How did she know about it?"

"I don't know. We didn't make any secret about it."

"Did your father touch you?"

"No, of course not," the witness said indignantly.

"Did you touch your father?"

"Absolutely not!"

"I take it then, that this was just an anatomy lesson?"

"Yes."

"How did you study the female anatomy?"

"With pictures."

"Your father had pictures of naked women?"

"Yes, they were pictures of women without clothes on like you would find in any medical book."

"Were they pictures from a medical book?"

"I don't remember."

"Did you ever think that there was anything about the lessons your father was teaching you or the way he was teaching you that was improper?"

"No, of course not."

"Do you, today, think they were improper?"

"No."

Errol Joyce was conscious that he had been involuntarily holding his breath. Jan had led the witness down the primrose path of cross-examination, scattering flowers on the grasses along the way. Her performance was, he thought, a magnificent example of courtroom technique.

She turned and looked out into the courtroom where Toli McLean was seated. The man was focused on her with a stoic expression. Jan turned and nodded to Errol and Hauck, then faced the judge. "Your Honor, with the permission of opposing counsel, I would like to interrupt my examination of this witness, by calling to the witness stand his father, Toli McLean."

Judge Clemens looked down at the counsel table. "Do either of you have any objection?"

Both lawyers shook their heads.

"You may step down; however, do not leave the courtroom," Judge Clemens said to Arlesen. Then, in a louder voice, she addressed the older man. "Mr. Toli McLean, will you please come to the witness stand?"

Toli passed his son without a word and sat in the witness chair. As Judge Clemens started to address the witness, there was a disturbance at the back of the room. Everyone's eyes turned to the sound.

The door in the back opened and Max and Alma Kadunce led Cubby and Niki McLean into the courtroom. Behind the four stood the sheriff, who had met Max's pickup truck and escorted them into town after having received a call from Sag Store. They stood inside the doorway, uncertain as to where to go. The sheriff whispered something. Max led them down the aisle, the girls holding hands, the old couple on each side.

Others in the courtroom were stunned by the unexpected appearance. Only Jan knew who the two adults were but there was no mistake as to the identity of the children.

Arlesen McLean turned on the front bench and said under his breath, "Thank God!"

Toli sat rigid in the witness chair. On the front row, Selma put her hands to her mouth to stifle a gasp and her face collapsed into a complex set of wrinkles. The others watched as, without a word, Arlesen rose and went to the children. They met halfway down the aisle. The father knelt and put his arms around their waists, and the girls grabbed and hugged him. Judge Clemens brushed her lips with her finger and let it rest lightly on her cheek as she watched the scene play out in her courtroom. There was no outburst, no crying, no shouts. Arlesen knelt and the trio clung together as the others looked on.

Judge Clemens finally spoke. "Mr. McLean. Mr. McLean."

Arlesen rose and turned to the judge's bench.

"I think we should complete this hearing," Judge Clemens said. "Sheriff, you were not aware of my ruling. I do not want the children to be in the courtroom. It will be just a few moments more. I think all of you should go into the jury room and wait there until I send for you."

Arlesen whispered something to the girls and Niki grinned.

The sheriff motioned for Max and Alma to take the children through the gate and around the witness chair to the door that led into the jury room.

Niki turned and waved at her grandmother. Selma smiled at the girls through her tears. The five-year-old also waved at her grandfather, but the man in the witness chair was not looking at her. He was looking into the eyes of Cubby McLean. Cubby drew back.

The girl stumbled against Jan Kiel, who was standing beside the jury box. Jan caught Cubby by her shoulders and steadied her. Cubby's whole body tightened. When the girl turned her face upwards, Jan saw something flicker far back in Cubby's eyes, a shadowy wariness, like an animal in a cage that, even if the door opened, wouldn't dare move.

Jan looked up at the witness. Beads of perspiration glistened on Toli's temples. For Jan, all of her inner warning systems went off at once.

In a short time, no longer than a breath, Cubby moved and sought out Alma's hand, and put Alma between her and the witness stand. They went through the side doorway, but before the chamber door closed behind the children, those in the courtroom heard Niki's plaintive voice.

"Alma, why is Cubby crying?"

The door clicked shut.

Judge Clemens turned to the court reporter. "Let the record show," she ordered, "that the minor children, Cubby and Niki McLean, were brought into the courtroom by the sheriff, along with two adults. Let the record also show that, at the court's direction, the children and the adults were escorted outside the courtroom and outside of the hearing of these proceedings. That no testimony was given in the presence of the children. No communications took place between any of the parties or the children that will prejudice this hearing, and there is no reason why the court should not proceed with this hearing."

Turning to Peter Hauck, the judge asked, "Mr. Hauck, do you agree that your client has not been prejudiced by the appearance of the children in the courtroom despite my earlier ruling that they not be present and not testify?"

He rose. "No objection on behalf of the McLean family."

"You, Mr. Joyce?" she asked.

Errol rose. "No, your Honor," he said and sat down.

"How about the Guardian Ad Litem?" The judge turned to the State's Attorney. Jan Kiel shook her head. "No objection," she replied quietly.

Turning again to the reporter, Judge Clemens said, "The court rules that there being no objection, the hearing will continue. Proceed on behalf of the Guardian Ad Litem."

There had been no change in the expression on the face of Toli McLean.

Errol stroked his chin. Where in the hell did they find the kids, he wondered. He looked back at P.M. Gregory seated in the shadows on the back bench.

The elderly lawyer, as if reading Errol's mind, shrugged to indicate that he had no idea where they had come from.

On the front row, Selma McLean grasped her son's hand tightly and held it at her side where her husband could not see her display of emotion.

The judge turned to the witness. "You understand that you are still under oath."

"I do," replied Toli in a firm voice.

Jan came right to the point. "Have you been present in the courtroom during the testimony of your son, Arlesen McLean?"

"I have."

"Did you hear your son testify that when he was in first and second grade, you were his teacher and he was taught in your home?"

"I did."

"Was that a correct statement?"

"It was."

"Were you present when your son testified that you taught him about human anatomy and about the conception of life?"

"I was."

"Was your son's testimony substantially correct when he told Judge

Clemens that as a part of your teaching, you had your son undress and you also undressed and were nude alone with your son, discussing anatomy?"

"It was."

"And that did happen?"

"It did."

"Did you also show your son pictures of nude women and use them for the purpose of explaining female anatomy?"

"I did."

"That was how long ago?"

The witness thought. "Twenty-two, twenty-three years ago."

"When he was about seven or eight years old?"

"About that."

"During these sessions, did you ever touch your son, or did your son ever touch your body?"

Toli McLean's face flushed. He leaned forward in the chair toward the lawyer. "Miss Kiel, I don't know what you are trying to imply, but if you're suggesting that there was ever any sort of misconduct or sexual contact between me and my son, I'll have a suit for slander filed against you before sundown. Because that would be a damned lie!"

Jan folded her arms and smiled patronizingly at the witness. "I take it then, Mr. McLean, that you are categorically denying that there was ever any sexual misconduct between you and your son when you were teaching him many years ago. And that you think it is a perfectly proper and acceptable teaching practice to have first grade students undress and examine their bodies and for you, as their teacher, to undress so the students can examine your body while you discuss anatomy?"

"I do," the witness replied emphatically.

She shook her head slowly. "Mr. McLean, to me it is absolutely incredible that you, a college professor, and your son, a trained educator, would say such a thing."

"Miss Kiel, you're a lawyer. You have been educated as a lawyer. The judge here is a lawyer. Peter Hauck is a lawyer," and pointing to Errol Joyce, he said, "and he's a lawyer. None of you is a scientist. None of you even thinks in terms of the analytical studies that scientists do. I dare say every one of you has attended an art class or has known of an art class in which students for hours study and paint the nude body of a model; or you've gone through museums and examined nude paintings and sculptures done by classic artists throughout history."

Toli turned to Judge Clemens and gestured. "All of you think that's a perfectly proper way to teach art. Or you read literature that is erotic; you defend the rights of students to have that literature in their libraries and to study it in their classes. And yet, you think that the scientific mind shouldn't be just as objective in its teaching by pointing to the nude body when we're trying to make the student understand the biology of man."

"Lord!" Jan exclaimed, "we don't show erotic literature or nude scenes to first graders."

"Ah ha! Now you're seeing my point! You're not disputing the value of using the human body as an educational tool when the student is studying anatomy. All you're doing is arguing about the age level at which it should be done."

"Would you clarify that?"

"I'll be glad to, Miss Kiel. Everybody is this room has seen the naked body, has read erotic literature, has seen nude sculptures. All of us would agree that those are acceptable educational tools at the college level and at the high school level. Some would disagree that they be used at the elementary level, and blind prejudice keeps the entire community from using them at the kindergarten or first or second grade level. And that's where they should be used!"

"That is one of the reasons you taught your son in your home before he started going to public school?"

"It is."

"And is that the reason you taught Cubby in your home rather than let her go to public school?"

The witness saw the thrust of the lawyer's question, but answered it. "It is," he said tightly.

"Mr. McLean, despite what anyone else thinks, it is your view that it is a proper thing for an adult to stand nude before a seven-year-old child or a seven-year-old child to stand nude before an adult if it is for the purpose of teaching them and is a part of their education. Is that what you are saying?"

"Yes. That's what I'm saying."

"You're not ashamed of that?"

"No, I'm not ashamed of that."

"And you are positive you are right?"

"I'm positive I'm right."

"Mr. McLean, in these teaching sessions you had with your granddaughter, Cubby McLean, did you have that child remove her clothes in your presence?"

"No," the witness said.

Jan was puzzled. "Your answer is no?"

"My answer is no. My granddaughter did not remove her clothes in my presence."

"Did you remove your clothes in her presence?"

Toli McLean stared blankly for a long moment before he answered. "One time."

Jan looked over at Judge Clemens. "So there will be no misunderstanding, in the presence of Cubby McLean, during one of the teaching sessions, you did remove your clothes, and you were naked in front of that child?"

"Yes. But you must understand that it was while we were studying one of the science lessons."

"I understand, but that is your testimony. Is that correct?"

"Yes."

"I have one other question."

The witness sat back in the chair and waited for the lawyer to pose it.

"Do you remember the incident several years ago when you were stabbed in the arm by your daughter-in-law, Kristen McLean?"

"I do."

"You testified earlier about that incident and said that was an example of the violent personality you believed your daughter-in-law to have?"

"I did."

"Will you tell the judge whether you were clothed or naked when that incident occurred."

The witness fixed Jan Kiel with a look of pure hatred.

"Will you answer the question?" She insisted. "When Kristen stabbed you, were you clothed or naked?"

"Naked. But it was my home!" shouted the witness.

Out in the courtroom, the statement sent a jolt through the frame of Arlesen McLean. He sat rigid, with an almost catatonic cast to his eyes. The significance of the admission caused his insides to shrivel.

Judge Clemens pounded her gavel.

"Court will be in recess," she announced. She pointed at the lawyers. "I want to see you three in my chambers right now!"

Check, thought Errol, wryly. Maybe check-mate, he reasoned, as he extended the chess metaphor. He looked at Jan, but she wore an expression of total innocence on her serene face. Yet, wasn't there the faintest trace of a victorious twinkle in her eyes?

CHAPTER 39

T HE JUDGE HELD THE DOOR OPEN and ushered the lawyers inside her chambers. The three took their seats. They sat in silence as the judge unfastened her robe and dropped it on the back of her chair. She sat down and leaned forward on her desk. "Well, what do you have to say?" she asked.

Errol looked at the other two lawyers, then spoke. "Respondent moves that the court dismiss the Petitioner's application for permanent custody."

"The Guardian Ad Litem joins in the Respondent's motion," Jan said softly.

"Counsel?" Judge Clemens asked, turning to Peter Hauck.

"I have nothing more to say on behalf of the Petitioner," he replied dully.

"All right." Judge Clemens picked up her pen and began to write. The three lawyers waited as she made her docket entry. When she finished, she read it aloud.

"The court, having heard the evidence and being fully apprised of the circumstances of the home in which Petitioner proposes to raise the minor children, is of the opinion that permanent custody should be denied to the Petitioner. The court sustains the Respondent's motion to dismiss Petitioner's application for permanent custody. The court orders that the custody of the minor children, Cubby McLean and Niki McLean, be temporarily placed with the Guardian Ad Litem, Jan Kiel, until such time as the court enters its final orders in this cause."

She looked across at Kiel. "Jan, I want you to use your discretion as to where those kids will live. I want you to arrange for someone to take care of them. I want you to see that the oldest girl is put in public school, and as soon as the mother's physical condition will allow, I will have another hearing so I can make a final determination as to who will have permanent custody of those two children."

Judge Clemens turned to Peter Hauck. "Do you have any objection to that, Peter?"

The older lawyer shook his head.

"Do you?" she asked Errol Joyce.

"No."

The judge tossed her pen on the desk. She leaned back in her chair and tipped her head back. "Christ! I'm going to get out of this office and go back to practicing law."

CHAPTER 40

O N THE COURTHOUSE STEPS, an enraged Toli McLean pointed a trembling finger at Peter Hauck. "You are fired!" he screamed. "You can walk home, and I'll be damned if I'm going to pay you a fee!" Turning, the professor ran down the steps to his car. His wife was already inside, waiting dutifully for him on the passenger's side.

Arlesen stood awkwardly by the rear door as if undecided whether he should go with his father or to the hospital to see Kristen.

"Get in," Toli said sharply.

Arlie hesitated. He winced under his father's withering glare, then reluctantly opened the door. He stood there, indecisive for a moment, then deliberately closed it, turned and walked across the parking lot.

Toli got in the driver's seat and slammed the door. He started the car with an angry twist of the ignition key.

The bemused lawyer watched his client drive away. "You'll pay my fee and with interest," Hauck called after him. He picked up his briefcase and started down into town to see if he could find a ride back to Duluth.

Max and Alma, holding the hands of Cubby and Niki, walked down the hospital corridor toward Kristen McLean's room.

The girls glanced around them in wonder as they walked along the hall. A nurse at the desk had told them they could spend the night with their mother, sleep in a nice, soft bed.

The old couple stood in the doorway and watched as the children broke loose and dashed to their mother's side. Niki ignored the nurse and climbed up on her mother's bed.

The sight of her children brought a pink glow to Kristen's face. She smiled through her tears and grasped the children.

Niki squirmed out from under her mother's arm and rose on the bed beside her. "Mother, guess what?" she said.

"What, honey?" Kristen whispered hoarsely. With tears in her eyes and a lump in her throat, she could barely talk.

"We saw a bear," Niki said. "And do you know what happened?"

Cubby, with her important voice, silenced her sister. "I'll tell her."

Cubby climbed up on the bed beside her mother and sister and began to tell their story.

Later that evening, Jan and Errol lay together on the four-poster bed. Their heads shared the same pillow.

"Errol?"

"Yes?"

"Why were you out by the lighthouse without your shoes on?"

After a long silence, he replied. "Most mornings I walk to the lighthouse to clear the cobwebs out of my head. I took Kristen's letter with me. I was on the lake side where nobody could see me, so I decided to go barefoot. The feel of those rocks on my feet does wonders for my spirit—makes me feel like a boy again. So I took my shoes and socks off and set them on top of the railing. Then this damn seagull came along. I don't know what the hell it was thinking about, but it swooped down to grab one of my shoes and knocked both of them over the sea wall into the lake. Like that, they were gone. I would have wrung the bird's neck if I could have caught it."

Jan raised up on her elbow and gazed down at his face. "Is that all?"

"Sure," he said. "Did you think I was some kind of an eccentric who went around with my shoes off just to get everybody's attention?"

Jan fell back on the pillow.

Errol covered her hand with his.

"It works," he said. "It really works."

"What works?"

"The law. You were magnificent, Jan. You filled in the cracks."

"Your mind, Errol. You saw Toli for what he was before anyone else did. I just followed your lead."

"God, I love it. I love the law!"

"And me?" she asked softly.

"I love you, too," he said squeezing her hand.

For a long while, the couple lay together, each with thoughts of the events that had transpired. The trial was over, but Jan's mind was still troubled by a secret thought. She nestled her face against Errol's chin and asked softly, "Do you like children?"

"Yes." The quiet response was immediate.

"Me, too. I mean I'm going to miss Cubby and Niki," she confessed. "For a little while they were my children."

"I know."

"I became their mother when we thought Kristen wasn't going to live," Jan said quietly. She lay back and stared at the ceiling. Errol could hardly hear her.

"I never got to be with them," she said, "but I thought about those two girls a lot during the trial. It was as if my very own children were missing."

With his fingertips, he gently stroked her arm.

"I want to have a baby," she announced in a barely audible whisper. When she finally spoke those words, tears began to trickle down her cheeks.

Errol pulled Jan to him. He put her head beside his on the pillow. He wrapped his arms around her, caressed her gently.

"I really do want to have a child of my own," she said. "I want to take the chance and see if I can do better than my parents did."

Errol squeezed her tightly.

"You will," he whispered.

Miles away on the windy reservation shore, the Whortleberry moon of August outlined a woman's figure on a black shelf of granite — the crying rock. Only the sobbing waters of Superior echoed the Ojibwa woman's *ancienne* lament:

It is time, Ninnimoshin, white man and friend,
it is time,
it is Autumn time, to give us the justice you promised
in your imperfect treaties.

The gently surging tide lapped at the crying rock, mingled with the Indian woman's tears, washing them back to the earth, back to the restless waters.

THE END